W9-BAV-566

Edited by
WILLIAM CULLEN BRYANT

Tales of Glauber-Spa
Volume 1

The American Short Story Series

VOLUME 37

GARRETT PRESS

512-00057-3

Library of Congress Catalog Card No. 69-11880

This volume was reprinted from the 1832 edition
published by J. J. Harper

First Garrett Press Edition published 1969

Reproduced from a copy in the University of Chicago Libraries.

The American Short Story Series
Volume 37
©1969

Manufactured in the United States of America

GARRETT PRESS, INC.
Publishers

250 West 54th Street, New York, N.Y. 10019

PROSPECTUS

LIBRARY OF SELECT NOVELS.

FICTITIOUS composition is now admitted to form an extensive and important portion of literature. Well-wrought novels take their rank by the side of real narratives, and are appealed to as evidence in all questions concerning man. In them the customs of countries, the transitions and shades of character, and even the very peculiarities of costume and dialect, are curiously preserved; and the imperishable spirit that surrounds and keeps them for the use of successive generations renders the rarities for ever fresh and green. In them human life is laid down as on a map. The strong and vivid exhibitions of passion and of character which they furnish, acquire and maintain the strongest hold upon the curiosity, and, it may be added, the affections of every class of readers; for not only is entertainment in all the various moods of tragedy and comedy provided in their pages, but he who reads them attentively may often obtain, without the bitterness and danger of experience, that knowledge of his fellow-creatures which but for such aid could, in the majority of cases, be only acquired at a period of life too late to turn it to account.

This "Library of Select Novels" will embrace none but such as have received the impress of general approbation, or have been written by authors of established character; and the publishers hope to receive such encouragement from the public patronage as will enable them in the course of time to produce a series of works of uniform appearance, and including most of the really valuable novels and romances that have been or shall be issued from the modern English and American press.

There is scarcely any question connected with the interests of literature which has been more thoroughly discussed and investigated than that of the utility or evil of novel reading. In its favour much may be and has been said, and it must be admitted that the reasonings of those who believe novels to be injurious, or at least useless, are not without force and plausibility. Yet, if the arguments against novels are closely examined, it will be found that they are more applicable in general to excessive indulgence in the pleasures afforded by the perusal of fictitious adventures than to the works themselves; and that the evils which can be justly ascribed to them arise almost exclusively, not from any peculiar noxious qualities that can be fairly attributed to novels as a species, but from those individual works which in their class must be pronounced to be indifferent.

But even were it otherwise—were novels of every kind, the good as well as the bad, the striking and animated not less than the puerile, indeed liable to the charge of enfeebling or perverting the mind; and were there no qualities in any which might render them instructive as well as amusing—the universal acceptation which they have ever received, and still continue to receive, from all ages and classes of men, would prove an irresistible incentive to their production. The remonstrances of moralists and the reasonings of philosophy have ever been, and will still be found, unavailing against the desire to partake of an enjoyment so attractive. Men will read novels; and therefore the utmost that wisdom and philanthropy can do is to cater prudently for the public appetite, and, as it is hopeless to attempt the exclusion of fictitious writings from the shelves of the library, to see that they are encumbered with the least possible number of such as have no other merit than that of novelty.

THEOLOGICAL LIBRARY.

I. LIFE OF WICLIF. By C. W. Le Bas.......................... 1 vol.
II. CONSISTENCY OF REVELATION. By Dr. Shuttleworth. 1 vol.

FAMILY LIBRARY.

I. II. III. MILMAN'S HISTORY OF THE JEWS................ 3 vols.
IV. V. LOCKHART'S LIFE OF NAPOLEON BONAPARTE..... 2 vols.
VI. SOUTHEY'S LIFE OF LORD NELSON..................... 1 vol.
VII. WILLIAMS'S LIFE OF ALEXANDER THE GREAT...... 1 vol.
VIII. NATURAL HISTORY OF INSECTS....................... 1 vol.
IX. GALT'S LIFE OF LORD BYRON........................... 1 vol
X. BUSH'S LIFE OF MOHAMMED.............................. 1 vol.
XI. SCOTT ON DEMONOLOGY AND WITCHCRAFT......... 1 vol.
XII. XIII. GLEIG'S HISTORY OF THE BIBLE................ 2 vols.
XIV. DISCOVERY, &c. IN THE POLAR SEAS AND REGIONS 1 vol.
XV. CROLY'S LIFE OF GEORGE IV......................... . 1 vol.
XVI. DISCOVERY AND ADVENTURE IN AFRICA............. 1 vol.
XVII. XVIII. XIX. CUNNINGHAM'S LIVES OF PAINTERS, &c. 3 vols.
XX. JAMES'S HISTORY OF CHIVALRY AND THE CRUSADES 1 vol.
XXI. XXII. BELL'S LIFE OF MARY QUEEN OF SCOTS..... 2 vols.
XXIII. RUSSELL'S ANCIENT AND MODERN EGYPT........ 1 vol.
XXIV. FLETCHER'S HISTORY OF POLAND.................. 1 vol
XXV. SMITH'S FESTIVALS, GAMES, AND AMUSEMENTS... 1 vol.
XXVI. BREWSTER'S LIFE OF SIR ISAAC NEWTON.......... 1 vol.
XXVII. RUSSELL'S PALESTINE, OR THE HOLY LAND ..... 1 vol.
XXVIII. MEME'S MEMOIRS OF THE EMPRESS JOSEPHINE 1 vol.
XXIX. THE COURT AND CAMP OF BONAPARTE .... 1 vol.
XXX. LIVES OF EARLY NAVIGATORS, &c. .... 1 vol.
XXXI. DESCRIPTION OF PITCAIRN'S ISLAND, &c. .... 1 vol.
XXXII. TURNER'S SACRED HISTORY OF THE WORLD.... 1 vol.
XXXIII. XXXIV. MEMOIRS OF FEMALE SOVEREIGNS... .. 2 vols.
XXXV. XXXVI. LANDERS' TRAVELS IN AFRICA........... 2 vols.
XXXVII. ABERCROMBIE'S INTELLECTUAL POWERS, &c... 1 vol.
XXXVIII. XXXIX. XL. LIVES OF CELEBRATED TRAVELLERS 3 vols.

Classical Series.

I. II. XENOPHON. (Anabasis and Cyropædia.)................. 2 vols.
III. IV. LELAND'S DEMOSTHENES........................... 2 vols
V. ROSE'S SALLUST.. . 1 vol.

Dramatic Series.

I. II. III. MASSINGER'S PLAYS.............................. 3 vols.
IV. V. FORD'S PLAYS.. 2 vols.

LIBRARY OF SELECT NOVELS.

I. II. CYRIL THORNTON.   XIII. XIV. THE CLUB-BOOK.
III. IV. DUTCHMAN'S FIRESIDE.   XV. XVI. DE VERE.
V. VI. THE YOUNG DUKE.   XVII. XVIII. THE SMUGGLER.
VII. VIII. ANASTASIUS.   XIX. XX. EUGENE ARAM.
IX. X. PHILIP AUGUSTUS.   XXI. XXII. EVELINA.
XI. XII. CALEB WILLIAMS.   XXIII. XXIV. THE SPY.

TALES OF GLAUBER-SPA.

BY

SEVERAL AMERICAN AUTHORS.

To seize the papers, Curl, was next thy care;
The papers light fly diverse, toss'd in air;
Songs, sonnets, epigrams the winds uplift,
And whisk them back to Evans, Young, and Swift.
POPE.

IN TWO VOLUMES.

VOL. I.

NEW-YORK:

PRINTED AND PUBLISHED BY J. & J. HARPER,
NO. 82 CLIFF-STREET,
AND SOLD BY THE PRINCIPAL BOOKSELLERS THROUGHOUT THE
UNITED STATES.

MDCCCXXXII.

ADVERTISEMENT.

THE letter from Mr. S. CLAPP which follows this announcement will sufficiently explain to the reader the manner in which the manuscripts from which the tales in these volumes have been printed came into the possession of the Publishers. Having obtained permission from Mr. E. Clapp to take time for consideration, they were inclined to believe on inspection that the handwriting of a portion of the collection was not new to them. But on applying to the quarter suspected, they obtained no admissions or information which threw any light upon the subject. They then submitted the whole to a select committee of five gentlemen, distinguished in private for their critical acumen. Their report was a singular one; inasmuch as each one unequivocally condemned, as un-typeworthy, four-fifths of the whole; but the single and separate fifths which separately pleased each of them, and on which each bestowed high commendations (no two of them agreeing), made up the entire fardel which Mr. Clapp wished to dispose of.

Under these circumstances they bethought themselves of procuring an inspection of the books kept at the Spa; and through the kind offices of a friend were enabled to ascertain that among those whose names were entered as having visited the new spring were Miss Sedgwick, Messrs. Paulding, Bryant, Sands, and Leggett. The name of G. C. Verplanck had been written, but a line was drawn through it, as if the entry had been made by mistake. There were no other names to whom suspicion could attach; and the Publishers have been unable, in reply to very polite inquiries, to obtain any light from the parties mentioned. They disclaimed, however, any right of property in the manuscripts, the contents of which are now given to the public; sanctioned, in the manner which has been mentioned, by the opinions of five gentlemen of discriminating taste. That they may afford pleasure to the reader, and some profit to Mr. Clapp, who is ascertained to be a man of exemplary character, and who has suffered so unexpectedly from the late painful affliction with which the land has been visited, is the sincere desire and hope of

THE PUBLISHERS.

₊*₊ The orthography of Mr. Clapp, Sen., has been scrupulously preserved.

INTRODUCTION.

To the Misters Harpers,

at their store in New-York City.

Glauber-Spaw, *July —.*

This letter my son, Eli Clapp, will hand you, along
with the parcel. I do not suppose you know me,
though I have advertised once in one of your York papers; and the only way I came to know you was by seeing in it that you printed all the books, and I take the
freedom of writing to you on the strength of it.

I have lived at Sheep's Neck since I was a boy, and
so did my father before me; but we have altered the
name lately to Glauber-spaw, and call the Old Ram's-
alley Epsom-walk, out of a notion of the doctor's and
my daughters. I will tell you how it happened, or else
you would not understand how I came to write to you.

I lived on the old homestead, man and boy, and was
married and had a family of children, for forty years and
rising, when my wife would send my daughters to a
fashionable school in Wetherville, to learn French and
darning-work and the forte-piano. I cannot say I had
much peace after that. From one thing to another, I
was obliged to build two new wings and a back-kitchen
to the old house; and when those were finished, that
was pulled down and another built, as they said it was
not in good taste. It tasted better to me altogether
than the new place; for I was obliged to raise money

on a mortgage to pay for the *willer*, as they called it, after they had cut down all the willers that were to be found upon it. They found the furniture, too, but I had to pay for it; and when it was in order, as they said, it was such a trumpery, bandbox-looking place, that I could not spit in it with any comfort.

The next thing they did, and by this time they had got my wife and youngest son all on their side (though Eli, who is a discreet lad, went and lived in the barn, and would not come inside of their shingle-shanty, as he called it), was to say that Sheep's Neck was no name at all for the farm. I told them they might call it Clapp's Folly, if they liked; at which they turned up their noses, and talked about St. Romans, and Tully-veal-and-lamb, and Mount-Peeler, and Bawl-town, and other names, to which I did not see no likeness in the premises.

Just about this time young Doctor Jodine, who had come to settle in the village, and soon got thick with my wife and daughters, began to analyze, as he called it, the waters of my spring, which we had all been drinking for ever, taking it to be plain water. But it was no such thing. The doctor made a memorandum of what it was, which he had published in a pamphlet, now for sale at the bookstore in Sheep's Neck Village. It had saline and gaseous properties, and was made out of different kinds of stuff, in which there was plenty of ox-hides and gin, as far as I can understand it, with a good deal of sulphur and soda. It is strange how the water did not seem to affect us any before the doctor had analyzed it. But after he had had the spring walled in, and let it off through logs so as to make it squirt up in a fountain, it is really astonishing how we came to find out its properties, and the kimistry of it. I take this opportunity of begging you to contradict a false tale which some of the neighbours who go to the second meeting-house got up, and which I have denied in my advertisement, that the doctor buried a barrel of salts and potashes under the spring, which I know not to be the fact.

The kimistry of this water, after it was found out, troubled me considerable. I suffered in body and estate; as the doctor's bill was highish, and I lost a fine heifer and two of my best hogs, who drank out of the fountain by mistake. There was little left of the poor things but the hide and bristles. The doctor said that the Spaw, as he called it, was medicine-like, and must only be taken by advice, as it was good for vallydinarians. We had a fine well on the farm, in which there is no flavour of hides or potashes that ever I tasted. I took to drinking that out of the bucket, to avoid mistakes; but my wife and daughters took half a tumbler of the Spaw every morning before breakfast, by the doctor's advice, as he observed they seemed to be in delicate health—which they did. They were almost as lean as the poor heifer and swine; and are not much better off in flesh now, though they have left off drinking the Spaw, and been taking what the doctor calls tunnicks.

It was not long after he had fixed up the spring, before my neighbour Woolley Lamb, who keeps the tavern and post-office at Sheep's Neck Village, sent his son Chris one evening to tell our folks that a carriage-load of people were asking him where the Spaw was, and whether they could get boarded there. My wife and daughters overheard the message, and very much to my surprise came fluttering out, like a clothes-wash in a gale of wind. I had boarded the Yankee schoolmaster, off and on, several years before; and some high-flying girls that had been at school with mine had come to see them for a spell, after they had reformed the house, as they called it; during which I spent the most of my spare hours in the barn, along with Eli. But I had no idea of taking regular boarders, though for that matter,

I did not see what else the new house was good for. Presently the doctor came up in the wagon, with my youngest son Cush, who had a load of unaccountable victuals and sauce, enough to last a whole winter. The doctor said that a member of Congress's family had come; and that two of the ladies were vallydinarians, who had been sent from away south to Glauber-Spaw, as the only place where they could get rid of their pulmonitory symptoms, and be saved from dying a natural death.

How my wife and daughters fixed it, I did not know, and hardly understand to this day. The party presently came up in a great coach and four, and a gig with two negroes a-horseback. I thought it was none of my business to help them in, as I was not allowed to hinder them from doing it. The carriages and all the cattle, as I found on coming back at evening, had been put into the barn, and poor Eli's chamber was broken up; and there was a great deal of clatter in the house, and my wife and daughters were so busy, and looked so airy, that there was no getting a word out of them. I was put down by being told by my woman, when I came to talk to her, that if I would only mind the farm, she would make a mint of money, that the girls would get well married, and that I need not trouble myself about the Spaw House, as Cush would see about it all.

Not to be too long with my story, I made myself as busy as I could with working the farm, and got my meals in the kitchen or in the fields, not troubling myself with the traps that they had up stairs, though I saw much coming and going, and some new faces. Cold weather came, and the house was empty; and some people that my wife had hired, unbeknown to me, were sent off. They looked as fine, almost, as the boarders, and had shown no more respect to me when they came straggling about, than if the land did not belong to me. As they were going out of the gate the sarciest one of the lot took off his hat in a contemptible kind of a manner, and said, " Good-by, daddy." I gave him a few kicks that sent him rather anyhow into Merino Creek, that they now called Magnesia Springs ; and Eli, taking his ox-goad to the balance of them, made them " walk Spanish," as they say here. They sued us for it, and the case is not tried yet. I don't see how they are to get any witnesses.

Eli told me he was going to be married to a neighbour's daughter, and live on his farm ; though he would help me to work mine for fair wages, and carry the stuff to market for me in partnership. He never asked his mother and sisters to the wedding, and so they don't speak. Presently my neighbour Colonel Cross, who had the mortgage, came for a year's interest, and part of the principal, which he had a right to ask for. My crops had been bad, and though I had cut considerable hay, what with mending fences when the high-flyers at the Spaw House had broken them, paying the hands, and getting little or nothing from the market for vegetables, as the most of them had been wasted in the house, I had not ready money enough to pay even the interest. So I went to my wife, who had all along been blarneying me, when she got time to talk, about her great prospects. But she opened her eyes, and asked me if I was crazy, to think she could catch money at once, out of the clouds, after all the expense she had been at ? I never heard her talk such hard words before, as she had picked up from the strangers she had been waiting on ; and I do not wonder at it, for I heard that some of them were Nullyflyers ; and I am told that those sort of people are not Christians, and are a kind of unnat'ral like. She talked about divestments, and futer returns, and the goose that laid the golden eggs. This was all I understood of her new-fashioned prose ; and I could not help saying rather passionate-like, " Burn my old clothes, misses, if you haven't di-

vested me of my farm, and I won't have no futer returns to it, that's flat.   You're a goose yourself, and
have made a gander of me, and where are the golden
eggs ?"   Then she showed me all the bills for furniture,
and groceries, and servants (she paid them vagabonds
more for a month than I can make off the farm), and
told me she had paid nearly half of them.   And she
said that next season she could make an estate, as all
the company had promised to come back and bring good
society with them, if she would make more room for
them.   And she showed me a parcel of trash that had
been given to the girls,—singing-books, and old clothes,
and poetry-works, and smelling-bottles, which she said
were invaluable proofs of regard from the genteel ladies
that would take care of Sally and Nancy.

I saw that I was in a hobbleshow, and I knew that
Colonel Cross was twistical ; but I did not know how
to help myself, when he came and said that he must
have money, and could not afford to wait for it ; but
that if I would give another mortgage for three times
as much as the principal and interest came to on the
whole farm, he would lift the other, as he knew a man
in Wetherville who would advance it if I would make
further improvements, so as to accommodate all the company that would like to come.   He said my wife and
daughters were smart and active ; and that, as I did not
know any thing about it, he would see to the improvements himself, if I would give him a commission.   I
did not know what he meant, and told him he must go
to the governor for that, but found out that he wanted
to be paid for his trouble.

I had a heavy heart enough when I signed the new
mortgage, and did not get a cent of the money ; which
the colonel put into the bank to pay for the improvements ; and I spent a melancholy winter, having no
good of my family, and being often driven out of doors
in cold weather by the everlasting strumming that was

kept up on the cracked piano, which, I was told for my comfort, was to be changed for a new one. The spring had hardly come when the whole place was covered with timber and carpenters. The colonel was boss, and I was told I had nothing to do with it, though I had made up my mind to that before. Another story was put upon the house, with long painted shanties, and sheds, and stables, and boxes with crosses and vanes upon them, all about the premises. They put one of these up on the hill we used to call Sheep's Misery, which they called New 'Limpus, over Merino Creek; and in the next general rain it limped down of its own accord; and it cost more, I was told, to put it up the second time than it had done the first.

They had not got every thing painted and varnished and gilded, and cleared away the chips, and got in the wagon-loads of curosities that they bought for furniture, before we heard that the cholera morbus had come over along with twenty thousand paddies and radikles into Canada, up to the north; and the people talked about nothing but whether it would come into these parts. The doctor had newspapers and tracts which he brought every day, and said he could cure it with the Spaw. Sometimes he said it was the real sphixy that had killed so many abroad, and then he said it wasn't. And he talked about premonitories, and made us show our tongues. He wanted me to take some pills; but I told him it was out of the contract, and I did not belong to the Spaw. But my wife and daughters took them, and a sorrowful time they had of it. I believe he would have gone on physicking them, and killed them, as he did an old maid in the village, if it had not been that he would have had no patients at the house if there had been no one to keep it.

We soon heard that the cholera had got into York State. We had then but a few boarders, who all drank regularly of the water, and yet had premonitories all the time. But when the news came that it was in the city, there was in a few weeks such a run of people that the house would hold no more, and they boarded about with all the neighbours. Among them was a town doctor, who said his nerves could not stand the sight of the disease; and he too talked about nothing but premonitories. Our doctor and he at first had a quarrel, and my wife talked of turning him out of doors, when he said it would be certain death to drink the Spaw. But the two doctors soon made it up, as they seemed to be likely to have business enough for both. Then our doctor gave notice that he would give a public lecture gratis about the disease, in the meeting-house, and we all went to it. I did not pretend to understand it, nor did I find any one who did; only it was fixed now that it was the real sphixy, and that a collapse couldn't be cured. I believed as much, for I was aboard of a steamboat when one of the flues bursted. They called it a collapse; and I am certain it was easier to make a new one than to mend that. When he came to talk about the premonitories and the spasms, there began soon to be a sighing and grunting, and finally a general groaning, for all the world like anxious meeting. Everybody, women and all, were putting their hands over their bowels; and my neighbour Slaughter, the butcher, who weighs twenty-three stone, clapped his on each of his sides, and getting up to give them a squeeze, set up a sort of a bellow like one of his own bullocks going to be killed. I felt a little squirmish myself, though I had not noticed it before. When he came to tell what was good to eat and drink, it was curious to hear him. I did not see that he left any thing for our victuals but beef and rice. Neighbour Slaughter stroked down his jacket as if he felt a little more comfortable, when he talked of beef; but I felt more uneasy than before, thinking what was to become of all my peas, and beans, and beets, and onions, and all kinds

of sauce, and corn, and watermilions, which he said it
would be wilful murder to eat. All liquids he said
must be avoided; and as for the Spaw, he explained
how the air was so peculiar-like, that what was good
physic in common times was poison now, and a kind
of worked backwards. But he said that as long as the
people staid quiet there, the air was better than it was
anywhere else; and if they minded the premonitories,
and sent for him or his friend Doctor Nervy when
they got them, there was no manner of danger. He
also gave notice that he would make out a list of what
was proper to be eaten at the Spaw House for the benefit of strangers.

For the matter of that, though I only saw what was
going on in the kitchen sometimes, they seemed to have
pretty much the same cooking that they had the year
before, when the Congress-people and Nullyflyers had
been there; except that all the beautiful vegetables,
which never looked nicer before, were left alone. I
was not sorry for this, except that I could not have them
cooked for myself without going over to Eli's, where I
soon made a bargain to get my dinner regular and comfortable. But after he had been to market a few times,
and come back complaining that he could not sell his
load to the huckster-women, he returned at last with the
whole load; saying he had been ordered off by the
mare's men in the market; that all the shops were shut,
and the streets whitewashed; and that everybody that
died had eaten some premonitory or another. And
being a hasty man, who has not yet got religion, he
damned the cholera morbus, and the mare, and the vegetables too, in a profane manner—though that you need
not mention.

Half the people were kept half-sick, and the rest did
not look well, and the two doctors had business all the
time; and I began to think my wife might make something of a spec out of the business, as the boarders

seemed glad enough to sleep anywhere, and fare as they could. Two or three times when I looked in by accident, at night, I saw a party in one room that were reading written papers aloud; and from what I heard my wife and daughters talking about it, I gathered that they amused themselves with it, and that it was made out of their own heads. I thought it as good a way of killing time as any, and better than strumming on the forte-piano, which was kept a-going from morning till night, till a child fell through the cover one day, and smashed all the wire-works. I was plaguy glad of this, for I didn't mind the fidells, and flutes, and tamby-reens that they got to dance to, half so bad as the nasty noise, to no tune at all, that they made with the piano. Luckily there was nobody to mend it, and the poor thing stays smashed to this minute. I don't believe it will fetch much.

But to come to the marrow of the matter, after these premonitories, one night, about two weeks ago, my old negro Samboney, who lives with his wife Dinah in a little old stone house near the Spaw, complained of a great many of them. I didn't see any good the doctors did, and Samboney was awful afraid of them. He said he had drunk nothing all day but hard cider, and eat no thing but salt pork and plenty of the nice vegetables Master Eli gave him (being some of the same that would have been wasted otherwise), and some water-milions, hard biled eggs, and nice green apples. Dinah said he had taken near a pint of spirits too, which was but natural in the poor neger; for after such a mess I should have taken some myself, for all Doctor Skinner and Doctor Nervy might have said. I told him to be quiet, and Dinah to kiver him up; but I had hardly sneaked into bed in the little room on the ground-floor, where my wife had put me since the company came, and begun to get asleep, when I heard Dinah screaming and thumping at the door, and bawling out,

" Cholera Morbish !—Samboney has got him !—He's a
kicking down the house !—Cholera !—Cholera !" loud
enough to wake the dead, and scare all the vallydinarians out of all the life that was left in them.   I got up,
while she kept on hollering ; and when I went out, it
was a curious thing to see and hear.   There was all
the people in the windows and piazzas to the back of
the house, in their night-clothes, some screeching as if
they had fits ; and there was the nigger-wench in her
white shimmey, dancing a rigadoon on the grass, and
pulling out her wool, and thumping herself like a possessed body in the New Testament.   And when she
yelled out " Cholera !—Cholera !" it put me in mind of
the cry of wo set up in the streets of the old Jerusalem
by a crazy man, which I used to read about in Josephus,
when I had a clean place to set down in and read any
thing.

There was a general mixture of noises and running
about the house ; but I could hear calls for Doctor
Nervy, and cries of " Send for Doctor Skinner," more
than any thing else.   Doctor Nervy at last came out
on the upper piazza in his flannel night-gown, with a
blanket over it, though the nights were as hot as Tophet
(as I had heard Eli profanely remark), with a bottle at
his nose, and a candle in his hand, to help him see the
moonshine.   When he heard and saw Dinah, he looked
flustrated, and said she was crazy, and must be tied and
taken away, till he could attend to her in the morning.
The wench was in a great passion to hear him say this,
and went on screaming, " You no tie me !—Comē tie
Samboney ! — Cholera got him ! — He kick down de
house and bedstead !—Cholera !—Cholera !—C'lapses,
spazemzes, and plemoneraries—he got um all !"

The doctor said if Dinah wasn't tied he could not
answer for the health of his nervous patients ; whom
he besought to get into bed, as he meant to do himself.
Some of the servants ran to the village for Docter

Skinner, and some went with me, at a respectful distance however, as I pushed Dinah ahead, and followed
her to the house.   Sure enough, poor Samboney had
kicked out the foot-board of the bed, and thrown off all
the clothes.   He was an awful spectacle, and roared
terribly.   We could not keep clothes on him, or make
him be quiet, until he became so of his own accord,
after an hour or more.   Then his nails were as blue as
indigo.   We could hardly say whether he breathed or
not, and he lay with his eyes open, quite resigned-like,
as if he had given up fighting the cholera, and meant to
leave the end to Providence.   He was just so when
the doctor came.   He did not know, I believe, whether
Sam was alive or dead.   He talked a good deal of
what he could do if he could get apparatus, and said he
must have a consultation with Doctor Nervy.   But he
wouldn't come, and had locked his door, ordering from
the window that no one should be let into the room who
had been near the case.   Doctor Skinner then stuck a
lancet into Samboney, but no blood came that would
trickle ; and he got the whiskey-bottle, and would have
crammed the muzzle into the poor fellow's mouth, but
his teeth were set so tight that he only spilled it all over
him.   The short and long of it was, that Sam died an
hour before daylight ; and the peculiarest part of all was,
that he began to kick again after he was a dead corpse.

When daylight did come, every carriage was ordered
up to the door, and such as had none were off on foot
to the village, some of them without remembering even
to ask for their bills.   My wife and daughters stood on
the steps with real tears in their eyes ; and I cannot
but say, that the two latter were served shabbily enough.
Mrs. Mullock had been pressing them hard to take a
short jaunt with her to the Falls ; and now they wanted
to go there out of pure fright.   But though there was
plenty of room in the carriage, she crammed it full of
bandboxes and unwashed clothes, to show the impossi-

bility of the thing, and said she depended on seeing them in Alabama next season.

Before breakfast-time not a stranger was left in the house. Doctor Nervy was one of the first who run off. And though there has been but one case in the neighbourhood since, and that five miles distant, not a soul has come to the Spaw.

What is to become of my farm and the fine house I do not know. I suppose neighbour Cross must have both.

On looking about the rooms, and at the various rubbish which had been left, I found, in one where the reading-party used to meet by themselves, a great pile of papers, making, I should say, many quires of foolscap. I thought, though they had been left as good for nothing, and were of no use to me, they might turn to some account. But I resolved to have the speculation all to myself; and on talking to Eli, he thought there would be no harm in seeing what the papers were worth. They have not been inquired after in two weeks, and I do not know whose they are ; so I conclude they belong to me. If you will give any thing for them, I will trust to you to fix the price. I am an unfortunate man ; and every trifle will help me that I can come by in an honest way. There were other scraps and blotted papers about the house, and some love-letters and verses ; but I take it for granted they are not worth any thing.

Your very humble servant,
SHARON CLAPP.

CONTENTS

OF

THE FIRST VOLUME.

LE BOSSU.

LE BOSSU.

CHAPTER I.

"Ah! luckless babe, born under cruel star
And in dead parent's baleful ashes bred,
Full little weenest thou what sorrows are
Left thee for portion of thy livelihed;
Poor orphan, in the wide world scattered,
As budding branch rent from the native tree,
And thrown forth, till it be withered."
  Fairy Queen.

THE brilliant reign of Charlemagne is, amid the dark ages, like the splendours of day preceded and followed by a starless night. History does not here disappoint, nor delude us. The men of letters with whom he delighted to surround himself, " the brightest jewels of his coronet," have left us minute descriptions and particulars, not only of the wars, edicts, and pilgrimages which rendered their sovereign the hero of warriors, the legislator of lawgivers, and the saint of the church, but they have introduced us within his palace, and seated us at his hearth. From Eginhard, his historian and secretary, and the lover (or, as he claims, the husband) of the emperor's beautiful daughter Emma, we learn the domestic habits, tastes, and affections of that great man with whose name the " decree of posterity has indelibly blended the title of *magnus.*" We are surprised to find that the chief of the western empire, who traversed his vast dominions, extending from the Ebro to the Elbe, with a celerity that has only been equalled

3 B

by the prodigy of our own times, condescended to direct
the planting of his gardens and the feeding of his
poultry; and that such is the enumerated variety of
his fruits and vegetables, that an amateur-gardener of
our own horticultural age could scarcely rival the
catalogue.

Charlemagne has been reproached with having been,
in the coarse plebeian phrase, a "hen-pecked husband." It may be so, for strength is ever condescending and gentle to weakness. It has been said by one
of nature's noblemen, the stature of whose mind and
heart corresponded with the six feet four inches of his
corporeal frame, that "all *good* husbands are hen-
pecked,—the women, poor creatures! ought to have
their way." Thus the lion regards the helpless little
animal that is thrown upon his mercy.

The softness of the great monarch's disposition was
as marked in his parental, as in his conjugal relations.
It is well known that he refused his beautiful daughters
to the most powerful suitors in Christendom, and for
the simple reason that governs a rustic, " sooth to say,
he could not bear to live without them." But the
emperor was destined to illustrate the old fable which
teaches us that even Jupiter cannot enjoy the pleasures
of mortals without first deposing his thunderbolts.
Domestic happiness is not the appanage of royalty.
It is by nature's decree free and spontaneous. It
smiles on the home of the subject, but with all his
"appliances, and means to boot, is denied to a king."
The emperor's daughters loved their father, but they
did not withhold their affections from their natural and
ordained channels, and the court was scandalized by
clandestine marriages, and secret intrigues, of which
the emperor (not willing to punish them) prudently
affected to be ignorant.

Aix-la-Chapelle was Charles's favourite residence.
He embellished this city with the riches of his south-

ern and more fortunate provinces, " being ambitious,"
says his historian, " that the capital he founded on the
confines of Germany should resemble magnificent
Rome."

The monarch himself marked out new streets,
caused wide avenues to be opened, and sumptuous palaces to be built. Churches, then the favoured objects
of architectural honour, were erected; costly bridges
were constructed, and all the art of the times exhausted
on the noble chapel, which, after being dedicated to
the Virgin, had the honour of incorporating its name
with that of the city, thereby changing Aix into *Aix-la-
Chapelle.*

Neither the decrees of a monarch, nor the wishes of
a hero, can countervail the laws of nature. Aix-la-
Chapelle soon dwindled into insignificance,—and what
is our city of Washington while towns are shooting
into life and consequence on every part of our conti-
nent! Charles's palace presented a singular mixture
and contrast of barbarism and refinement. It was
enriched with sculptured marbles and precious vases
transported from Ravenna, and embellished with statues
and paintings that were reckoned chef-d'œuvres of the
arts, while it was destitute of the common articles of
convenience that are now deemed essential to the dom-
icile of the humblest mechanic. There was a like
ill-assorted and startling variety in the guards and attendants of the palace. They were composed of men
from all the different provinces of the vast empire—
Romans, Gauls, Saxons, Franks, Huns, Avars, and
numberless others, each speaking the language, wearing the costume, and bearing the arms peculiar to his
own province. The emperor himself, elevated by his
genius, caught a ray from the lights of distant ages, while
he was in part immersed in the darkness of his own.
The accomplished Alcuin was his poet-laureate, and
the learned Eginhard his secretary and friend; but

though, as they boast, he had learned both Greek and
Latin from oral teaching, he never acquired the art of
writing.   A rare art and expensive luxury it was, when
blank parchment was quite as rare and almost as dear
as paper written over with good poetry is now.

Should our fair readers be inclined to substantiate
the following narrative by their own investigations, we
would refer them to any accredited history of the age
of Charlemagne, and particularly recommend the recent and still unfinished " History of the French," by
the most philosophic, purest, and truest of historians,
M. Simonde di Sismondi.

We must forewarn them, however, that they may
explore far and wide without finding some of the particulars we shall relate, and which we confess to have
been derived from sources less authentic, and quite
inaccessible to others.

It was late in the eighth century, and in the afternoon of a mellow October day, that Charles was
seen entering the palace gates, attended by a gay
retinue of court lords and ladies on their return from a
hunting excursion. His social and domestic tastes
were a singular feature in that barbarous age.   Even
now, in the golden age of the sex, the presence of
ladies on occasions when Charles deemed them indispensable would be esteemed rather an impertinent
intrusion.

The emperor was preceded by Frank soldiers, his
chosen men-at-arms. He was without any emblem
or insignia of royalty, save that which nature had
stamped upon his lofty frame and noble countenance.
In dress and language he adhered tenaciously to the
usages of his forefathers, and now, as usual, he was
dressed in the simple costume of the Frank soldiers,
with the addition of an otter-skin over his breast and
shoulders, a Venetian cloak, a gold sword-belt, and

his good weapon "joyeuse." On his left rode his
eldest and illegitimate son, Pepin, called *Le Bossu*,
from a slight deformity of the spine, occasioned by an
accident of his infancy which had spoiled one of nature's masterpieces. He was the son of Himiltrude,
the most beloved and most lamented of all Charles's
favourites. From her he had inherited the rich dark
eye and jetty locks of the south, which, though he
bore a striking resemblance to his father, gave to his
face more of the beau-ideal,—more of the bright and
changing lights of imagination and passion. In Pepin's
youth Charles had employed the skill of Christian
and infidel leech, and had commanded the prayers and
penances of holy men, to remedy his misfortunes ; but
when it was found there was no exemption to royalty
from the lot of humanity,—that that beautiful head
must be borne by a bent and stinted trunk, every measure was taken to alleviate the misery. Pepin was in-
structed in athletic and graceful exercises. His health
was fortified and his vigour increased by field-sports,
and every ingenious art was employed by which his
person might be managed and sheltered. In his boy-
hood he submitted to this discipline, and was eager to
profit by it, but as he advanced to manhood he disdained
the arts that seemed to him unavailing ; he affected indifference to an incurable misfortune, and carefully
closing the natural outlets of an irritated and dejected
mind, and the inlets to compassion and sympathy, he
shut up his grief in his own heart, till it became a spirit
that ruled him, and could be ruled only by one celestial
influence—still there was nothing in his demeanour that
betrayed his feelings to a common observer. In spite
of the imperfection of his person he was foremost in
all manly exercises, and repeatedly, while the future
heir of the empire, Louis le Debonnaire, was indulging
in the soft pleasures of his palace in Aquitaine, Pepin,
at the head of his father's forces, or by his side, drove

back the barbarians from one frontier, and repelled the Saracens from another, and then returned to Aix-la-Chapelle to reap his father's favour. But, alas! a false hand had begun to mingle tares with that well-earned harvest.

At the emperor's right-hand rode his queen, the crafty, cruel, and still beautiful Fastrade. Her buskined ankles, the bent bow and quiver at her back, and the brilliant crescent that sparkled on her hunting-cap, showed that she had chosen to represent the goddess Diana; and though her person was somewhat too mature and matronly for the forest divinity, yet her rare gracefulness and classic beauty helped out her royal right to violate the letter of mythology.

The emperor's beautiful daughters and the other ladies of the court composed her train of nymphs, and were attended by lords and lovers, bearing cross-bows, and fantastically decorated with antlers, skins, and other emblems of the chase. Among them, before, or behind, as his horse willed, for he seemed not to interfere with the animal's discretion, rode Alcuin, the unconscious butt and laughing-stock of the gay lords, as an awkward savant of the present day might be of a knot of court soldiers or city dandies. But while he cowered over his horse's mane with such an aspect of awkward timidity, his thoughts perchance were absorbed on some of those treatises on theology, philosophy, or rhetoric, which caused him to be venerated even in those barbarous times as the finest genius of the age, and which have transmitted his name to us, while century after century has heaped oblivion on the proud names of contemporary warriors. Who was she who rode so gracefully at the queen's right-hand, in a green hunting-dress exquisitely fitted to her nymph-like form, with her face modestly shaded, but not concealed, by a black hunting-cap turned up at the side and fastened with a golden arrow instead of the

wreath of white poppies (the insignia of Diana's nymphs)
worn by the other ladies ?

Was it her rich brown tresses where the golden sunbeams seemed to linger—her eye of the deepest violet
hue—the rose opening on a cheek of infantine delicacy,
or those lips that seemed carved and died as if sculp-
ture and painting had tried their rival arts upon them—
was it matchless colouring and form that riveted the
eye to the orphan Blanche of Aquitaine, or did her spirit
beam through its mortal veil, and make her approach
that ideal beauty that the arts have laboured to impart
to their representations of immortals ?

The figure, character, and mysterious fortunes of
Blanche, all conspired to stimulate the imagination.
She was the last relict of the Merovingian race, and
nature had stamped on her unrivalled tresses her descent
from the "princes *chevelus.*" She was the last too of the
house of the renowned Hunold of Aquitaine, who with
all his family, save this delicate scion, had been pur-
sued to cruel death by the unrelenting hatred of the
queen. Blanche was preserved from the general fate
by the ingenious affection of her nurse, Ermen. But
when the fact of her existence, which Ermen had sedulously concealed, was betrayed to the queen, she, instead
of causing the infant to be put to death, as was expected,
commanded that she should be brought to the palace,
nurtured there, and treated with the most marked favour.
This singular departure from the terrible consistency
of the queen's conduct was long a matter of speculation to the courtiers. Some believed that her malignity was controlled by magic, others that the orphan's
tutelar saint had worked the greatest of all miracles in
her behalf—had converted diabolical hate into generous love, had filled her with kindness, who was,

> " From the crown to the toe, top-full
> Of direst cruelty."

But a keen observer might have discerned in all these
profuse manifestations of favour the constrained air of
unwilling kindness.   One spring of the heart, one tone
of the voice, excited or modulated by the movement or
melting of love would have been worth them all.

There were some other peculiarities about Blanche
that were mysteries to common observers.   As she
grew to womanhood, though solicited by the allure-
ments of a brilliant court, and though her beauty was
so striking as " ne'er seen but to be wondered at ;"—
though the homage of all eyes, and the vows of captured
hearts awaited her, she was rarely drawn from the nun-
like seclusion of her own apartment, but by the command of her royal mistress.

Our readers must forgive the prolixity of our ceremony of introduction, remembering, in our behalf, that
court presentations cannot be brief, and return to the gay
company, who were now approaching the palace, up an
avenue, enclosed on one side by a marble wall.   The
queen had addressed Blanche in a low voice.   Blanche
did not reply, but at the instant, Pepin's inquiring
glance met her eyes suffused with tears.   " Curse on
that demon's tongue," thought he, " it never moves but
to send off a poisoned shaft."

" My lord," said the queen, addressing the emperor
in a voice which she affected to depress, but whose
clear shrill tone she well knew reached Pepin's ear,
and cut to his very soul, " my lord, I was just admiring
your shadow on this marble wall, somewhat lengthened
by the descending sun, but it still retains its symmetry.   But Blanche, didst thou not say it was pity to
set off the noble proportions of our lord emperor by the
contrast of Le Bossu's shadow."

" Nay, that I did not, Madam ——; but truly I
marvel that my royal master's shadow has not a virtue
like to the holy apostle's—or at least if it cannot

cure those on whom it falls, I marvel, as I said, that it does not protect them."

"Spoken boldly! my pretty Blanche," exclaimed Charles, whose generous spirit was roused by the sarcasm on his unfortunate son. "I think it is ever the weakest animal that is most courageous in defence."

"And what craven animal is that, my lord, who is willing to be defended by the weakest?" asked the queen in a voice tremulous with the passion she betrayed in her affected irony.

The emperor saw the angry spot on his wife's brow, and as usual he sheltered himself in silence, which he had often occasion to find a friendly shield from similar conjugal attacks. Blanche, however (the only person who never felt, nor feigned fear of the queen), replied to her interrogatory, "I think, madam, I have heard that the eagle will remain passive while the little sparrow-hawk drives an ignoble enemy from his eyrie."

"Ha, my lord!" exclaimed the queen, "heard you that?—The golden arrow won to-day by Sir Pepin's superior shaft, has plumed my Lady Blanche's wing for a bold flight indeed."

This was an artful reference of the queen to the arrow that was attached to Blanche's hunting-cap, and which was won for her at the expense of some mortification to the emperor. A golden arrow had been offered in guerdon for the best shaft that should be shot during the sports of the day. Charles and the prince had arrived at the same instant within bowshot of a stag at bay. The emperor, as of grace he ought, had the first trial. His arrow touched, and glanced off. Pepin's followed, and was buried in the victim. The emperor was vain of his excellence in sylvan sports, and could not brook to be surpassed, even by his son, and this little successful rivalry, managed by the crafty queen, was an important step to the fatal issue between the father and son. So much more are even the great (alas for human

greatness !) governed by their " idol vanities," than by
those reasonable motives which the grave historian sets
forth with such imposing dignity. Blanche saw the
emperor's eye turn angrily towards Pepin—she felt
that she had ventured too far, but while she was mus-
tering words to excuse or conciliate, they turned an
angle of the wall, and were in front of the grand entrance to the palace.

" In the name of the holy martyrs, what have we
here ?" exclaimed Charles. In front of the steps that
led to the vestibule, on the mosaic pavement, stood an
ambassador from Haroun al Raschid. In his right
hand he held the standard of Jerusalem, and in his
left, the keys of the holy sepulchre, the caliph's magnanimous gifts to the western monarch. Near the
ambassador stood a black slave, beside a huge elephant
whom he held, or rather seemed to hold, by a gold chain
which was wound round the animal's neck, and care-
lessly thrown over the attendant's arm. The chain, as
if to show the elephant's docility, was so delicately
wrought that a child of a year old might have broken
it asunder. The slave was dressed in white and scarlet
silk intermingled, and his naked and jet-black arms were
encircled with bracelets of gold set with precious stones.
Dispersed around were the ambassador's attendants in
their picturesque oriental costume. As Charles advanced, the envoy proclaimed his errand, waving on high
the holy ensign, and bending forward till his lips almost
touched the pavement. His inferiors imitated and thrice
repeated his *salaam*, and the well-taught animal evolved
his trunk, and knelt, as if with instinctive homage,
before the great monarch. The horses in the emperor's train were startled by the novel exhibition, and the
retinue was thrown into disorder, of which Charles
was unconscious, while eager to express his reverence
for the sacred emblems of the restored rights of Christendom, he pressed forward and dismounted,—knelt

before the holy standard, crossed himself, kissed the
ponderous keys and placed them in his belt. He then
turned towards the queen, who had not yet dismounted.
" Still in thy seat, Fastrade !" he exclaimed ; " By my
faith, I thought thy heart and foot would have leaped at
sight of these holy symbols."

" My heart, my lord, has done them reverence, but
you see—I must wait till my lady Blanche is served."
The emperor turned towards the prince, who was standing beside Blanche holding the bridle of her palfry.
Charles drew his sword, and raised the hilt to strike
him. A mortal paleness overspread the face of the
prince, his lips were livid, but he did not speak, nor
even involuntarily flinch from the menaced blow, which
was arrested by Blanche, who, springing from her palfrey, stood between the father and son. " Nay, my
lord emperor," she cried, " touch him not—blame him
not—it was my fault that he did not his duty to my
royal mistress—my palfrey started at the sight of that
monstrous beast, I shrieked, silly girl that I was, and
Sir Pepin sprang to my aid. But indeed, my lord, I
would rather have died than he should have provoked
thy displeasure. Oh say you pardon him," she continued with more earnest entreaty, " he cannot bear
your anger." Her manner expressed what she too well
knew—he *will not*. The king was touched by her
generous intercession, and good-naturedly putting aside
the curls that half-veiled her mantling crimson, with
the weapon he had destined for a harsher service,
and kissing her, he replied, " For thy sake, my pretty
Blanche, and for this kiss on thy blushing cheek, Sir
Pepin is forgiven."

" And now, young man, atone for thy offence—kneel
down before the queen, and let her honour thee by
making a footstool of thy hand, while she permits me
to lift her from the saddle."

The prince did not move. Fastrade bit her lips, and

then suddenly turning her horse's head towards the re-
creant son, and affecting to believe he was dutifully
complying with his father's bidding : " Nay it were
superflous for Sir Pepin to kneel," she said, " your hand
my lord." Charles extended his arms. She laid her
hands upon them, and Pepin at the same instant stooping to avoid her, she placed her foot on his shoulder,
and for a half moment, but long enough to touch the
spring of hate and revenge, her foot rested on that
projection which procured for the unfortunate prince
the descriptive appellation of *Le Bossu.*

Pepin sprang from the insulting touch, but the indignity had been inflicted. The queen had been permitted
to insult and degrade him in the presence of the nobles—of his sisters—of the lady of his love. His
father's hand had been raised to strike him for a petty
offence offered to the queen. A fire was kindled in
his bosom destined to be fed and cherished by those
who were seeking an occasion, and a fit instrument to
avenge their own wrongs.

The whole party now proceeded to the grand saloon
of the palace. It was never safe to offend the queen;
and those who had been betrayed into an involuntary
expression of indignation, if it were only by one of
those exclamations in which the swelling soul finds
vent, were most obsequious in their demonstrations of
respect. The prince seemed lost in gloomy abstraction;
and even the soft inquiring glance of Blanche's eye
met no return from his. " Alas !" she thought, " I
have offended him—I have passed the bounds of maid-
enly reserve, and exposed to public scrutiny the feelings
that were for him alone. I have fallen to the level of
these court ladies who tell their loves to the passing
winds." Ah, poor Blanche ! she fell into a woman's
common error in believing that her lover must be occupied with the sentiment that always occupied her.
Love is to a man like the sunshine of a stormy day,

bright, short, and fitful ; beautiful and pervading while
it lasts, but succeeded by more potent and more enduring passions. The prince was possessed by burning
thoughts of wrong and vengeance, and even Blanche's
influence did not penetrate the thick clouds that were
gathering about him. Happily they both passed unob-
served, for as the party entered the grand saloon, a
beautiful novelty, the production of the superior arts of
the East, attracted every eye. In the centre of the
apartment stood a table that was long afterward preserved as an illustration of the arts, and of the barbaric
taste of the age. It was formed of three burnished and
embossed silver shields. On this table was placed another
gift of the munificent Haroun, a water-clock made of
gold and precious stones. The work-shops of Geneva
and Paris now produce every day more complicated
and perfect mechanism, but then the most polished
court in Europe stood as if entranced gazing on this
wonderful timepiece, and lingering hour after hour to
watch the advent of the little automata who were made
to appear on the dial-plate, and tell the hour by ringing
a bell.

"By St. Denis !" exclaimed the emperor, while he
gazed at the clock with the delight of a child with a
new toy, "this surpasseth the wonders described in
Eastern tales. Tell me, Eginhard, have you ever found
in all your thousand volumes that treat of Rome, and
Greece, and elder Egypt, any thing so curious, so inex-
plicable as this."

"Never, my lord emperor," replied the court-bred
historian.

"And you Alcuin, declare to me, hath any thing
been wrought by science, imagined in poetry, or dreamed
of by philosophy, that matches this marvellous little
creature, who stealeth away our time even while we
watch its passage."

"Nay, my lord emperor, but that seeing is believing,
4

I never would have credited that the skill of man could have produced a piece of mechanism in which beauty and utility are so combined, and carried to such perfection that each seems to have been the only aim of the artist."

"Ah!" exclaimed Charles, delighted to be assured that ignorance made no part of his admiration, "you are right, my wise and learned friends, neither art nor nature ever produced any thing so perfect."

"There, my liege," replied Alcuin, who was accused of the susceptibility to female beauty that seems a part of the poet's nature, "there, my liege, I crave your leave to dissent. This production of Eastern art is indeed wonderful; but how poor, how dull, how insignificant, compared to one of nature's masterpieces!" As he finished speaking, he fixed his eyes on Blanche, who stood leaning pensively against a statue of Ceres,—the comment could not be misunderstood—every eye had followed the direction of Alcuin's, and a murmur of assent ran round the circle. Blanche started from her revery, looked up, and a deep blush suffused her cheek.

"Each look, each motion waked a newborn grace."

The assent became applause, and the caliph's envoy, as if to ratify the truth of the poet's sentiment, advanced, and nearly prostrated himself at Blanche's feet, saying, as he did so, "By our holy prophet, the mighty caliph will deem too much honour done to the most cunning work in gold and precious stone, that it be compared to this masterpiece of Heaven's creation."

It was afterward remembered by many who were present, that at this moment the impatience which the queen's countenance betrayed at Blanche's having become the object of exclusive attention, gave place to a glow of pleasure. It seemed as if a sudden light had flashed upon her. She looked at the Eastern stranger, then at Blanche, and then seemed lost in her own thoughts. The emperor again reverted to the clock, and ordered the pages to place it in the queen's apartment.

" I pray it may not be sent thither," cried the queen, devoutly crossing herself. " I think naught less than the spell of the magi, or the craft of their great master, the evil one himself, could make these images so marvellously to appear and disappear. Or perhaps they are not images, but the little people, the fairies we hear of in our northern provinces ! If my lord would do me grace, let him order it to Blanche's apartment."

" It hath been thought," replied the emperor, but in a tone so doubtful that though the words were afterward weighed in the courtier's nice balance, it could not be decided how much he ventured to imply, " it hath been thought that Blanche had power over *evil spirits ;* but there are none here to try her art, and this matchless gift from our most noble ally would too much honour any subject in our empire. By my faith it shall not be removed from the place where it now stands— these shields of renowned warriors are a worthy pedestal for it. And now, my lords, we must separate to devise some fit return to our brother Haroun, and it shall be our care that he does not surpass us in generosity; albeit we cannot match him in skill."

Late in the evening, Fastrade, who was superstitiously exact in her devotions, retired to her private oratory, a small apartment lighted by a single silver lamp hanging beside a crucifix. Nothing could better illustrate the impotence of external religion than this proud woman, reeking with crime, and teeming with cruel purposes, worshipping the image of perfect benevolence and meekness.

Father Bernard, her spiritual guide, was awaiting her. The emperor tolerated no pampered luxurious priests at his court, and Father Bernard appeared strictly conformed to his edict, which declared it to be " suitable that the soldiers of the church should be inwardly devout, externally learned, chaste in life, and erudite in speech." Father Bernard wore a mask, and had always worn one, in obedience to a vow made by his parents, who had dedicated him in his infancy to a religious profession. With this exception his dress was the uniform of his order ; and according to its strictest rule, there was no approach to embellishment nor superfluity ; and his attenuated person, sickly ·complexion, and faded eye indicated that his life was as austere as his profession. His demeanour was that of a man accustomed to independent and direct proceeding—more knightly, than priestly. Still he had tasked himself to the study of the human mind till he had mastered his subject, and could adroitly thread the subtle passages of that mysterious labyrinth—subdue its strength, and manage its weakness. He had been confessor to the queen for fifteen years ; the depositary of the secrets of a conscience never for a single day void of offence towards both God and man.

Always self-abasing and sycophantic to her priest, Fastrade was more than usually so this evening, and Father Bernard soon suspected that she had sins of more than ordinary magnitude to confess. But whatever solicitude her manner betrayed, it was not indicated by her words when drawing near to the priest, and fixing her dark brilliant eyes on him, she said, " I have summoned you, father, to consult you on a point touching the honour and advancement of our most holy faith." She paused, stammered, and seemed quite at a loss how to proceed.

" Speak on, daughter," said the priest, " the heart is ever bold in a good cause, or, as saith the Scripture, ' the righteous are bold as a lion.' "

Fastrade cast down her eyes and looked much like a detected criminal, but she proceeded—" You have heard of the splendid gifts my husband has received from Haroun al Raschid?"

" Yes."

" You speak coldly. But though Father Bernard, 'not being of the world, worldly,' may despise the costly masterpiece produced by the arts—perchance the magic of the East,—he cannot be indifferent to the unrequitable generosity that has remitted to us the holy standard of Jerusalem, and the sacred keys of the tomb of God?"

" Vain and bootless symbols, madam—the sullied standard of a vanquished power, and the keys of an inaccessible and violated sanctuary! And so far from unrequitable, that they are designed by the wily caliph to purchase the services of the emperor against the Saracens of Spain. These Mahometans resemble us Christians in preferring even infidels to those of their own faith, who differ from them concerning an incomprehensible dogma, or useless rite. But proceed, daughter, your zeal is just in that our monarch should not be surpassed in chivalric courtesy by the caliph."

" Ay, father, but what have we to return?"

" Bauble for bauble—why not the clasp of diamonds that sparkle in native lustre on our master's imperial mantle?—the richest gems of Christendom."

" Of Christendom they may be," replied Fastrade, suppressing a smile at the priest's ignorance, " but the caliph's envoy, now in our palace, wears far richer stones than these."

" Then, why not the silver disk that hangs in the banqueting-hall, which, though graven with all the learning of our astronomers and geographers, is useless here; for, sooth to speak, our warriors can sooner traverse and ravage a province than read its name."

" My lord did speak of this, but Alcuin says that albeit inscribed with all the knowledge of our empire in these sciences, it would but expose our ignorance to

Haroun's learned men, taught by their magicians, doubtless, father, else how should infidels in aught excel Christians ?"

" I commend thy pious inference, daughter, but in this matter of the presents I cannot assist thee farther with my counsel. The treasures of the palace have never arrested my thoughts, nor even attracted my eye. These matters do not pertain to my office, and I cannot see how, as you hinted, they can in any way affect the holy cause of our religion."

" I have not yet fully explained myself. I was willing you should first see our perplexities, in order that you might the better comprehend the relief and pleasure the emperor derives from the device his royal mind has adopted." Once more the queen faltered, and then proceeded with an air of resolution, as if she had nerved herself for a dreaded task : " It is now, I think, holy father, fifteen years since the reputation of your sanctity induced me to select you for the place you have ever since held—I was prostrate with a malady that seemed to be drying up the fountain of life."

" I remember, daughter—your mind had passed from the exaltation of victory to sore conflicts of fear and remorse."—

" Truly, father, but was not the fault—"

" Fault !—call it crime, daughter—things are not changed by names."

" Was not, then, the crime necessary—was not Hunold in open rebellion against the emperor ?"

" Was it *necessary*, madam, that you should cause the royal faith solemnly pledged to Hunold and his confederates to be violated ? Must I remind you that after they had lain down their arms, and received the emperor's pardon on condition that they would pass from shrine to shrine, doing heavy penance at each, you caused them to be seized, their eyes plucked out, their tongues torn away by their roots, and every species of torture inflicted till they were done to death—was this *necessary ?*"

" Spare me, holy father—remember how afterward I repented me ; and that when I discovered that one child of Hunold survived, I revealed the secret to you, and promised to be governed by your counsel?"

" Ay, daughter, and after a night's vigil and ceaseless prayers, I gave you the response of the Deity, that the innocent helpless orphan should be brought to the palace—that she should be your *shrine of expiation*— and that for every good deed done to her you should be assoilzied of one crime, in the black list committed against her father's house ; and that for every wrong of word, or act, a score should be marked against you, that neither prayers, alms, nor masses could efface. This was the inspiration I received, and truly delivered; did I not ?"

" Yes—yes. But why repeat it ? Have I not been obedient to the celestial voice ? has not Blanche been the chief object of my care and bounty ? Have I not seen, as she rode by my side, the eye even of the churl forget its loyalty and fix on her ? and yet have I not put down my queenly rights and womanly vanity, and ever given her the place of honour ? Have I not borne that she should gainsay me when none other dared ? Have I not granted to her intercession, what I refused to all others ? Have I not decked her with gems and costly apparel ? and though her nature resembles the humble flower by whose name the fair beauty is designated by the caliph's envoy"—

" Haroun's envoy ! Has he seen Blanche !"

" Ay, and marked her as the lily of our court. Holy father, if ever criminal did faithfully the appointed penance, I have fulfilled mine. It is for thee, the worthy servant of God, now to strike the balance in which my deeds to the house of Hunold are weighed."

" Madam, the balance cannot be adjusted till death

closes the account. Blanche is still in your power—still to receive good or evil at your hands."

"Good—naught but good, father, as you shall hear."

"Then proceed plainly to the point; for remember, daughter, all self-delusion and hypocrisy vanish before God, as the mist melts away in the eye of the sun."

"Father, I have no fear of communicating to thee, but that thou art always somewhat over-jealous for Blanche."

"Thou knowest, daughter," replied the priest, in a voice that penetrated the queen, "that as it respects the orphan Blanche, I am as a shield appointed by God to defend thy soul from crime, and as a leech to heal it of the wounds that have but one cure—but one, remember. My jealousy is for thee. Proceed, daughter."

"Then, father, hear me, and I call God to witness that what we purpose for this girl is, as I at first declared, for the advancement of our most holy religion; and if we fail in the blessed end we seek, our motive I deem should sanctify our purpose."

"Proceed, madam."

"The great Haroun has ever shown a preference for blonde beauties, delighting to place them beside the dark-eyed girls of the East, and thus to heighten the beauty of each by contrast. The favourites of his haram are the blue-eyed Saxon and the fair Circassian. The caliph's queen has just died, and Haroun has appointed an extraordinary term of mourning to manifest his sincere and uncontrolled grief. Till that has expired, none may hope to succeed to the place of the deceased."

"I see—I see. It is for this place that Blanche is destined."

"I crave thy patience, father. The character of the superb Haroun al Raschid cannot be unknown to thee: generous, enlightened, magnanimous, his only misfortune is to have been born a follower of the false

Mohammed—his only sin, that he tolerates all religions —that he extends an equal favour to the fire-worshipper of Persia, and the servants of the Cross."

"In that doth he truly resemble the Divinity," murmured the priest. The unpriestly remark was either not heard or not understood by the queen, and she continued, "Thou knowest, father, the matchless beauty of Blanche, much as she shrinks from the public gaze (and truly she hath a Turkish love of veils and seclusion), is the theme of every tongue, and hath been sung by minstrels, and far celebrated by the paladins of our court."

"Yes,—and I know that her spirit is fit for its excelling temple, and that wisdom, humility, love, and all the sweet messengers of God dwell there. I know she lives in your licentious court unscathed as were the faithful in the Babylonian's furnace—fragrant and unsullied as the peerless flower to which you have compared her, albeit, like that, rooted in a rank soil."

"True, true, most true, father; and doth not this rare union of outward beauty and inward grace point her out as a fit instrument to convert the caliph to our most holy faith? and it may be to exalt the cross above the crescent in all his wide dominion?"

"And for this doubtful end the child of Hunold is to be expelled from Christendom—to be degraded to the level of the minions of the haram? Madam, the vengeance you poured on Hunold and his nobles was mercy to this. It is better that the eyes should be torn out and the tongue out-rooted than that the whole body should be cast into hell."

"Sir Priest—Sir Priest—you exceed your office, you pass the bounds of my forbearance. You have already made me pay dearly for the vengeance I visited on Hunold and his vile band of conspirators. You have closed up the natural outlet of my hate, and there is a festering and gangrene pool within my heart that can no longer be endured. I might have strangled the chicken in its nest, but you have made me foster the bird to peck at me !"

" Be calm, madam : remember I am but the humble interpreter of the Almighty's will. Thy salvation, or perdition, eternal and irremediable, depended and still depends on thy nurture of this innocent bird."

" Be it so, be it so. I have done well, and now purpose well,—I call all saints to witness for me ! Blanche shall be sent to the caliph with a royal retinue of knights. The emperor wills it,—the safety of the empire demands it :—for know, Sir Priest, that this foolish girl, who has refused the hands of the proudest nobles in the land, loves—nay, dotes on Le Bossu !"

" Ha !" exclaimed the priest. It is sometimes difficult to comprehend the bearing of an exclamation. The queen interpreted Father Bernard's in accordance with the suggestions of her own evil mind.

" It is monstrous," she said, " that perfection should desire to be mated with deformity ; but so, on my faith, it is. I have before suspected she returned his passion,—to-day she betrayed herself in the eye of the whole court. Le Bossu has lain under his father's displeasure for the last month, and to-day he has received indignities that his contumelious spirit will not brook. In brief, there are disaffected, rash, and impetuous youths, such as Baudouin, Arnolphe, and Berenger, the sons of Hunold's confederates, who are ripe for revolt, who are ready to peril their lives to place Le Bossu and the daughter of their renowned leader on the throne. Our warriors worship this misshapen dog ; their silly brains are dazzled with his victories, and they deem his deformity but the sign of preternatural power. Now, holy father, once more I appeal to thee. Is it not prudent to thwart this dangerous union ?—is it not pious to prevent hostility between the son and father ?—to save for holy church the gold that would be spent in most unholy warfare ?—to give this young devotee opportunity and subject for her zeal ?"

"Madam," replied Father Bernard, in a tone of bitter contempt, "if thou art reasoning to convince me, thou art wasting thy breath; if to silence the voice of thy conscience, believe me, thy labour is equally vain. Answer me one inquiry—truly as if thou wert at the confessional: Has the emperor decided to send Blanche to the caliph?"

"He has."

"Then, Fastrade, my ministry with thee is impotent —thy soul is sealed with double damnation; for, as holy church saith, he who repenteth himself of his repentance, and turneth back from the good he purposed, sinketh into remediless ruin, and none can help ·him."

"Nay," exclaimed Fastrade, "I will not believe this, —the church has penances and masses to outweigh the heaviest crimes, and the royal coffers shall be emptied but I will obtain absolution."

"Miserable woman! delude not thyself with this lying doctrine of a perverted religion and false priesthood. I tell thee the soul can only be purified by its own act; the prayers and penances of the universe could avail thee naught. '*Work out thine own salvation*' is the unalterable law written in the word of God, and wrought into the nature that he hath given thee, which makes thee incapable of any other heaven than that within the recesses of thine own soul."

"Within the recesses of my soul!" exclaimed the queen: "*there* is indeed hell!"

"Ay, woman," replied the priest, changing from a slow and somewhat ecclesiastical manner to a tone of deeply excited and personal feeling,—"Ay, woman, a hell of insatiable cruelty—of revenge for unrequited passion—revenge that died not with its victim, but must still be wreaked on the innocent orphan."

" What meanest thou, Sir Priest—have the dead appeared to thee ?"

" Nay, lady, the dead tell no tales, as thou didst well believe when thou gavest orders to thy emissaries to extinguish the last spark of life in Hunold. He never told your secret : his was not a spirit to betray, even to the ear of his merciful and abused sovereign, the folly of the woman who vainly tried to seduce him from his loyalty to the idolized mother of Blanche. Ha, madam! thou stoopest to the ground, and art struck with terror, even as was the guilty king when the prophet appeared to him. Shall I tell thee more ?"

" Nay—hold—it is enough—leave me—"

" To commune with thine own heart !" And with these parting words, uttered in a tone of irony and exultation that ill suited their tender character, Father Bernard withdrew.

Fastrade, when left to herself, and recovered in some degree from the shock and confusion of mind occasioned by the discovery that the secret which she believed to have been buried in Hunold's grave was known to her confessor, vainly endeavoured to account for this mystery. Father Bernard, she knew, had been dedicated to a religious life in his earliest youth, and had never left the recesses of the cloister till, by her command, he was called to the court. He had declared to her that Hunold never told the tale of her dishonour, she had a moral certainty that none but Hunold knew it, and she came to a conclusion, natural to a superstitious mind, that her confessor was endued with supernatural power. It soothed her pride to believe this ; for by managing her religious terrors, and by the more legitimate authority of a superior mind, he had governed her, and made her feel in his presence something like the awe that is inspired by an element over which we have no control   The restraint he imposed had become intol-

erable to her. She would not have scrupled at any
moment, by the foulest means, to have rid herself of
Blanche, but for the belief infused by Father Bernard,
that her own destiny was indissolubly inwrought with
the beautiful orphan's. When the scheme of sending
her to the caliph flashed upon her, it seemed to promise
a compromise with her conscience. Blanche might be
exalted from her lowly dependence to the most magnificent station in the East. This she whispered to
her conscience. Her passions said that she should
deliver herself for ever from the presence of Blanche,
who annoyed her almost equally as a youthful and sur-
passing beauty, and as the living memorial of Hunold.
She should break Le Bossu's heart, too, whom she
hated for his lofty disdain of her, and dreaded as the
future rival of her sons. She had flattered herself that
she could artfully commend this plot to her confessor ;
but some secret misgiving induced her, before making
the communication, to deprive herself of the power of
retracting by putting the cards into the emperor's hands
to deal, having well shuffled them herself.

Pepin, after the insult he had received from the
queen, had felt himself to be a disgraced man, and
avoiding every eye, he had remained solitary in his
own apartment. Till now, love had been the master-
passion of his soul ; its melting influence and gentle
thoughts had pervaded his existence, and seemed to
constitute his life. Now he passed the night in brood-
ing on his own degradation ; and though, when the
image of Blanche glanced athwart the deepening gloom
of his mind, she seemed to him a messenger of heaven,
it was a heaven for ever lost to him. His gallant spirit
had caught the first ray of dawning chivalry, and he
spurned the thought of allying himself to the lady of
his love while he was dishonoured by an unavenged
insult. And how was it ever to be avenged ? His
enemy was a woman—the wife of his father, fenced

5   C

about by his father's power, and guarded by his over-
weening affection. "I might," he thought (misery
opens the door to temptation, and evil thoughts eagerly
rush in), "I might raise a standard of rebellion : I have
many friends, and should soon have many followers :
I know there are unquiet spirits abroad that fear
not even the great emperor's power. My father has
wronged me of late : he has misinterpreted my motives
and misconstrued my actions, and—oh, shame, even to
think of it !—he has raised his hand to strike me. But
get thee behind me, Satan—it is all that fiendish woman.
Till within this last month my father has been godlike
in his unalienable love and unwearying kindness to me.
Oh, I must endure it till Heaven shall grant me deliverance by death !" From these and bitterer thoughts,
a thousand times revolved, he was roused late on the
following day by a note from Father Bernard, requesting the prince's immediate presence in his dormitory.
At first he threw it aside with careless indifference ; but
then his consideration returned to it, and he felt a little
curious to know what the queen's confessor, a priest
whom he had regarded as absorbed in the strictest services and gloomiest abstractions of his religion, could
have to say to him. When the mind is engrossed with
any subject of overpowering interest, it seems as if
every occurrence may have some relation to this subject. Impelled by this feeling, the prince obeyed
Father Bernard's summons.

Father Bernard's name had long been embalmed in
the odour of sanctity. Before leaving the monastery he
had acquired the title of saint, a title seldom accorded
but by the decree of posterity, and after the tomb has
barred out alike the gratitude and the envy of man. At
court he had maintained the seclusion of his monastic
life. He was never suspected as the author of the
queen's mysterious kindness to Blanche ; and as she
continued audacious in her crimes, it was believed that

her confessor's indulgence was commensurate to her demands. The mischievous and exploded dogma of political economy, " that private crimes are public benefits," then exactly adjusted the scales by which the church was made to profit by the sins of the offender; and it was believed that the confessor heavily assessed the emperor's coffers to redeem his queen's lapses.

The prince found Father Bernard impatiently awaiting him; and after bolting his door, and securing himself from every mode of intrusion, he proceeded, without preface or apology for betraying the secrets of the confessional, to impart the communication he had received from the queen. The prince heard him in silence, but his deathlike paleness, his fixed eye, and his quivering lip betrayed the indignation and anguish that overpowered him.

The priest paused for a moment and then said, " If I mistake not, my lord, in believing that you have a feeling more tender than pity for this helpless maiden, you will make an effort for her rescue!"

" An effort! Sir Priest I would give my life to save her from a thousandth part of the evil that threatens her—but what can I do? I have lost my father's favour —the meanest churl in the empire has more weight in his councils than I—I am a disgraced and fallen man."

" Nay, my lord prince, disgraced you cannot be but by your own act, and if you are fallen, why rise and return tenfold the blow that cast you down."

" Holy father, do you remember against whom you counsel resistance—true the queen is the instigator of this mischief, but is she not protected by an unassailable barrier?"

" Ah well!" replied Father Bernard, in a tone of mingled pique and disappointment, " I was deluded—I believed you loved Blanche."

" Loved her! and so I do, with a devotion that the imagination of a cloistered priest never conceived. But

think more justly of the Lady Blanche than to believe
she would accept a lover stained with crime."

" Crime, my lord ! Circumstances alter our relations,
and modify our actions. He who takes the life of
another in defence of his own is not accounted a mur-
derer.   And is he criminal who resists the malice and
tyranny that crushes him ?—who rescues the innocent
and helpless from the most accursed fate ?"

" Ah !" exclaimed the prince, " my sword almost
leaps from the scabbard at the thought of it—but the
way !—the way ! My father, till these few days past,
has always been kind and generous !"

" Kind and generous !" retorted the priest with a
scoffing smile, " while you fulfilled and never opposed
his wishes—while your hand, never weak nor unwilling,
fought his battles—while you were content to return
from the hard-fought field and live in his eye without
honour or reward—to be a waiter-on of the court—to
be called *Le Bossu*—to ride beside our lady Fastrade on
gala days, and patiently take her insults,—and doubtless he will again be kind and generous if you will
tamely be trodden under foot of the queen, and quietly
sit with your hands folded, and see the helpless lady
depart for the caliph's haram."

" No more, Sir Priest—tell me what may be done—
I will think on't."

" Nay, you must not think—the bold resolve and
bolder act must go together—the present fortune must
be taken at its flood. All is prepared to your hand—
the emperor has issued orders for reorganizing the
forces just disbanded. Many of his leaders are disaffected. They have been outraged by the audacious
queen, and are burning for revenge. The Saxon
provinces are in open revolt. They have burnt their
churches, driven off their Christian priests—sacrificed
the bishops to their divinities, and returned with pas-
sionate devotion to the worship of their gods. The

Saracens, led by the infidel hero Abdelmélec, have passed the Ebro and the Pyrenees—have daringly advanced to Narbonne and burned its fauxbourgs. The spoils of the emperor's richest provinces decorate the mosque of Cordova, and his Christian subjects are the captives and slaves of the infidels. There was a time when the emperor would have beaten down these rebels and enemies at opposite extremes of his empire, but his vigour is now touched by advancing age, and relaxed by long prosperity." Father Bernard spoke with the rapidity and decision of a man accustomed to govern the decisions of others. The priest seemed as utterly gone and forgotten as if the character had been the light masquerade of an hour. " If," he said in conclusion, " if, my lord Pepin, you remain passive, your ruin is certain—it is resolved on—what remonstrance can turn the queen from a purposed mischief? She knows too well the story of your noble grandfather to risk subjecting her sons to your rivalship? She knows that Charles Martel, left by his father immured in a prison, without the legal inheritance of one rood of land, superseded his legitimate brothers, and extended his dominions far beyond his father's limits.

" You are the son of the great Charles—this is all our warriors demand—you have his eagle-eye, his front, his voice—this to them will be the signal of victory and glory. What care they if your brothers can boast a legitimate birth! This is a matter for priests, not warriors. It is enough for them that you can traverse a province, while our young master, Louis le Debonnaire, is counting his beads. What say ye, my lord ? This night the sons of Hunold's confederates—would to God he had a son to revenge him—but they were all strangled by the queen's order—all his brave boys !" For the first time the priest faltered, his voice was choked with emotion—" Pardon me, Sir Pepin," he said, " will you meet these young men at the altar in

the great chapel, and there receive their oaths of
fealty ?"

It was for Blanche's sake alone that Pepin had at
first listened, but as the priest had proceeded he had
touched the spring of ambition, and of that love of power
that is the master passion of most men's minds. It was
the possible master of Charles' great empire, whose eye
and cheek were now lighted with a brightness from the
kindling fires of his soul. Still he hesitated to speak
the word that must sever him from the parent stock.

"We waste time, my lord," urged the priest. "Are
you for this noble enterprise, or must I seek another leader
who will dare to rescue Blanche—and deserve her ?"

"And who are you," exclaimed Pepin, all the passions in his frame aroused, "who are you that dare to
speak to me of giving Blanche to another ?"

The priest replied with perfect calmness, for he had
been schooled in the fires of a living martyrdom.
"Come near to me, young man, and you shall hear a
name that these walls must not echo." Father Bernard
pronounced the name.

"Righteous Heaven !" exclaimed the prince—"Is
this so—can it be so ?"

"Do you doubt it ?" asked the priest, with the assured
smile of one who can command belief.

"Nay, I cannot; it furnishes the key to a mystery,
insolvable till now—I am yours—I submit myself to
your guidance with one single condition—our friends
shall swear to hold my father's life inviolate."

"Your father's—granted—but not Fastrade's. May
I live to see the dogs eat that Jezebel ! You meet us in
the chapel, my lord ?"

"Yes."

"You now know, my lord, why you received so im-
perative an order from the emperor this morning, to
hold no communication with the Lady Blanche, public
or private. He feared to have the decree against her

reach your ear. He knew your noble nature too well to believe you would submit passively to it. But go now to her saloon ; the night is so dark you may escape observation. Ah, how often have I watched your steps thither, when you thought the eye of Heaven could scarcely penetrate your secresy. But be cautious. On your life do not betray my secret. Remember that in fifteen years no tone of the voice, nor cast of the eye has answered to the gushings of my heart, though there have been moments when I have felt as if every drop of blood was drained from it. Farewell, my lord. Inspire the poor girl with courage. Assure her that her safety is first to be cared for—to-night we will consider the means. I will remain at the altar till the last lingering devotee has left the chapel, and then, by Heaven's good aid, we'll weave a fatal mesh for our enemies !"

CHAPTER II.

"Amo te solo, te solo amai,
Tu fosti il primo, tu pur sarai
L'ultimo oggetto che adorerò."

Metastatio.

FASTRADE had, to quote the language of Father Bernard, made the Lady Blanche her "shrine of expiation ;" and like many others who render a forced homage, she had loaded the altar with gifts, while she neglected the spirit of the giver. A saloon and contiguous bedchamber were assigned to the beautiful orphan, arranged according to her own taste, and luxuriously furnished by the queen. At one extremity of the saloon was a deep recess, lighted by a window that extended from the ceiling to the floor, and filled with rare plants arranged on semicircular steps. Before these was a silver fountain which was supplied by an aqueduct, and could be made to play at pleasure into a marble basin, over which a statue of one of Flora's nymphs was bending, apparently in the act of filling a watering-pot. Suspended from the ceiling by silver chains, and half hidden by the flowers, were cages, whose little prisoners sent forth such a wild harmonious chorus, that it seemed as if their gentle warder must, by the artful position in which she had placed them, have beguiled them into the belief that they were in their own sweet woods. Opposite this sylvan scene, and reflecting it almost as distinctly as the more perfect reflectors of our own time, was a polished silver mirror, hung on each side with embossed sconces of the same precious metal. Instead of the ottomans and sofas of a modern drawing-room, piles, or couches of cushion were placed at convenient distances, covered with silk " from farthest Ind," richly embroidered with flowers and imitations, and fantastic caricatures of animals. Beneath the silver mirror was a marble slab, supported by sea-nymphs, and covered with the choicest shells ; and in the centre of the apartment was a small ivory table inlaid with silver, with an oriental lamp in the centre constantly burning, and diffusing sweet odours ; beside it an hourglass, in which the sands of time were literally golden ; and dispersed around, a few manuscript books beautifully illuminated.

Our readers must imagine the apartment we have described occupied by a single tenant, Ermen, the faithful nurse and serving-woman of the Lady Blanche, a hardy, frank, good-humoured looking person of the certain age of forty. " Nothing more uncertain than the certain age ;" but not with those of low degree. Time had notched its revolutions on Ermen's honest face, and with less agreeable records of its progress, had impressed there acute sense and kind dispositions.

" I marvel that my lady does not return," thus she soliloquized—" it takes but short space to say yes—but heaven help us ! still shorter to say no. He will not say that word to her—bless his great heart—he never yet spoke it to aught of womankind—after all, if worst come to worst, it would not be so bad if my poor lady would make the best of it—but it's only little folk, and not great ones, that have the skill to make the best of a bad bargain. If all that our minstrels report is true, this renowned caliph is of a right noble temper —but then he is a *paynim*—and our royal queen is a *Christian !* Truly, there is much virtue in a name !" Here Ermen's cogitations were broken by the opening of the door, and her mistress entered, her person enveloped in a veil, which having cast aside, she threw herself on a couch, pressed her hands to her temples, throbbing with repressed emotion, which now burst forth without control. " It was in vain then, my lady ?" said Ermen.

" Oh, utterly in vain, Ermen !"

" You were not admitted to the private audience room ?"

" Yes."

" But the queen was there ?"

" No."

" You were faint and faltering then, and did not press your suit ?"

" Nay, I poured out my very soul—I entreated—I knelt—but it is of no use, Ermen. The emperor is resolved—his word is pledged. The cries of the victim for succour, who is already delivered to the executioner, are bootless."

" St. Genevieve aid us ! It passeth my comprehension that the emperor should deny you, my lady—you whom no one can deny—not even the queen ; so that it is currently said in court that you wear a talisman

that can unfiend the fiends. But the devil, that has
ruled her in all things else, has now got the upper
hand in this too. Our good lord emperor deny you,
indeed! Nay, it is the queen. There is no mischief
abroad but she brews it. Why were the fifty cottages
burnt at Mens, but because a poor churl refused to
the queen the hawks she had trained for my Lady Bertha! And the artisans of our city must all be thrown
into dungeons, forsooth, because one of their number
had offended my lady queen. I marvel at our great
sovereign! Though I am a woman that says it, no
good or honour ever came to a man, high or low, by
being ruled by a woman. Has not he suffered the
noblest in the land to have their eyes plucked out at
the queen's order, and now my Lord Pepin has offended
her, and that is to be wrested from him that is far dearer
than eyes or soul either. Think you the prince is acquainted with this journey of ours, my lady?"

"I believe not, Ermen—it is yet a secret."

"I believe not, too, or we should have heard from him
before this. He has a bold heart and a quick hand.
Beshrew me! if he submits without striking a blow."

Blanche rose for the first time from her disconsolate
position; "You do not mean, Ermen," she exclaimed,
"that he would attempt resistance—he cannot be so
foolish—so frantic!"

"I do not know what you count foolishness, my lady,
but my Lord Pepin is not of a spirit to sit down and
weigh his strength before he resists attack."

"But, Ermen, his father's power is as irresistible as
the tides of the ocean."

"It may be; but do you think my Lord Pepin would
let the waves of the ocean overwhelm him without buf-
feting them. He never quietly submitted to any injustice. He is lion-hearted, and, as they say of that royal
beast, kind and fostering to every thing weak and powerless. Ah, he is noble and gentle, and save in that small

matter of the rising on his back, perfect, soul and body ; and there, I verily believe, he was smitten of a demon, who could not bear the world should have the pattern of a perfect man."

Ermen's praises were fallen on an ear attuned to them, and though the keys were struck by an unskilful hand, Blanche had gradually subsided into the silence of a greedy listener. Ermen, like a careful nurse, who has tried the admission of a little light upon an afflicted vision, and found it to solace rather than irritate, ventured a little more. " Cheer up, my blessed young lady," she said ; " it seems pretty dark now, but I, that have lived to more than twice your age, have seen many a cloudy morning turn into a bright day,— Ah, I remember that time your father's beautiful house was burned, and all his pleasant places laid waste. I thought life would be one wail and sad lament, but we have had many a bright hour since. Now, my lady, I must leave you, and I pray you to take my counsel,—hope for the best—nay, expect it—that will keep down the black vapours."

Poor Blanche, when left alone, found it (as others have) far easier to approve advice than to be governed by it. She rose from her seat and went to the window —the night was shutting in dark and threatening. As she turned her eyes towards the heavens she saw one planet shining through the parted clouds with undimmed lustre. To a thoughtful mind it is natural to perceive a relation between the outward and the inward world. " The clouds have hidden all but this one beaming light from me," she said. " Beautiful image of the love of God, that penetrates the thick darkness around me, and will sustain me in my utmost need." She might have been mistaken, at this moment, for a saint holding communion with Heaven, or rather for a spirit of heaven, that had just touched upon the sorrows, but never known the sins of humanity. Her rich tresses,

wreathed in curls, and infolded by many a braid, were
fastened by a cross of pearls, so as to define perfectly
the Grecian outline of her brow and head.   Her white
muslin dress, fastened by a girdle of the same pure
gems, harmonized with a celestial character, and gave
to her figure, relieved as it was against the deep crimson window-hanging, a spiritual aspect.   Her thoughts
were soon brought back from their heavenward flight,
and weighed down by the cares of earth.   " But for
the dismal memory of his loneliness, she said, I might
endure it—who shall console *him* when I am gone?
who shall sooth his irritated spirit? who shall watch
against the demons that torment him?—it was my
mission?—"

" It is not finished, Blanche," said a voice that re-
sponded to her low but audible tones, and turning round
she saw, by the light of the little lamp, that the prince
had entered without rousing her from her abstraction.

" Oh, my lord, it is," she replied, in a voice almost
choked with emotion—" and you have yet to learn
the cruel decree—and to endure it."

" Nay, my love, not yet to learn it, nor would I endure it, if all the fiends of hell, instead of one, had
decreed it.   What! suffer you to be driven out of
Christendom, and delivered up to be the minion of the
infidel caliph.   Did you deem that my soul had been
trampled out of me, Blanche ?"

" My lord, you know I never had one evil or demean-
ing thought of you ; but who has dared to inform you
of what I have been so sternly commanded to keep a
secret ?"

" It signifies not who—be tranquil on that head, and
Blanche, my love, keep down your womanish spirit,
and listen to what I have to tell you—that she-wolf
has well stirred the stream, but she will yet find herself foiled of her victim."

" Ah me ! my lord, do not raise hopes that must be

crushed. The darkness will only be more terrible after the flash of light has passed—but hark—some one knocks—it is not safe for you to be seen here."

The knocking was repeated, and proved to proceed from the faithful Ermen, who being in nothing excluded from her mistress' confidence, was immediately admitted.

She whispered to her lady, " I have a private message to you from the emperor."

" Speak it aloud, Ermen, my lord Pepin knows all."

" Blessings on the free tongue that told him. I fear not now to tell you the emperor's behest. My heart did sorely misgive me, for I know it the nature of the timid deer to fly to the covert. But my lord will counsel bolder measures."

" I know, my good Ermen, you would fain have a stouter spirit than your poor mistress, to rely on," said Blanche, with a faint smile. " But tell us quickly, what message do you bring from the emperor ?"

" As I left you, my lady, I was met by a page from the emperor, who commanded my presence. As we went along the gallery I fished from him, that since you left the audience-chamber no person had been admitted—the queen herself had been put off, and the emperor had been heard walking up and down, as I, or any of the commons would, with a worried mind ; so I thought to myself this augured well for my dear lady, for when the emperor gets in a ferment, and is left to himself, he works off pure, like good liquor."

" Proceed to the message, honest Ermen," said the prince.

" He bade me tell you, my lady,—Heaven grant I may not forget the words—he tried to write them, but everybody knows that, for all his getting up o' nights to practise, and Master Alcuin's teaching, he is yet not the clerk to do it."

6

"The message, Ermen," repeated the prince, impatiently—"the message."

"My lord, I crave your patience: I must tell a story my own way,—if I drop a stitch the whole ravels out. Where was I? ah! at the writing. Well, he scrawled and scribbled, and spoiled parchment enough for one of my lady's heartfull criss-crossed letters to you, my lord. I had a great mind to snatch it from the floor and smuggle it into my pocket against a time of need. Now I have got to the right place, and I'll make even work of the rest of it. The emperor bade me tell you there is still one—oh skies above! I have forgotten the word—alterative—no, that is not it. I'll leave it out. If the great people would leave out half their words, we simple folk could understand them far better."

Patience was like to have her perfect work; but Blanche, who well understood her woman's infirmities, cast a deprecating look at the prince, and she was permitted to proceed without interruption.

"The upshot of it is, my lady, that the emperor says he will take back his royal word to the ambassador, provided you will profess yourself a nun"—

"Now the blessing of our holy mother Mary be upon him!" exclaimed Blanche.

"Nay—nay, Blanche"—

"My lord, and you, my lady, hear me out. There is something far harder for you to do than to drop the but half-lifted veil between you and the world: you are to persuade my Lord Pepin to retire to the monastery of Pruim, of which the emperor will make him Abbé. You are allowed to-morrow to make your decision whether you will be the bride of Heaven—or of the caliph."

"My decision is already made. My lord—my dear lord—hear me. Away from you, it is all exile—desolation, but not all degradation. In leaving the world I leave only you—for you are the world to me. We but end this brief life a little sooner: at the best it would have been a few more hopes—blighted, it may be; a few more years—a past and useless dream when they are ended—Nay, if you will not hear me out," she concluded, covering her face with her hands, " think from what I escape !"

" Blanche, this is idle; your vows are plighted to me, and I swear by all the saints in heaven, that Omnipotence alone shall wrest you from me ! Leave us, Ermen."

" I'll come again for your answer, my lady, shall I not ?" inquired Ermen, while she indicated by a slight compression of her under lip her secret and very satisfactory conjecture as to which of the lovers was like to obtain the victory in the pending controversy. Her mistress bowed assent, and she withdrew.

" Think you, my beloved," said the prince, passionately pressing Blanche's hand to his lips, " that I will supinely yield this, after it has been promised to me again and again, in smiles and in tears ? Never !"

" Oh, I well know, never voluntarily; but our fate"—

" Pardon me, dearest, for cutting off the words from your sweet lips,—but I read far differently the book of our fate. I see inscribed there banded friends, trusty followers, a crushed enemy, victory and empire, and my peerless Blanche sharing with me the throne of the West."

There was a fearful ecstasy in her lover's eye, that shot terror through Blanche's gentle soul. " My dear lord !" she said, in a voice of such deprecating tenderness that the prince saw he had alarmed her.

" Pardon me, dearest Blanche," he replied; " I should more cautiously have disclosed to your timid spirit the bright future that is opening upon us; you are confounded by the sudden light."

" I do not comprehend you, my lord."

" My gentle girl, you could not comprehend the

means, were I to detail them, by which your freedom
and safety are to be secured till you permit your lover
to put the bridal ring on your finger, and Heaven and a
good cause shall enable him to place a crown on your
head."

" A crown, my lord! Has insult and wrong vanquished your virtue ?—do you purpose rebellion against
your sovereign—your *father ?*"

" My ties to my sovereign, Blanche, have become
weak as my obligations have diminished. My father
severed for ever the bond that united us when he saw
me suffer the touch of that fiend's foot, and was silent."

" Ah, my lord, human imperfection should be borne
with and forgiven. Your father is blinded and perverted
from his noble nature by the queen."

" But he *is* perverted, Blanche, and he, or you and I
and others, must suffer the consequences. On whom
should they fall,—the guilty or the innocent ?"

" Leave that to Heaven's judgment. But be assured,
that nothing God reckons evil can fall on him who is
shielded by innocence. Do not part with that defence,
my lord."

" Oh innocence ! it is only for the sucking babe and
you, sweet saint, who live at the gate of heaven. As to
right and wrong, how can we, who are groping in the
dark and tangled passages of life, say what is right and
what is wrong ? We can only discriminate colours
accurately, Blanche, in full light."

" My lord, we are only perplexed when we look
without, where men impose false colours to confound
our enslaved senses. Within is God's own light—
always clear and bright unless we sacrilegiously dim
it with our evil passions."

" This is useless, my love. He who is driven to the
brink of a precipice, must not be over-nice in discussing
the only mode of escape. What would you have me
do ?—quietly submit to see you the proffered bride of

the caliph? I am not yet the poor slave to suffer that !"

"But remember, we have an alternative—the peace and sanctity of the cloister. Oh, my lord, it is both sin and folly to reject it."

"Blanche! Blanche!" replied the prince in a tone that betrayed the irritated pride of the lover. "It seems right easy for you to transfer your heart to the cloister. But thus it ever is with your sex: your affections are so soft and fusible, that they can be recast at any moment; religion offers the mould, and the change is at once perfected: the lover of this hour is the devotee of the next."

"My lord, you do us much injustice. The disappointments, the reverses, the struggles, the anguish of a woman's love must be pent up in her own heart—no human eye may see it—no human ear may hear it. Man proclaims his, and it escapes in its publication,— and he follows some new idol: it may be wealth, or fame, or power, or glory. But she who truly loves, never loves but once; and it is because her affection is pure, disinterested, and self-devoting, that it may be— not transferred, my lord, but succeeded by a sentiment holy, illimitable, and eternal."

"My dear Blanche, on my bended knees I pray your forgiveness for my slander. But do you think, while you are convincing me of the value of my treasure, you are preparing me to acquiesce in being rifled of it? What do they offer us? My peerless Blanche, the most beauteous flower that ever opened to the eye of the sun, may be permitted to wither in the cloister's tomb—perchance to wear out vigils in prayers and penances for my Lady Fastrade! And I, who have led hosts to victory, and will again—so help me, God— I am to be promoted to the abbacy of Pruim! Or, if I would play the saint, I may, perhaps, like my meek uncle Carloman, tend the sheep of the monks of Mont

Cassin, dress the food for their pampered palates, hide
my royal birth, and be scourged by every valet in the
monastery. Nay, by the mass! I will rather follow in
the footsteps of Charles Martel, and snatch the crown
destined for my legitimate brother's brows, though,
after I have won, deserved, and enjoyed it, the kind
priests shall say of me, as they say of him, that my soul
is doomed to eternal torments, not only as the recom-
pense of my own sins, but that I may burn for the good
of others, who step to heaven over my head! But my
dear Blanche," added the prince, changing his voice to
a mild and affectionate tone as he caught the sad and
half-reproachful expression of her face, "I should not
cloud these last moments—this is our last parting—our
last separation: to-morrow you shall be apprized of the
means by which your safety is to be secured till He
who has willed that our hearts should grow together
in adversity, shall reunite us in prosperity. Then,
dearest, you shall see him swaying multitudes who has
hitherto been the slave of another's will. Oh, Blanche,
will it not be sweet to share together wealth, power, and
honour?"

"Ah, my lord! your love was enough for me; other
wealth, power, or honour I never coveted, nor do I now.
Alas! that little stream that flowed so freshly and so
quietly, giving forth no sound to others, but making
such music in our ears, and nurturing flowers always
blooming and always sweet—that little stream will soon
be forgotten—my lord hath launched on the ocean of
ambition. Man may wile away his unripe youth on
that pure stream; but once embarked on that tempest-
tossed ocean, he never returns. Alcuin has read me of
such things in the old poets: now I believe it, for I
feel it." Blanche laid her head on her lover's bosom,
overpowered by feelings that silence and tears only
could adequately express; and he, for a few moments
at least, felt that a love like hers, that disdained all

accessories, was sufficient for him, and he told her so.
"My dearest Blanche," he said, "if there were a spot
in the wide world whither we could fly and remain un-
molested, not a thought or desire of mine would stray
beyond it. But there is no such haven for us: nothing
remains for me but resistance, or submission to have my
sole light extinguished. Then what would life be to
me?—the bitter draught it was before you made me
love it. I felt myself degraded below the standard of a
man: you have raised me above my fellows—you
have made *Le Bossu* the envy of the handsomest and
noblest paladins of our court." Never, in all the tenderness of their confidence, had the prince before
alluded to his deformity. Blanche perceived that his
frame thrilled at the word. "You wrong me, Blanche,"
he continued, "to doubt my exclusive devotion to you.
I have enlisted in this very enterprise you so deprecate
for your sake."

"For mine, my lord? Oh, then abandon it, for no
good can come of it. If, as the heathen priests of Odin
hold, the temple is desecrated in which a lance has been
permitted to enter, is not the filial bosom polluted in
which one disobedient thought has risen? In sooth,
it is far better to yield to evil than to inflict it—to embrace the cross than to be crushed by it."

"These are a woman's timid thoughts: dismiss them,
Blanche. Our affairs are complicated with others—I
have embarked, and cannot turn back if I would. But
the victory achieved, and my Blanche shall be to me
what the image of the goddess Bertha is to the Saxon—
no evil passion shall confront you—hate and revenge
shall vanish before you—and spears and shields fall to
the ground!"

It is not in the nature of a tender, devoted woman
to oppose long the bold decision of a resolved man.
Her power must be reserved for his hours of happiness
or suffering. Blanche ceased to resist her lover's deter-

mination, even by her meek persuasion, and their conversation soon subsided into those interchanges of
expressions of deep and eternal love, beautiful to them,
but untranslatable into the vulgar tongue.

While they were imprudently protracting their in-
terview, Ermen was killing the time in walking up and
down a gallery that communicated with various apart-
ments of the palace. There she met her gossips, managed the easy key to their confidence, heard all their
mistress's secrets (and, in the licensed court of Charlemagne there was as abundant materials for scan-
dal, as in the French courts of a later date), but never
indulged them with a hint of her lady's affairs.   As it
is difficult to decide which is most agreeable to a real
scandal-monger, hearing, or telling tales—there is no
reason to suppose Ermen's companions were dissatis-
fied, though one after another dropped off and left her,
wishing that lovers would bethink them that there were
more than two people in the universe.   Suddenly her
attention was arrested by hearing her mistress' name
pronounced by a voice that issued from a guard-room,
at the extremity of the gallery.   No one, Ermen
thought, had a right to speak aught of her mistress,
that she had not a right to hear ; and she instantly
placed herself in a convenient position for her ear to
do its duty.

" I doubt the queen mistakes," said one of the
parties, "in supposing the prince to be in the Lady
Blanche's saloon, but for all that we must maintain our
watch."

"Ah, Valdrad and Hardouin !" thought Ermen, "well-
chosen men for spies."

" You have a snug warm birth here, Valdrad," continued the first speaker.   " I am chilled through in the
court.   There is a snow-storm without—a pretty time
of year to begin winter, truly.   Come, change posts
with me for a little while."

" With all my heart, though on my faith, Hardouin, I like not this trust of our gracious lady. I had rather make love than mar it. I had rather the prince would escape than be caught in a net of my spreading."

" Curse on that cowardly fashion of yours, Valdrad, as if you could lighten a sin by lamenting it, when you have not the virtue to eschew it. Now I take quite another way to hush my conscience. There must be a certain amount of sin enacted on this mortal stage, and he is the boldest fellow who cheerfully bears his part of the burden. For example, somebody must do this villanous duty for the queen. The prince cannot escape her. She has stirred up the emperor's heart, which is of itself as clear as this cup of Rhenish, against him ; and without our means, and even if she does not now detect the prince in this violation of the emperor's commands, she will contrive some mode to provoke him to resistance—his ruin follows of course."

" I am not sure of that. There is nothing that, if left to himself, the emperor will not remit to Le Bossu. But come, Hardouin, lend me your watch-coat, and I'll to the outer post." Accordingly he sallied forth, but immediately returned, saying, " It's as dark as Erebus. How am I to depose to the emperor that I have seen the prince issue from the Lady Blanche's saloon, when I cannot see my hand before my face ? Stay, a lucky thought strikes me. This damp snow—as clever a material to take the measure of a man's foot as can well be contrived—covers the court two inches deep. Not an impress will be made upon it till morning, unless it be by the prince. He shall betray himself. The emperor is the lark of the palace. The queen has nothing to do but to point to the footsteps from her window,— a hint to her is enough."

" Bravo, Valdrad ! They say the devil deserts his followers at their utmost need, but our lady queen finds him as true as steel. Here is a fall of snow to befriend her, and a witty-pated fellow to teach her how to profit by it."

Ermen had heard enough. She left the friends to quaff their Rhenish, and hastened to her lady's apartment, where she immediately communicated the amount of her information. The prince perceived his danger, and saw no way of escaping it. An arrest, at this stage of his affairs, would be fatal. Blanche, habituated to depend on the fidelity and experience of her serving-woman, appealed to her. " Dear, good Ermen," she said, " can you devise no way to save my lord from this peril ?"

" Indeed, my lady, I cannot. Would that he had that winged horse our minstrels sing of, that touches never a hoof to the ground, but posts through the welkin like an eagle——stay, let me think."—Ermen paused, tasked her wits, and a bright gleam shot through her little gray eye, as she exclaimed, " Yes, there is a way." She opened a door that led into a vestibule, and an outer door. " It is still as dark as Egypt," she said, and then, after a moment's awkward hesitation, she added, " you must pardon me, my lord. The manliest and noblest must condescend to their necessity. The royal lion was helped out of the net by the mouse. Say your parting words, my lord, and come hither ; but you, my lady, stay there." The parting of the lovers seemed to Ermen needlessly protracted——to them, fraught as the future was with uncertainty and danger, it was most brief, and such as seems to " press the life from out young hearts."

Blanche, in spite of Ermen's counsel, which had a woman's wit in it, would have followed her lover to the threshold ; but Ermen hastily closed the inner door, and left her mistress to guess at the modus operandi by which her lover's safety was to be effected.

Effected it was, and the prince kept his appointment in the chapel, and was animated by the zeal and harmony of his confederates. Father Bernard, who still maintained his incognito, was the soul of the conspiracy. All deferred to his superior knowledge, and agreed to be governed by his bold, yet prudent counsels. The plan of the conspirators was, not to attempt to overthrow the power of the emperor—this did not enter into the hope, perhaps not the wish, of the boldest among them; but to elevate a standard under which the wronged and disaffected might rally. To establish, under the prince, their favourite leader, a rival and independent government, and to secure to him wholly, or in part, the succession of the empire.

CHAPTER III.

"Though an ill mind appear in simulation,
And for the most, such quality offends,
'Tis plain that this, in many a situation,
Is found to further beneficial ends."

Rose's Orlando Furioso.

FORTUNE, always delighting to ensnare human credulity and play with human hopes, seemed to lavish her smiles on the conspirators. The queen had received the report of her emissaries, and was eager to enjoy her malignant triumph at the detection of the prince in a violation of his father's commands. She went earlier than usual to the emperor's dressing-room, which overlooked the inner court of the palace. He was dressing while, according to his daily custom, he was listening to the reading of one of the learned men of his court. Charles was avaricious of time, and of time only, and appears, from the brevity of his toilette, to have thought with a witty anti-Brummel of our own day, that the

poorest employment a man can have, is that of looking
at his own face. Fastrade found a pretext to dismiss
the reader. "Rely upon it, my lord," she said, as soon
as they were alone, "you have acted with your usual
wisdom in striking at the root of this love-affair of your
son with my ungrateful Blanche. The Scripture saith,
wind, rain, and snow are God's messengers, and I think
this snow is sent thus untimely to inform you Le Bossu
has violated your command—his love has overruled
his duty: look there, my lord!" The emperor made
no reply; his keen eye was fixed on the traces of
the footsteps to which Fastrade had directed it. She
deemed her point secured. "It is most certain," she
continued, "that Pepin has abused your confidence :
but do not be harsh with him. An arrest for a few
weeks, till Blanche is far beyond his reach, will prevent any further rashness on his part."

The emperor still made no reply, but sounded a
bell: a servant appeared. "Send Eric hither," he said.
Eric was the court shoemaker, and, like all the other
masters of the domestic arts then in use, he lived within
the palace walls. He was instantly in waiting. "Eric,"
said his royal master, "go measure me the prints of yon
footsteps on the snow. Return and tell me, as I think
you can, whose shoe has made them."

"If it can be told, my lord emperor, it is I that can
tell it, for I have fitted every foot at your majesty's
court for the last ten years."

"I rely upon you. Fear not to report truly,—fear
nothing but to deceive me."

"It is right, where justice demands punishment," said
the queen, "to proceed, as you ever do, my lord, with
scrupulous caution; otherwise we might surely in this
case trust to our eyes: no one can mistake the track
of Le Bossu's almond-shaped foot."

"Almond-shaped! I know not what you mean by
almond-shaped, my lady; but if in aught to disparage

the shape of Pepin's foot, by the mass you greatly err.
His foot is as fairly formed, and as well set on, as any
lord's, or lady's either, in the court. It is like his
mother's, and that was never matched in beauty by any
foot of flesh and blood."

Fastrade reddened with vexation (her own little
foot was her pet idol), but she knew too well the art of
managing, to chide when she was chidden; and reserv-
ing her resentment for some more auspicious moment,
she remained rather awkwardly silent. Eric soon re-
appeared, with a last in his hand, which looked like an
unshaped block of wood, as broad as it was long.
" The track, an please your majesty," said Eric, " is
Ermen's, the Lady Blanche's Gallic serving-woman. I
have measured it with her last: you see, my lady, there
is no other woman's like it—so broad, and flat on the
instep—short-vamped and square-heeled."

" Enough, Eric," said the emperor, evidently agree-
ably surprised. " I am satisfied—here is gold for your
trouble—say nothing of the errand I sent you on. And,
good Eric, I commend you for being at your stall at this
early hour: I like no drones in my hive. My Lady
Fastrade," continued the emperor, when the menial
had left the apartment, " you have been somewhat over-
alert with your suspicions."

" If so, my dear lord, it was an over-zeal in your service: I ask no obedience from Le Bossu—he violates no
duty to me."

" Nor to me either. On my soul, I believe I have
wronged him—and in matters far more serious than
this love-passage. By Heaven! I had rather be a
duped and credulous fool, than a tyrant father. Leave
me, Fastrade—I have business with my secretaries."

" I will leave you, my lord, but not in anger with me.
You must first forgive me for loving you too well, and
serving you too anxiously. Simpleton that I was! I
deemed it my duty to tell all that was in my heart to

my royal lord and master, but, in future, so far from troubling you with my sad suspicions of Le Bossu, whatever outrage and obloquy he may heap upon me, I will remember that the lot of woman is on me—that I must live—suffer—and be silent!"

"Oh woman, woman!" thought Charles, "what a power of words you take to express your vow of silence;" but he vouchsafed no reply to her meek resolution, uttered as if she were the most oppressed and enduring of women. His feelings had taken a new and strong direction, and he suffered her to depart without one apologetic word or look. His generous spirit was stung with a sense of injustice to his son, and he determined to repair it on the instant, by giving him a signal proof of his confidence.

One week earlier this step would have saved Charles from everlasting regrets, and the prince from crime and sorrow; but neither monarch nor subject can control the consequences of evil actions. "As ye sow, so shall ye reap," is the just and immutable law.

The reader must readily have conjectured the mode by which Ermen evaded the peril that menaced the prince. He was allowed no choice of the means, and scarcely time to feel how much more ludicrous than heroic was his position. The night that followed he had passed without sleep, and in anxious deliberations, and when he was summoned to his father's presence, his pale and haggard aspect alarmed the emperor. "Are you sick, my son?" he inquired, in a kinder voice than had fallen on the prince's ear for many weeks.

"No, sire, not sick, but—"

"But what? my dear Pepin."

"Heart-sick, my liege. Is it strange that I should droop, and grow pale, in the cold shadow of my father's displeasure?"

Pepin's noble heart was unschooled in artifice, and

he felt its true blood rush to his face, at the first evasion he had ever used with his father. The emperor saw only in his flushed cheek the expression of filial feeling, wounded by his injustice.

"My dear Pepin," he said, "there has been something wrong between us. We have both been to blame —have we not?"

"I believe so, my lord."

"Nay, Pepin, do not so be-lord and be-liege me: have you not always called me father? It is the title God has made, my son, worth all others of man's creation. I would not be a common king, and live far up in the frozen regions, above the sweet and melting breath of nature. Call me father, my dear son; and henceforth let us maintain the natural offices of our relation. You shall be my support and hope, and I will be your protector and benefactor." The impulse of Pepin's heart was, to throw himself at his father's feet—to swear to him eternal gratitude and fidelity—but the solemn oaths he had plighted in the chapel still vibrated in his ear, and withheld him; and when the emperor concluded, by saying, "Is not this our compact, Pepin?" and offering him his hand, the prince gave him his, but it was as cold and nerveless, in his father's warm grasp, as if it were death-stricken.

"So mute and cold, my son!" The emperor gazed at him for a moment, piercingly. "Ah, Pepin," he continued, "I see how it is with you. Duty, honour, glory, all weigh light against love. But believe me, my boy, this will pass away—it is the plaything of our youth—the mist of the morning, certainly to be dispersed by the fervid sun of manhood. As to this pretty Blanche, she is a rare gem, I grant you, and fit for a monarch's cabinet; but I have given her away, and I cannot retract my royal word."

"But why was that word given, sire?"

"Why, in part, young man, to place her far beyond

D 2

your reach—think you it were well to reward treason and rebellion by giving the daughter of the rebel Hunold to my favourite son? Let that pass—let us not look back, but forward—you have glorious work before you —no time for a lover's sighs—the Saxon provinces are in revolt—the barbarian forces have already passed our eastern frontier. I am bound, as you know, to the succour of the Pope against his insurgent Romans,—and as a proof of my restored confidence, I shall give to you the supreme command of the forces already levied and now levying for this eastern war. And further, my son, name to me your friends, those that you would have appointed to stations of trust and honour under you, and their claims shall be considered."

Pepin was overpowered. He saw placed in his hands, by the blind confidence of his father, the certain means, as he believed, of achieving his designs. A vision of love, independence, and power floated before his eyes ; but he recoiled from himself at the thought of abusing a trust so nobly and generously proffered. He made an effort to express, in general terms, his gratitude, but he abhorred hypocrisy, and the words died away on his lips. A nervous tremulousness seized his whole frame. He was exhausted by long-continued excitement, fasting, and vigils, and torn by the conflict of opposing passions. The emperor believed his agitation to result from a spirit grieved by injustice, and overpowered by unexpected kindness. " Now God forgive me !" he exclaimed, as he rang for assistance, " for ever distrusting him." The prince attempted to rise ; he again essayed to speak, but the power of motion and utterance failed him, and when the attendants appeared he was conveyed, unconscious, to his own apartment.

The scenes that followed may be imagined. His faltering and changing purposes—the whisperings of unappeasable resentment to the queen—Father Bernard's stern, unyielding onward pressure—the indignant remonstrances of his confederates, and above all, and finally prevailing, the soft pleadings of a love that melted every subordinate affection in its fires.

In a few days he was at the head of his father's forces, marching towards the eastern frontier of the empire. In a few days more he had unfurled an independent standard, and declared that he would never lay down his arms till he had secured a participation in the government, and an equal succession with his brothers. Success everywhere attended him. The emperor was on his progress towards Rome. There was no loyal force to oppose the prince, and he marched victoriously from city to city.

Where was the gentle Blanche while these events were shaping her destiny? The prince had been compelled by his military duties to leave Aix-la-Chapelle without delay. He had previously concerted a plan with Father Bernard for Blanche's clandestine removal to a place of security, where she might await the moment when their happy destinies should be achieved, and for ever united. In the mean time Father Bernard remained in the palace to watch, with his untiring eye, over the safety of the orphan. For this end he curbed his haughty spirit, and still stooped to play the priest to the queen; and kept down, as well as he might, his impatient desire to unsheath his sword in a fair field. Through Ermen's agency he effected a communication with Blanche, and every measure was appointed to secure their secret and safe release from thraldom. The appointed hour was at hand, when their hopes were suddenly dashed by an order from the queen, who ruled the palace in the emperor's absence, to remove the Lady Blanche to an upper apartment, where she was to be strictly guarded, till she could be sent off with her retinue, without danger of being intercepted by the prince. The queen, still influenced by the

7 *

superstitious notions respecting Blanche that had been
so deeply stricken into her soul by the priest, treated
her with no discourtesy that she deemed unnecessary.
She assigned to her use the emperor's private sleeping-
room, which communicated on one side with a gallery,
guarded day and night, and on the other with her own
bedroom; the passages to which, in the emperor's
absence, were always jealously guarded. The third
day of Blanche's removal had passed, and was succeeded by a quiet starlit evening. The busy and the
happy were either reposing or revelling, and no sound
was heard in the streets of Aix-la-Chapelle, save the
half-stifled groan of the houseless vagrant—the slow
step of the penitent returning from midnight prayers, or
the whistle of the soldier who did the watchman's
duty. Blanche was sitting at her casement-window,
absorbed in sad and tender thought, while Ermen was
pacing up and down the room, performing superfluous
services, keeping time with her tongue to her movements; complaining, expostulating, and entreating, half
to herself, and half to her lady : thus letting off the
accumulating steam that, being restrained from its proper channels, must find a safety-valve or explode.

" Our bodies might be as free as our thoughts," she
said, " if my lady had taken my advice."

"What advice ?" asked Blanche, rather to humour
Ermen's tongue than for information of what had been
already repeatedly rung in her ear.

" What advice ! sure, my lady, you know—but it's
easy going over it again, and maybe you'll think differently—pardon me, my dear young mistress, but they
say wit had better come late than never. It is but to
give the ten gold pieces to our warder—his honesty,
a plague on him ! is not worth half the sum, but he
swears by St. Denis he'll not take less—then the
Saxon churl at the other end of the gallery is easily

disarmed by a cup of drugged Rhenish—after that our only hindrance till we get to the private passage to the chapel are the two Gallic sentinels below the first flight of stairs. And one glance of your eye—one word from your tongue, my lady, will move all the bars and bolts at their command, for the loyal blood of Aquitaine is in their veins, though my Lady Fastrade knows it not. Once in the chapel, we might trust to holy mother Mary to help her own servants out of her own temple —that is, if we help ourselves; beyond that, I'll trust to my own wits alone,—for once in the free air, they'll rise like steam from a boiling pot when the cover is taken off."

" Consider once more, my good Ermen, by what means we should escape : first, by corrupting the fidelity of our keeper—"

" Pardon me, my dear lady, the faith that is to be bought for ten pieces of gold is not worth speaking of."

" Be it so then. But in sorrow, I must confess there is no human virtue but has its price, since my good Ermen is willing, for the doubtful chance of liberty at last, to expose to cruel punishment two of her kind-hearted countrymen. Oh it is the bitterest drop in my sorrows, that I involve my best friends in crime, as well as misery. You, Ermen,—this kind mysterious priest, who is playing a treacherous part for me, and my dear lord, whom the doom of treason certainly awaits."

Blanche's voice expressed her utter hopelessness, and Ermen forgot all her plans and pique, in the desire to console her. " Now, my blessed lady," she said, " do not talk so despairingly ; I had a dismal dream of the dead last night, and that's a sure sign you'll hear good news of the living. Do not lay your head so droop-ingly on your harp, as if you were never again to wake it to a joyous measure—nay, do not rise from it till you have once more played that Gallic song, that my fathers sung ere they had passed under the yoke of barbarian, or Roman either. Ah, well I remember how your little hand and foot kept time to it, while you were yet a baby in my arms. There it is!" continued Ermen, as Blanche, to gratify her, boldly struck the chords. The wild heroic air called up the dead and the distant, in the faithful creature's memory. "It is too much!" she said, with streaming eyes, when her mistress had finished. "I see those vine-covered hills—and the white cottage—and the pear-tree—my father—my mother. I hear the viol, and the flute, and the shouting chorus of us young ones, as we stopped to join them—but hark—is that the echo of my memory, or are you answered from below?" Both listened intently, and heard these words repeated, in the lowest audible tone:

> "Fear is for the willing slave,
> Triumph waits the true and brave."

Blanche grasped Ermen's arm, while Ermen exclaimed, 'It is the prince's voice!"

"Hush, Ermen, for the love of Heaven, hush!"

"Ay, my lady, but look, look!" At this moment a procession of priests and attendants, bearing the host to a dying man, were seen to issue from a monastery on the opposite side of the street. By the torches they carried, two persons were distinctly descried passing from beneath the palace wall, and deliberately crossing to the opposite side. They were muffled in the long hooded russet cloaks worn by the pilgrims of Jerusalem, whose order was designated by a broad white cross wrought on the back of the cloak. As the host passed them, the pilgrims dropped on their knees; and then rising, exchanged a salutation with the priests. The procession passed on rapidly, and the pilgrims appeared to be slowly following in their train, till they turned a corner, and disappeared. Blanche was certain, that one of these seeming pilgrims was the prince; but while she wondered what wild hope could have led him to such a rash exposure, and held her breath, and strained her ear for what she fancied was the sound of rapidly returning footsteps, she heard voices in the gallery at her door. The bolts were turned, and Father Bernard entered. "Now, holy father," said the warder, as he admitted him, "for the love of mercy shrive the lady quickly; for as I hope St. Peter will turn the key of heaven for me, I scarcely dare to break the strict order of the queen, even at the word of her confessor."

"No more words, good fellow. Here is gold for thee. If thou hast unabsolved sins do some act of mercy with it. Now get thee out—lock the door, and thou shalt have notice when I have done my office with the lady."

The man obeyed. Father Bernard turned towards Blanche, who approached him with an expression of the most earnest inquiry. He would have replied to it, but his heart was swelling, and his pulses throbbing; the tide of long-repressed feeling overwhelmed him like a flood, and he was on the point of stretching out his arms to her, when the thought that he might ruin all renerved him, and he said, in a voice so tremulous as scarcely to be intelligible, "I have come to attempt your rescue—there is not a moment to be lost—silence, caution, and celerity alone can save us. Do you follow, Ermen. Obey any signal I may make, but speak never a word. We must first pass through the bedchamber of the queen. She is at her prayers in the adjoining oratory. Her jealous ear will catch the least sound. Off with your shoes, Ermen—they creak like a rusty hinge. But, woman, what are you doing?—there is no time for other preparation."

"Beshrew me," thought Ermen, "if my life were worth saving if I left this," and she hastily finished

D 3

tying on a petticoat, into which she had providently
quilted her mistress' gold and jewels.

Blanche wrapped herself in her veil, while the priest
was cautiously unlocking the door, with a key which
he had drawn from his bosom.   As he opened the door
he recoiled at an unexpected obstacle.   Here it will
be necessary to pause for a moment, to present some
particulars that materially affected the safety of our
fugitives.   On their left was a window, in a deep recess, before which hung a curtain that had been dropped
for the night.   On the opposite side of the apartment
was an open door that led into a small bathing-room,
lighted by a suspended silver lamp, and dimmed by the
soft fumes of a perfumed bath, prepared for the queen.
The object that had startled the priest was the queen's
tire-woman, who sat in the middle of the room,
awaiting her mistress' protracted devotions ; her drowsiness had overcome her, and she had fallen asleep.
As she was a plump young creature, seemingly full-
fed, her sleep was profound, and like to continue so,
as was indicated by the nasal sounds she emitted, and
which fortunately drowned any inevitable noise our
passengers might make.   But there was a vigilant little
spirit that could not be eluded, in the shape of a German
poodle, lying on the maid's lap, with his head peering
over her shoulder.   His prying eye was strained
towards the door, but he made no sign of molestation
at the accustomed sight of Father Bernard.   Blanche
too, who had often caressed him, was permitted to enter
without a greeting ; but no sooner had poor Ermen
passed in, and the priest closed the door, than the
poodle, who felt that she was " a questionable shape,
and he would speak to her ;" set up that petulant and
continuous barking peculiar to this species of animal ;
and which neither menaces, nor bribery, nor any thing
but the voice of the master can still.   A sound was

heard from the oratory. It was too late to retreat, and impossible to go forward, as there was a guard at the outer door, who was to be passed by force, or artifice. In this strait the fugitives glided behind the curtain already mentioned. Here they stood, breathless, while the queen unbolted her door, opened it— looked round, saying, "Ha ! my pet, is it only you?— hush—hush, I'll soon be with you." She reclosed the door. The priest gavé her time to recommence her prayers, and then darted from his retreat, hoping they should reach the outer door before the poodle could renew hostilities ; but at the first glance at Ermen he again set up his relentless din. Ermen now took her defence upon herself, and answering to his challenge, seized him by the throat, and dashed him into the bath, and before the little creature had time to recover his breath from the suddenness and fright of the immersion, they had gained the gallery, and closed the door behind them. Here they were challenged by the sentinel, who, however, supposing they had just left the queen's presence, and were going forth at her pleasure, permitted them to pass. There was probably something hurried and stealthy in their manner, that awakened his suspicions, for he immediately followed them, and then checked himself, saying mentally, " I am a fool ! It is impossible the priest should have taken the Lady Blanche out of durance without the queen's knowledge. And if he has he must return. The devil himself cannot cheat the Hun guards at the foot of the grand staircase !"

This was too true : Father Bernard knew that with those wary and resolute guards, who never wavered from the letter of their orders, neither force nor artifice would avail, and he had taken his measures accordingly. After making two turns in the gallery, they descended a short flight of steps to a platform, where there was a window that overlooked the street, and was about

twenty feet above it. The priest cautiously opened the
window, and made a signal, which was returned from
below. He whispered to Blanche, " Now, my child,
be of good courage. I must leave you, but as true a
heart, and a stronger arm than mine awaits you."

" The prince ?"

" Ay, ay, Blanche, the prince, and one faithful aux-
iliary. I remain here to do one more duty, and
then, all perils past, God grant we may meet again—
his shield be over you."   He then drew a ladder of ropes
from beneath his cloak, uncoiled, and having fastened it
to a staple in the window, dropped it.   It was received
below, made fast, and Blanche descended, and was in
her lover's arms.   The past, the present, the future,
were blended, in one brief instant, of fear, joy, and hope.
Such instants outweigh hours of peril and months of
suffering.

In the mean while Ermen mounted the ladder, which,
though it had scarcely felt Blanche's fragile form,
stretched beneath Ermen's ponderous frame, swaying
backward and forward.   " It's the weight of my petticoat," thought Ermen, and most heartily she wished her
riches had their usual quality of wings, and would fly
away with her, or from her.   " Mother of mercy save
me !" she cried.

" Be silent, woman, and hold fast," said a stern
voice from below.

" Hold fast, indeed ! does he deem me such a fool
as to let go, while I'm flying like a kite here between
heaven and earth, and t'other place gaping under me ;"
but this response and prayers to every saint in her memory, were thought, not spoken.   Not a sound escaped
her till her foot touched terra firma, when her feelings
were relieved by one long satisfactory groan.   She and
her mistress were immediately enveloped in cloaks
and hoods, similar to those worn by the prince and his
attendant.

These disguises were the best security against dangerous scrutiny. Priests and pilgrims might allege a holy motive to account for the irregularity of their hours; and it was not safe to scan too narrowly the profession of sanctity which secured to them their immunities.

Scarcely had the fugitives passed beyond the palace walls, when they heard, issuing from its portals, the cry of "Treason! treason!" An instant after the palace-bell sounded, and in the space of a few flying moments responsive alarms rung from church and convent-bell. The earth seemed to have given up its dead. The streets, so silent a few moments before, now teemed with swift feet and eager voices. "Keep close to me, and fear nothing," whispered the prince to Blanche. "All depends on our going calmly forward;" and in the next breath, accosting a passenger—"What meaneth this uproar, sir citizen?" he asked.

"They say the queen is murdered!" was the reply.

"Amen!" cried several voices, not loud, but deep. The involuntary prayer was scarcely uttered before the peal of a herald's trumpet was heard, followed by his voice, demanding silence, attention, and prompt obedience from the emperor's liege subjects. He then proclaimed that the rebel prince was within the walls of the city, and had effected the escape from the palace of the Lady Blanche of Aquitaine, a damsel easily known by her famed beauty, and attended by a serving-woman, brown, short, thick, and elderly—loyal subjects were forbidden to give them harbour or aid. Every house and sanctuary was declared to be open to search, and a munificent reward was offered to him who should apprehend and deliver up the fugitives.

"Elderly, indeed!" whispered Ermen to her lady; "they'll not know me by that description. I am but forty my next birthday, and that's a month off yet."

The prince communicated for a moment with his associate, and then said, "My dearest Blanche, my

8

presence but endangers you. If sagacity and good
faith can avail aught, you are safe with your conductor.
Heaven and all saints guard you—farewell, we shall
meet ere the dawn."

"Farewell!" replied Blanche, in a voice that expressed the terror and shrinking of her spirit; and as
the prince glided away and disappeared from her sight,
she, for the first time, felt the horror of her position.

A moment before and his presence was peace and
safety, and seemed to breathe around her a sheltering
atmosphere; now she felt that she had passed from a
nun-like seclusion into the midst of a clamorous mul-
titude, and was the hunted fugitive among them. "Oh
that we had never embarked in this perilous, desperate
enterprise," she thought. Still she was not quite desperate. Her spirit was buoyed up—her strength sustained by the hope of possible escape, and she kept
pace with the regular and rapid strides of her conductor. He had just said to her, "Courage, lady! we
are near the barriers," when they were overtaken by a
detachment of the queen's guards, mounted, and bearing
flaming torches.

"Stop, Sir Pilgrim," said their leader, "cloaks and
hoods are of no avail to-night!" and suiting the action
to the word, he stretched out his lance, and with its
point drew back the hood of Blanche's protector.
Blanche shrunk back, and clung to Ermen, expecting
the next moment would reveal her features to her
pursuers. But they were checked when they saw on
the shaven head of the pilgrim the voucher for his claim
to that sacred character with which, not even a court-
soldier might trifle with impunity; and they were over-
awed when the pilgrim said, in a voice that had more
of authority than inquiry, "Shall I proceed, soldier, or
will you further profane the holy garb of our order, by
searching under the hoods of my young brothers for the
runaways from your court?"

"Nay, good pilgrim, God forbid we should farther offend—we were over-zealous in our duty, and we will gladly expiate our offence by whatever penance you shall appoint."

"Son, we leave that duty to your confessor; but, if you would make his task the lighter, do us the courtesy to give us your protection beyond the barriers. We had appointed to reach the monastery of St. Denis of the rock before the dawn, and we have already suffered much hindrance from the tumult of the city."

"Right gladly will we lessen our offence by doing thee this service, holy pilgrim; and with the more pleasure that, but for this rencounter which, God forgive us! began with sacrilege on our part, you could not have passed the barriers. We are now on our way to the eastern portal to direct that none be permitted to pass out till further orders be received from the palace."

Nothing more was spoken during the short space they traversed preceded by their duped escort. Every one gave place to the queen's guards. The portal was thrown wide open at their leader's command, and as the pilgrims passed out, "Farewell, good soldier," their conductor said, "for the grace thou hast done us we give thee many thanks, and full acquittance for thy fault, and will fain remember thee in our prayers at St. Denis' shrine."

"Heaven reward thy sanctity, most holy pilgrim! What a besotted fool I was," continued the soldier, dropping his voice, "not to know from a glance at the step and mien of these holy brothers, that they were no counterfeits. Look, comrade," he continued, pointing towards Blanche, "at that little low youngster that sticks so close to his fat brother; you see by his dainty steps that he has been convent-bred, and only used to pattering over the cloister's floor at the sound of matin and vesper bells. I marvel if those little feet carry him half way to the Holy Land. Come," he concluded,

raising his voice to the key of authority, " shut the gate.
It is the queen's command that, till further orders, none
be permitted to pass the barriers in any garb, or under any pretext."

These words had scarcely died away on the ears of
our fugitives when they turned from the highway into
a wood that skirted it, and was intersected by footpaths
diverging in every direction. The most obscure and
involved was selected, and they were soon in the intricate depths of a forest, amid huge old trees whose
mossy branches were so interlaced as to exclude every
ray of the feeble starlight. Their conductor was happily accustomed to the tangled and devious way, and
he led them with unerring certainty to a path that followed the course of a little brook, around the bared
roots of trees, over stones imbedded in moss, and down
sharp declivities till it ended in a rich forest-glade.
Here man had selected one of God's first temples for
his worship. A little hermitage stood on the verge of
the green sward, just peeping from the enfolding
branches of the trees. Every refreshment that could
be obtained had here been provided for our fugitives,
and Blanche, oppressed with fatigue, which the delicate
habits of her life made utterly overpowering, after a
slight repast, and while Ermen was finishing a meal
that ill suited an anchorite's cell, lay down on a pallet
and was soon in profound sleep.

Early on the following day they were joined by the
prince, who, having happily escaped the dangers that
menaced him, came to assure himself of Blanche's
safety, and to conduct her to the place where he had
appointed an ample military escort to meet and attend
her to the monastery of St. Genevieve, of which an assured friend of Father Bernard was the superior.

At the end of their first day's journey they were met
by the news that the emperor had been recalled, and
was already at the head of his forces. Their imme-

diate parting was inevitable. Blanche did not speak
—no words could speak the anguish of her heart.—
" My life—my dearest Blanche," said the prince, " do
not fear the future. Victory, that has hitherto clung to
my banner, will not, cannot desert me now."

" But now you have to combat against your father !"

The prince's eye fell, and a momentary shade passed
over his face ; but again the fire of confident hope flashed
from his eye. " Ah, Blanche !" he exclaimed, " is not
your life cast upon the issue—our love—freedom—
honour—power ?—Nay, if there were forty fathers,
they should not unnerve my arm, nor abate my courage
one jot ! Farewell, dearest ; when we meet again, we
meet to part no more."

" In heaven, then, my lord !"

The words struck on the prince's heart like the prophetic words of the dying ; but, repelling the thought,
he replied, " It will be heaven to us, Blanche," and tore
himself away.

While we leave our heroine to arrive safely, as she
did in due time, at the monastery, we must return to
the palace.

The queen, on issuing from her oratory, found her
poodle in a most piteous condition, running about the
room, whining, and shaking his streaming head and
sides. Immediately, a suspicion flashed into her mind.
She went towards Blanche's door to listen—all was
still. She opened the door, and found the room deserted. The alarm was instantly given, and at the
same moment a secret messenger, who had demanded
an audience, was admitted. He proved to be a false
wretch from the prince's army, who, having been trusted
with the secret of his leader's having rashly ventured
within the city, had come to obtain the price of betraying
him. In the confusion of the moment the guards had
not been examined, of course they volunteered no disclosures, nor was the manifest passage through the

8 *

queen's apartment immediately remembered; so that it was concluded the prince had scaled the wall to the Lady Blanche's window, and Father Bernard's agency was not even suspected.

The alarm bells had roused every inhabitant of the palace; and lords and ladies, soldiers, guards, pages, and servants had flocked to the great hall, first to learn the cause of the disorder, and then to discuss it. The queen was on the dais at the upper extremity of the hall, chafing like a tigress whose prey has been wrested from her, while a few of her courtiers were trying to sooth her with

> " Mouth-honour, breath,
> Which the poor heart would fain deny, but dare not."

Father Bernard entered. The crowd opened a passage for his reverend figure, and he proceeded to the vacant space before the queen. " I crave an audience, madam," he said.

" Ha, father! dost thou bring us news of Blanche ?"

" Madam, I ask your patience, and yours, noble lords and ladies." He paused. A breathless silence answered him, and he proceeded—" There was a descendant of the Merovingian race who had twin sons, the one so like the other that their mother could not discriminate them ; the one was bred as the descendant of a royal stock should be—the existence of the other was concealed from the world, and, to avoid the evils that might arise from his resemblance to his brother, he was dedicated to St. Stephen, and immured in a cloister, his face being hidden by a steel mask."

" What means this ?" thought the courtiers; " the holy father surely speaks of himself." " What means it ?" thought the guilty queen, and her heart sunk within her.

" In due time," proceeded the priest, " he that was

knightly-bred appeared at the court of the sovereign who had usurped the throne of his fathers. That sovereign had a soul befitting royalty—he could honour even him whom he had injured—the knight was trusted and cherished—the wife too of the sovereign graced him with favours." Here the queen's emotion became apparent, and nearly uncontrollable, but she dared not speak, lest she should identify the persons of the narrative. The blood burst from her bitten lip, still she suffered the priest to go on. "It suits not to tell more in the modest presence of these ladies, save that, faithful to his wife, the knight spurned the woman false to her royal lord. Her guilty love turned to hate. The knight was outraged; he rebelled, was vanquished, and pardoned by his sovereign on condition that he should make a pilgrimage to Rome, doing penance before the relics of the saints at every intermediate shrine. He arrived sick and exhausted at the monastery of St. Stephen, near Ravenna, of which his masked brother was abbé. The brothers met. The abbé, to relieve the miserable broken man, volunteered to finish the pilgrimage for him."

Here a shriek, half-subdued, but piercing, came from the queen. The priest paused—the stillness of death followed, and he proceeded : "The abbé received on his own innocent body tortures destined for his brother, and inflicted by emissaries sent by the treacherous queen. The supposed abbé—mark ! was summoned to the court to direct the conscience of the queen. She told him that an infant daughter of the knight survived. She would have offered up this last victim on the altar of insatiate revenge, but that the Almighty now visited her with disease, and the terrors of the sure hereafter. The confessor grasped her conscience in this first weakness of humanity, and he has since ruled it. For fifteen years that woman daily unveiled her polluted soul before him she deemed her victim : her very pulses

were governed by his word. She was the dupe, the
willing, trembling instrument of him whose name she
would have effaced from the earth, while he, the minister of Heaven's mercy to his child, watched over her
innocence and safety. This night he has delivered her
from the house of bondage, and now," he concluded,
unclasping his mask, and throwing it aside, " *Hunold
of Aquitaine* is avenged."

While the queen listened there had mingled a whisper of incredulity with the storm of her passions ; but
when the priest cast away his mask, and revealed the
noble and well-remembered features of Hunold, hys-
terical convulsions seized her, and she was borne off,
shrieking, in the arms of her attendants.

In the confusion of the moment, and perhaps favoured
by the forbearance of those who had listened in mute
wonder to his tale, Hunold glided through a side passage, and escaped from the palace, and was never again
seen within the walls of Aix-la-Chapelle.

CHAPTER IV.

"Oh that the desert were my dwelling-place,
  With one fair spirit for my minister,
  That I might all forget the human race,
  And hating no one, love but only her."
                                        Childe Harold.

THE Lady Blanche was still in the secure asylum
of the Abbey of St. Genevieve.   Here, in safety, and in
tranquil devotion, she might have worn out life, had
that fire never been kindled in her bosom which, once
lighted, cannot be extinguished without making a waste
and ruin of the tenderest affections.   Heavily as her
forebodings weighed on her heart, she could no more
envy the calm safe sisters of the monastery, than the
living, feeling, throbbing form can envy the mute cold
statue.   The storm might sweep away her last hope,
but who that dwells in the land of blossoms, fruits,
and *hurricanes*, will exchange with the natives of the
safe and frigid north !   Even so thought Blanche, while
every day was bringing some agitating rumour from the
scene of conflict.   By the latest accounts the hostile
forces were not far from the valley-lands, overlooked
by the abbey.   The emperor was at the head of his
army, and at the approach of the great sovereign,
Pepin's forces were sensibly diminishing.   Still he
kept the field, without any apparent abatement of hope
or activity.

Affairs were in this position when, at an early hour
of the morning, the repose of the abbey was disturbed
by a rumour of the near approach of the hostile armies.
The abbess, with her nuns, according to the letter of
her duty, hastened to mingle with her matin prayers,

petitions for the downfall of rebellion. Blanche, with her faithful Ermen, stole to a tower of the abbey, where she was destined to endure what a martyr might suffer at the stake, who had a threefold portion of life and sense in every nerve.

The valley, or glen, if it might so be called, broken as it was at intervals into ridges and abrupt descents, was encompassed by hills, and intersected by a narrow, deep, and impetuous stream, with precipitous and impracticable banks, which were connected by a single plank-bridge thrown across the stream, where it dashed over a ledge of rocks. At the eastern extremity of the valley, on a declivity, stood the abbey overlooking the domain attached to it—its garden, farms, and the whitewashed cottages of its artisans which were clustered together at the extreme opposite, under the shadow of the hills that appeared there to wall in the valley, and were only separated where the bold little stream had forced its passage. The peace of ages was, for the first, to be broken in this sylvan scene, where even now the stillness was so profound that the chirping of the cricket, and the rustling of the fallen autumn-leaf, under the squirrel's fleet foot, might be heard. The trees, save where the firs glittered with dewy webs, were stripped of their summer glory; but, like a youthful face, " touched, not spoiled" by grief, they looked cheerful in their adversity ; glittering dewdrops studding their branches, and the glossy bark brightening in the flush of the rising sun. The stream, that leaped and " danced to its own wild chime," was fringed with the last gay flowers of autumn—those bold little heroes that hang out their colours even on the very frontiers of winter. The windings of the stream, far off among the distant hills, were marked by the light warm mist which rose from it, giving a bluish tint to the atmosphere, and nearer, and immediately under Blanche's eye, settled in dense fog, over the coves, or rolled up the mountains in fleecy clouds.

Scarcely had Blanche and Ermen taken their stations in the tower, when the silence was rudely broken by the braying of a war-trumpet that pealed over the valley, waking a thousand echoes among the hills ; the tramping of horses followed ; and the prince, at the head of his gallant followers, was seen descending rapidly to the valley. His war-cry was shouted and answered by the clamour of the hostile army, that appeared to Blanche like birds of evil omen, darkening the opposite plain. As the prince had the inferior force it was of vital importance to him to command the passage of the bridge ; and he gained it by so rapid a movement that Ermen had scarcely time for an exclamation, before he seemed to be disposing his force about it, so as most effectively to repel an attack.

" What means that ?" said Blanche, pointing to a standard-bearer. " That surely is the banner of my father's house. A fiery sun emerging from a cloud, on a field of white."

" But look, my lady, close beside it, at the knight in black armour, with the black plumes. It is your father in shape and bearing, with a little stoop of the shoulders, as if he had some added weight of years ; but otherwise the same."

" Ah, Ermen, our fancies cheat us ; it is the banner that has conjured up this image in your memory. It is an evil augury, this banner of a fallen house."

" Think not of auguries, my lady, fortune is on the side of the prince. See how gallantly he rides. His white plumes even him with the tallest. Any one may see he was born to rule, though his poor mother did stand on the emperor's left side. Now he salutes his soldiers. Ha ! hear their acclamations—God bless him ! he had always the hearts of the commons. Heaven and all saints stand by him, I say, be he right or wrong !"

The "amen" *did not* stick in Blanche's throat, though conscience would have kept it there; and Ermen proceeded, "Beshrew me if I think it handsome in the abbess and her nuns to be throwing their prayers into the scale of the strongest; they ought to stand aside and let 'em have fair play." Whether Ermen meant that Heaven or the abbess should not interpose, it is difficult to say;—an untutored conscience is very docile —she probably had some secret misgivings of the righteousness of the prince's cause, and preferred there should be no appeal to a celestial tribunal.

The manœuvres of the two armies continued for some time without an assault from either party. The emperor had not yet arrived on the field of battle. Meanwhile the forces on both sides were concentrating at the bridge. The prince had concealed a reserved corps behind a hill in his rear, in order by his seeming weakness to tempt the enemy to the perilous passage of the bridge, where their numbers would rather embarrass than aid them. They perceived the disadvantage at which they must attack, and hesitated to encounter it.

"Ah!" said Blanche, "it is a proud sight to see their steeds prancing, their banners and pennons flying, their lances gleaming in the sun, and those gallant knights unblenching before the face of death, if we could forget what they may be before the sun sinks behind yon hills."

"They forget it, my lady, or they would be as very cowards as we women are. I have seen these lordly men who throw down their lives upon the battle-field as if it were but a cast of the dice, I have seen them shrink from a twinge of the tooth-ache, and, if death did but peep at them through the curtains of a sick-bed, their hearts would die away within them. But they have a brute's instinct to fight, and when that is roused they forget pain and death, and all that comes after.

Truly, I think, after all their boasting and blustering, we women might dispute the palm of courage with them, for we bravely meet and triumph over those natural enemies of our race, pain, and poverty, and death, which Heaven has made it our necessity to encounter; while they, for the most part, are only brave in meeting dangers of their own creation. I marvel they do not begin—they stand there on each side of the bridge, looking like wild beasts, ready to spring the moment the barrier is withdrawn."

Ermen's wonder was scarcely expressed when some of the youngest and most daring of Charles' paladins, unable any longer to brook delay, or endure the defiance and stinging taunts of their antagonists, dashed over the bridge, were encountered, and repelled, or overthrown. Many a daring onset and gallant rescue followed. Suddenly a cloud of dust was seen rising in the distance. The oriflamme was descried. The emperor's battle-cry was heard, and, at the conquering sound, his soldiers, like a pack of hounds at the voice of their master, rushed upon the bridge. They were met and driven back. Pressed forward by their own column, they became pent within the narrow space. Carnage and horrible confusion ensued—men were slaughtered in masses—horses and riders were overthrown, and when the command for retreat was given, the bridge was piled with trampled, struggling, and dying men. "See, see, my lady," cried Ermen, "my Lord Pepin's men toss those carcasses into the stream as if they were sheep slaughtered for the shambles. No wonder you cover your eyes; it pierces my old heart to see those bodies, that one minute ago were full of life, strength, and hope, so broken and dishonoured."

" God forgive them !" ejaculated Blanche.

" But look once again, my lady ! See how daringly the knight of the black plume advances, just so my Lord Hunold would have done; he passes the bridge !

9   E

See, with his few followers he dashes on the retreating
column—Ah! they turn on him—now, St. Denis aid
him!—there goes the prince to his rescue!"

"Heaven help us," cried Blanche, "he is lost! Oh,
what rashness to pass the bridge! Shame on the cowards, now there are myriads against him, how they set
on him—he is surrounded!—his retreat utterly cut
off!" Blanche clasped her hands and fixed her eye in
breathless apprehension on that frightful melée, "Ah
me! Ermen, my head is giddy; I can see nothing, look
if you can see him?"

"No, my lady, no."

"Look narrowly, Ermen, do you not see the top of
his plumes?"

"No, no, indeed!—nothing but glancing lances and
gleaming shields. What can that waving mean? they
fall back! Ah, there he is, side by side with the black
knight. See, they burst through the close ranks of the
enemy—ha! how they trample them down. Mother
Mary! how they tread the life out of them—they are
already at the bridge—the black plume passes it, but
ah! the broken planks fly from beneath his horse's feet.
What a horrid gap he has opened for the prince—his
steed recoils—his pursuers are on him! Now, Heaven
save him from falling with his back to them! their
lances almost touch him. Bravo! the leap is made—
he is safe."

"Surely," said Blanche, as her heart heaved from
the suffocating pressure that was upon it;—"Surely
Heaven's shield is before him."

"And behind him too, I think, my lady; and a lion's
heart within him. See how the enemy seem cowering
on their side the bridge, like frightened hawks, afraid
to stoop to their prey; and my lord's men, bless them! I
see by their bearing, that each one feels as if he had
the strength of ten men in his single arm. There comes
a messenger to the prince with good or evil tidings."

"Heaven grant them good," replied Blanche, "but I fear, for my lord rides hastily off with him."

"I marvel the brave paladins endure the taunts of the black plume," resumed Ermen. "Hark! how he dares them to follow the example he set them. Ah! there is my lord emperor—his spirit will not brook being thus kept in abeyance. He calls on his guards to shame the loitering cowards, and follow. I doubt if he knows of that yawning abyss. Ah! now he sees it. But it is too late—he cannot turn back—his fiery steed leaps over. A few follow him—rather death than to desert your master! but every hoof that touches the bridge widens the gap. Mother of mercy, they fall through— the generous youths!—they are crushed on the rocks —horse and rider!"

Shouts rent the air. Ermen's voice might be heard, like the shriek of an owl, mingling with and heightening the clamour.

"Think you, Ermen, the victory is won; that the emperor's mistake is fatal?" demanded Blanche.

"Assuredly, my lady: the emperor sees it himself, but it is too late. See how his brave paladins gather round him. They seem to feel no more than their senseless shields, the blows they receive in his stead. They fall, one after another—the last is gone! He is single-handed against a host. What a salvation is a brave spirit! See how he gives them thrust for thrust, and fights as if he were backed by thousands. But, oh!" continued Ermen, her interest naturally shifting, as the inequality of the contest became more manifest, "It is in vain, as one assailant drops, another takes his place. It is too much! Our noble master against such odds! The craven wretches, why do they not give him a fair field! Right royally he still defends himself! Ah! he wavers—his shield has fallen—his left arm hangs like a lopped branch—he must fall !— see, they press on him. Now God have mercy on

E 2

him!—Ah! there comes the prince again—how furiously he rides. Must his hand give the finishing stroke? I cannot look on that—"

Blanche sunk on her knees. "Merciful Heaven!" she cried, "let him not lift his hand against his father —save him from parricide!"

" Oh, look up, my lady, once more look up! The prince is striking down the lances of the assailants, and shouting, 'Back, villains, back—touch not his sacred life!' "

Their arms fell as if they were paralyzed, and they recoiled a few paces, leaving a vacant space, where the steeds of father and son met, bit to bit. The prince dismounted, threw down his lance and shield, and kneeling in the dust, cried, "My liege—my *father*, forgive me!"

Ermen broke into a wild hysteric laugh, and turned to her mistress, but her gentle nature was overpowered, and she had sunk down in utter unconsciousness. Neither saw nor knew, till many hours after, what followed. That the tide of fortune had turned in the em peror's favour, and deliverance from the perils that beset him was near at hand, at the moment the interposition of his son saved him from certain death. A detachment from his army had been guided by one of the loyal abbey tenants, to a fordable passage through the stream. They had wound unperceived around the hills, fallen on Pepin's reserved corps, and cut it off completely; and at the moment the prince was surrendering himself to filial duty, his followers were surprised by superior numbers falling on their rear. He could not look on and see his faithful friends falling in a cause he had abandoned; and giving orders that the hlace where the emperor stood should be considered neutral ground, and sacredly guarded as such, he plunged into the thickest of the fight. Many a long-remembered deed of desperate valour did he achieve; but it was of no avail : long before the day closed, the din of arms had ceased ; the prince, and the handful of his followers who survived were prisoners, and the victorious army was retiring towards Aix-la-Chapelle.

The wounded and dying left on the field of battle were, in obedience to the benevolent orders of the abbess, conveyed to the cottages of the peasants, where all that leech-craft could do was done ; and when that was unavailing, the last offices of humanity were faithfully rendered. On the spot where the conflict had ended was found the body of the warrior who had been distinguished by the black plume. Though he was quite unconscious, life still tenaciously held its grasp ; and the badges of priestly office being discovered on the removal of his helmet and armour, he was deemed worthy to die within the consecrated walls of the abbey ; and accordingly he was carried thither. There he was destined to find not only a cure for the wounds of his body, but the skill that could pluck from his memory its rooted sorrows.

To women, old Homer (with the spirit of the golden age of gallantry) assigns the art of compounding the nepanthes. And, if there is a human hand skilled to prepare the sweet draught, oblivious of grief, sorrow, and care, it is that of a daughter.

Hours of tumultuous passion—years of gloomy self-annihilation were in the memory of Hunold, like a dismal and fading dream, while his eye reposed on Blanche ; and he felt, in her assiduous devotion, the healing efficacy of filial love.

For the present they were secure from molestation ; and of the future they hardly yet dared to think. The apprehensions that racked Blanche's heart were visible in the mortal paleness that settled on her cheek ; in her nervous starts at any unwonted sound ; and in the touching contrition which she manifested for the frequent abstractions of her thoughts from her father.

9*

The ultimate fate of the prince remained yet unde-
cided. Rebellion is the unpardonable sin in the creeds
of absolute monarchs ; and in this case justice, as well
as the almost uniform practice of the times, demanded
his death. Still the decree came not, and it was evident that there was some wavering in the sovereign's
mind—some leaning towards the milder punishment of
the tonsure, and seclusion in a monastery, a penalty
equivalent to our " state prison for life ;" a convenient
mode of shutting out of the world those who were *de
trop* in it. The partisans of the vindictive queen urged
that the death of the prince was essential to the present
tranquillity of the emperor and to the secure succession of the legitimate heirs. But the emperor seemed
cold to whatever proceeded from the queen's counsels.
He had received some faint intimations of Hunold's
disclosures ; and though he was too discrete a husband
to dive into a well because truth was at the bottom, yet
it was evident that the spell of her influence was dis-
solved—that her royal consort was disabused, and that
some change had passed, like that which reduces the
seemingly-beautiful enchantress of a fairy-tale to the
reality of an ugly old hag.

At length the intrigues of the courtiers were ended,
and the speculations of the gossips of the city silenced
by the publication of the emperor's decree. It ordained
that on a certain day the prince should receive the tonsure publicly, at the altar of the great chapel. That
after this rite of initiation, he should be escorted in state
to the monastery of St. Alban, where he was adjured by
the strictest prayers and penances to expiate the sin of
rebellion.

The ambitious prince was for ever to be severed from
the world. The purest, tenderest, and most ennobling
of human passions was to be converted to sin. The fire
that was kindled to gladden social life, was to be for ever
shut up in the bosom, there to burn and consume. Strange

that man should have been so long permitted to countervail the benign designs of Providence ! that he should have been suffered to condemn to waste and mouldering the affections that were bestowed to sow the wide harvest-fields of the world with joy and beauty !

The day arrived appointed for the ceremony. Early in the morning the gates of the city were thrown open. Nobles with pompous retinues, and rustics with their families, crowded the avenues. Greediness of spectacle has been common to all ages of the world, from long ere David danced before the ark of the Lord to this present moment, when the park of our city is a living mass, gazing at the beautiful illuminations for this centennial celebration of the birthday of our immortal Washington.

Church and convent-bells were tolling. Processions of the religious orders filled the streets with the sublime anthems appointed by the church ; and the Gregorian chant resounded from the choir of the great chapel.

It was remarked by those court observers of *straws*, who were watching the decline of Fastrade's sun, that the emperor on this day had given the final decision to the great musical controversy that had agitated the empire. The queen had favoured the Gallic or Ambrosian party, but the emperor, who had inclined to the muse of Italy, finally adopted the Gregorian chant ; justifying his decision publicly, by the pious illustration that, " as a river is purest at its source, so Rome, being the fountain of all divine wisdom, ought to reform the Gallican music after the model of her own."

The emperor and his court, in their ceremonial costume, entered the chapel by a private door, and occupied seats at the right of the altar ; the emperor and queen were in a position a little elevated, and in advance of their attendants. There was an unquietness in Charles' manner, and a heavy shade on his brow, that indicated the yearning of his heart towards his son ;

and the reluctance with which he had submitted to the
usage that imposed the humiliation of a public ceremony.   The state smile the queen had assumed did
not veil her gratified malignity, while her sallow cheek,
and restless and falling eye, fully betrayed her consciousness that she had fallen from her high estate—
that the emperor was no longer the duped husband,
flexible to the purposes of her insatiate cruelty.

The doors were thrown open, and the eager crowd
of spectators, marshalled by officers, were conducted
to the seats assigned them, according to their rank.
The chapel-bell struck, and the prince, preceded by men-
at-arms, and followed by a procession of the monks of
St. Alban, entered the grand aisle.   His dress resem-
bled that worn by his father on high festivals.   A golden
diadem, set with precious stones, bound in its circlet a
head that looked as if it were formed to ennoble even
such an appendage.   His buskins were thickly studded
with gems, his tunic was of golden tissue, and his purple mantle fastened by a clasp of glittering stones.
This royal apparel was meant in part to show forth the
ambition that had o'erleaped itself; and in part to set
the splendours of the world in overpowering contrast
with the humility of the religious garb.

The prince advanced with a firm step.   His demeanour showed that if he had lost every thing else, he had
gained the noblest victory; victory over himself.   There
was nothing in his air of the crushed man; on the contrary, there was his usual loftiness, and more than his
usual serenity.   As men gazed at him, and saw the impress of his father on his mild majestic brow, they felt
that nature had set her seal to his right of inheritance.
He paused as he reached a station opposite his father,
signed to his attendants to stop, and turning aside he
knelt at his father's feet.   Their eyes met as tenderly
as a mother's meets her child.   Charles stretched out
his hand, Pepin grasped it, and pressed it to his lips,

The spectators looked in vain for some sign of sternness in the father, and resentment in the son. Little did they dream that the father and son had met that morning, with no witness but the approving eye of Heaven; and had exchanged promises of forgiveness and loyalty never to be retracted in thought, word, or deed.

As the prince rose to his feet his eye encountered the queen's, flashing with offended pride; but hers fell beneath the steady overpowering glance of his, which said, " I am not yet so poor as to do *you* reverence." The emperor did not rebuke, or even seem to notice the omission. His eye was riveted to the gracious tears his son had left upon his hand.

The prescribed devotions and pompous preparatory ceremonial of the Romish church were performed. The prince then laid down his glittering crown, and exchanged his gorgeous apparel for the garb of St. Alban's monks, a russet gown fastened at the waist with a hempen-cord. It was noticed by the keenest of his observers that he did not lay aside his sword; but, he might have forgotten it, or a soldier might be permitted to the very last, to retain the badge of his honour and independence. A glow of shame shot over his face as he bent his head to the humiliating rite of the tonsure; and the eyes of the truly noble were instinctively averted, as his profuse and glossy locks fell beneath the razor of the officiating priest. This initiatory rite performed, a hood was thrown over his head, and the soldier-prince was lost in the humble aspect of the monk of St. Alban.

A court order had declared that the prince should be escorted to the gates of the monastery by the emperor, the lords and ladies of the court, and the paladins and chiefs assembled at Aix-la-Chapelle.

The troops of the late victorious army were stationed in double lines on each side of the course, along which the procession was to pass. The emperor and his son rode first, side by side. The queen, at an intimation from her royal consort, that savoured strongly of command, had withheld her presence. The bright skies, and transparent atmosphere of one of the earliest days of winter, gave lustre to every object, and clearness to every sound. Banners and pennons were streaming in the light breeze. The burnished shields, and unspotted lances of gala days, reflected from a thousand points the sunbeams. The proud step of the war-horse—the gay prancing of the palfrey—the glittering decorations of the court-ladies—and the state costume of the lords gave to the grand cortége the aspect of a triumphal procession. But how little like a victor looked the prince, whose diminished form seemed shrinking beneath the russet folds that enveloped him; and bending, in dejected attitude, over the fleet and fiery steed that had so often borne him to victory ! How the pealing anthems struck on his ear like a funeral dirge, hymning him to his tomb,—and the trampling of his horse's hoofs as they rung on the pavement ! " Oh, my generous unrivalled steed," he thought, " were we but once alone beyond the barriers, I would doff this cursed hood, and cast all upon a single chance ! Oh, Blanche, were I but with thee in some lone isle, in mid-ocean, or on some far spot of the desert—the world forgotten !" The past, the future, the possible floated before him in perplexed and maddening vision. His breath came gaspingly. It seemed to him that his pulses beat audibly—his eye " devoured the distance." The procession was within sight of the barriers, and not far distant from them. The gates were wide open, but the way to them was guarded by men with drawn and upraised weapons. " It is but the soldier's death," thought the prince, " instead of mouldering away within the cloister's walls. I violate no duty to my dear father. In every issue I am dead to him—it is *possible !* Does Heaven, or do the fiends inspire my purpose ! Heaven, surely Heaven, for oh ! Blanche, it is for thee, and thee alone !"

This last thought gave the irresistible and effective impulse. He threw off his hood, drew his sword, roused his horse's mettle with a single word, and beating back the spears of the amazed guard, he darted at full speed towards the gate. He cleared the barriers, his horse flew onward as if " the speed of thought were in his limbs ;" and before the cries of alarm and pursuit had passed along the ranks, he had disappeared.

Clamour, consternation, and confusion ensued. The zealous and officious were posting to the pursuit, when they were arrested by a peal from a herald's trumpet, followed by a proclamation, commanding the emperor's liege subjects to return quietly to their homes, and in future to refrain from any pursuit or quest after the fugitive, as that important duty was to be confided to private emissaries. The measures that were to be adopted, and the success that ensued, never transpired beyond the cabinet councils of the emperor.

The ingenious monks, at no period at a loss for the interpretation of an event that baffled common sagacity, maintained that the prince had been spirited away by St. Alban, that worthy saint being indignant at his admission into their immaculate fraternity.

But according to our modern creeds, the powers that superstition imbodied in the fancied favourites of Heaven, are within the mission of mortals ; and all-enduring, and all-conquering affection, works more miracles than the whole corporate body of calendared saints.

A saint there undoubtedly was in the case, for according to traditions long after familiar on the lake of Constance, a creature of beauty, so excellent that it seemed suited " t' envelope and contain a celestial spirit," dwelt on the little island of Meinau, in that lake. She had come thither from some far-distant province, with her father, her husband, and an ancient

serving-woman.   From the time of her advent, poverty
and misery disappeared from the shores of the lake, as
shadows fly before the sun.   The little waste isle became a paradise; and in due process of time those
young enchanters appeared, who repeat to the parent
the joys of his youth, and strew his path of life, even
down to the gates of death, with solaces and hopes.

As ages passed on, these traditions assumed a more
questionable shape; and, as is usual, a larger propor-
tion of fable was mingled with truth.   The knights
of the Teutonic order, afterward established at Meinau,
pointed visiters to a spot where, as a legend told, stood
a chapel in the reign of Charlemagne.   The officiating
priest was so far superior to the surrounding peasantry
that he would have seemed to them all celestial, but
for a slight deformity of the back, which stamped him
of mortal mould.   His devotional services, the legend
said, were assisted by an angel, surrounded by cherubs.
On Sundays and holydays the chapel was open to the
peasantry, and a special service was performed for the
emperor Charlemagne.   The legend farther intimated
that the long and prosperous reign of that great sovereign was mainly owing to the holy services of these
mysterious worshippers in the little chapel of Meinau.

CHILDE ROELIFF'S PILGRIMAGE.

CHILDE ROELIFF'S PILGRIMAGE;

A TRAVELLING LEGEND.

> Childe Roeliff was a citizen,
>   Thorough ye citie knowne,
> Who, from hys wealthe and dignitie,
>   Had ryghte conceited growne.

ROELIFF ORENDORF,—or, as he was commonly called, Childe Roeliff, on account of a certain conceited simplicity which caused him to be happily insensible to the sly ridicule called forth by his little purse-proud pomposities,—was a worthy man, and useful citizen of the queen of cities—I need not mention the name,—who having got rich by a blunder, had ever after a sovereign and hearty contempt for wisdom. He never could see the use of turning his head inside out, as he was pleased to call it, in thinking of this, that, and the other thing; and truly he was right, for if he had turned it inside out, he would, peradventure, have found nothing there to repay him for the trouble. But, for all this, he was a very decentish sort of a man, as times go; for he subscribed liberally to all public-spirited undertakings that promised to bring him in a good profit; attended upon all public meetings whose proceedings were to be published in the newspapers, with the names of the chairman, secretary, and committee; and gave away his money with tolerable liberality where he was sure of its being recorded. In short, he was wont to say, that he did not mind spending a dol-

lar any more than other people, only the loss of the
interest was what he grudged a little.

The Childe's father was an honest tinman, in times
which try men's pedigrees,—that is to say, some forty
years ago ; and Roeliff being brought up to the same
trade—we beg pardon, profession,—became, as it were,
so enamoured of noise, that he never could endure the
silence of the country ; was especially melancholy of
a summer evening, when all the carts had gone home ;
and often used to say that Sunday would be intolerable
were it not for the ringing of the bells.   Yet, for all
his attachment to noise, he never made much in the
world himself, and what little he did make was in his
sleep, he having a most sonorous and musical proboscis.
It was thought to be owing to this impatience of repose,
or rather silence, that he caused his daughter, at the expense of a great deal of money, to be taught the piano,
by a first rate pianist, whose lessons were so eminently
successful, that Roeliff was wont to affirm her playing always put him in mind of the tinman's shop.

His early life, until the age of nearly forty, was spent
in plodding and projecting schemes for growing rich,
but without success.   Having, however, contrived to
amass a few thousands, in the good old way of saving
a part of his earnings, he was inspired to purchase six
acres of land in the outskirts of the city, in doing which
he made a most fortunate blunder—he bought in the
wrong place, as everybody assured him.   In process of
years, however, it turned out to have been the right one,
for the city took it into its head to grow lustily in that
quarter.   Streets were laid out lengthwise and cross-
wise through it; one of which was called after his name.
The speculators turned their interests that way, and
Roeliff came out of his blunder with a great *plum* in
his pocket ; nay, some said with a plum in each pocket.
"Where is the use," said he to his friends, "of taking
such pains to do right, when I have grown rich by what

everybody said was wrong ?"   His friends echoed the sentiment ; for what man of two plums was ever contradicted, except by his wife ?   So Roeliff ever afterward took his own way, without paying the least regard to the opinions of wise people: and if, as we have often read in a book, the proof of the pudding is in the eating, he was right, for I have heard a man of great experience hint, that one-half the mistakes we make in this world come of taking the advice of other people.   " Every man," he would say, " is, after all, the best judge of his own business.   And if he at any time asks the opinion of others, it should only be that he may gather more reasons for following his own."

The period in which a man grows rich in his own estimation, is the crisis of his fate ; and indeed the rule will apply equally to nations.   Every day we see people who don't know what to do with themselves because they have grown rich : and is not this unlucky country of ours on the eve of a mighty struggle, merely because she is just getting out of debt ; and, forgetful of the old proverbs, about reckoning your chickens before they are hatched, and hallooing before you are out of the wood, is in a convulsion of doubt and uncertainty as to what she will do with her money afterward.   So it happened with friend Roeliff.

He was more puzzled a hundred times to know how to spend, than he was in making his fortune ; and had it not been for his great resource of standing under the window of a neighbouring tinman's shop, enjoying the merry " clink of hammers closing rivets up," he would have been devoured by the blue devils, which everybody knows are almost as bad as printers' devils.   At first he was smitten with an ambition to become literary ; accordingly, he purchased all the modern romances : fitted up a library in an elegant style, and one morning determined to set

10*

to work improving his mind. About an hour after he was found fast asleep, the book lying at his feet, and his head resting on the table before him. It was with considerable trouble that Mrs. Orendorf at last shook his eyes open; but such was the stultification of ideas produced by this first effort of study, that Roeliff often declared he did not rightly come to himself until he had spent half an hour under the tinman's shop window. This disgusted him with learning, and he turned his attention to the fine arts; bought pictures, busts, casts, and got nearly smothered to death in submitting to Browere's process for obtaining a fac-simile of one of the ugliest faces in the city. He rode this hobby some time with considerable complacency; and covered his library walls with pictures christened after the names of all the most celebrated masters of the three great schools. One day a foreign connoisseur came to see his collection; and on going away, made Roeliff the happiest of men, by assuring him he had not the least doubt his pictures were genuine, since they had all the faults of all the great masters in the highest perfection. "It is of no consequence," thought Roeliff, "how bad they are, provided they are only originals."

But to a man without taste the cultivation of the fine arts soon loses its relish. Affectation is but short-lived in its enjoyments, and the gratification of one vanity creates only a vacuum for the cravings of another. Roeliff was again becalmed for want of some excitement, and the tinman, unfortunately, removed to a distant part of the city, leaving, as it were, a dreadful noiseless solitude behind him. At this critical period, his favourite nephew, an eminent supercargo, who had made the tour of Europe, returned like most of the touring young gentlemen, who go abroad to acquire taste and whiskers, with a devouring passion for music. He had heard Paganini, and that was enough to put any

man in his senses out of them, in the quavering of a
demi-semi-quaver. Under the tuition of the regenerated
man, Roeliff soon became music-mad. He subscribed
to musical soirées ; to musical importations from Italy ;
to private musical parties, held in a public room, in the
presence of several hundred strangers ; and enjoyed
the treat with such a zest, that it is affirmed he was
actually more than once roused from a profound sleep,
by the crashes at the end of some of the grand over-
tures.   " Bless me ! how exquisite ! it puts me in mind
of the tinman's shop," would he exclaim, yawning at the
same time like the mouth of the great Kentucky cavern.

One summer came—the trying season for people of
fashion and sensibility, and the favourite one of Roeliff,
who could then sit at the open windows, and enjoy the
excitement of noise, dust, and confusion, to the utmost
degree possible, in the paradise of Broadway, just as
our southern visiters do.   But it is time to say something of Mrs. Orendorf, who had a great deal to say for
herself, when occasion called for the exercise of her
eloquence.   About this time she made the discovery,
that though she had spent every summer of her life in the
city, for more than forty years, without falling a victim
to the heat and the bad air, it was quite impossible to
do so any longer.   In short, the mania of travelling
had seized her violently, and honest Roeliff was at
length wrought upon to compromise matters with her.
Mrs. Roeliff hinted strongly at a trip to Paris, but it
would not do.   In the first place, he considered his wife
a beauty, as she really had been twenty years before ;
and felt some apprehensions she might be run away
with by a French marquis.   In the second place, he
could not bear the idea of parting for so long a time
from the music and dust of Broadway ; and in the
third place, he had some rational doubts whether he
should cut any considerable figure in the saloons of
Paris. Mrs. Orendorf, however, insisted on going

abroad somewhere, and the worthy gentleman proposed
Canada. The lady, on being assured that Canada was
actually a foreign country, assented to the arrangement; and it was determined that they should stop a
few days at the Springs, on their way to foreign parts.
Accordingly, Mrs. Orendorf, and her only daughter,
Minerva, went forth into the milliners' shops to array
themselves gorgeously for the approaching campaign.
It was settled that the travelled supercargo, for whom
Roeliff entertained an astonishing respect, and in whose
favour he had conceived a plan which will be developed
in good time, should go with him, as Minerva's beau.
Young Dibdill, so he was called, abhorred such notorious
things as a family party; and was at first inclined, as
he declared, to "cut the whole concern;" but as Minerva
was a very pretty girl, and an heiress besides, he at
length made up his mind to be bored to death, and accorded his consent, with the air of a person conferring
a great favour.

That our travelled readers may not turn up their
noses at Mr. Julius Dibdill for such a barbarous dere-
liction of the dignity of his *caste*, we will describe our
heroine, before we proceed with our legend. She had a
beautiful little face, rather pale, and reflecting—a beautiful little figure, round, and finely formed—a beautiful
little foot and hand—and the most beautiful little pocket
ever worn by woman. It held two plums,—for be it
known that Roeliff Orendorf had but this only child,
and she was heiress to all he had in the world. She
was, moreover, accomplished, for she danced, sung,
dressed, and walked according to the best models; and
what is greatly to her credit, though rich, handsome,
and admired, she was not more than half-spoiled. It
is not to be denied that she was a little sophisticated,
a little affected, and a little too fond of the looking-
glass and the milliners' shops; but there was at bottom
a foundation of good sense, good feeling, and pure sen-

sibility, which, it was obvious to an attentive observer, would, under happy auspices, in good time, redeem her from all these little foibles.

Minerva, though scarcely eighteen, had many admirers, and might have had many more, had it not been for her unfortunate name, which put the young gentlemen in mind of the goddess of wisdom ; and kept some of them at an awful distance. Among these admirers were two who claimed and received particular preference in different ways—her cousin Julius she despised more than any other, and Reuben Rossmore she cherished above all the rest in her heart. Yet, strange to tell, she preferred a walk in Broadway at noon with Julius, before one with Reuben ; and a walk with Reuben on the Battery of a moonlight evening, to one with her cousin Julius. Would you know the reason of this odd inconsistency? Julius was one of the best dressed and most fashionable young men in the city. He smuggled all his clothes from London and Paris by means of a friend in one of the packets. Whereas Reuben was generally about twelve hours behind the march of improvement in his dress, and wanted that indispensable requisite of a modern Adonis, a muzzle *à la Bison*. So far as nature's workmanship went, Reuben was Apollo to a satyr, when compared with Julius ; but the tailor cast his thimble, his shears, and his goose into the scale, and restored the balance in favour of the latter. Not one of the charming divinities who emulate the waddle of a duck in their walk, and the celebrated *Venus de Monomotapa* in their figures, but envied Minerva, when escorted by Julius ; yet not a single one of them all would have cared, had she walked from Dan to Beersheba, and back again, with Reuben Rossmore. Such is the influence of the example of others on the heart of a young girl, that our heroine sometimes would turn a corner when she saw Reuben coming, while she always met Julius with

smiling welcome, or at least something that answered
the purpose just as well. To sum up all in one word,
Julius was most welcome in public, Reuben in private.

" She is ashamed of me," said Reuben to himself,
when he sometimes thought she wished to avoid him in
Broadway ; and he would refrain from visiting her for
several days. But when at length he overcame his feelings, and went to see her, the manner of her reception
in the quiet parlour of the worthy Roeliff banished
these throes of pride, and he forgot his suspicions in the
joy of a smiling unaffected welcome.

It was on the 29th of June, 1828, that the party,
consisting of Roeliff, his lady, daughter, and nephew,
two servants, six trunks, and eight bandboxes, embarked
in the steamboat for Albany. Minerva recommended
the safety-barge, on account of the total absence of all
danger, and the quiet which reigns in these delightful
conveyances. But Roeliff hated quiet, and loved his
money, and, on Mrs. Orendorf observing the fare was
much higher than in the other boats, like honest John
Gilpin—

> "Childe Roeliff kissed his loving wife,
>   O'erjoy'd was he to find,
> That though on pleasure she was bent,
>   She had a frugal mind."

So they embarked on board one of the fast boats,
and away they went up the river as swift as the wind.
It ought to have been stated before, but it is not too
late to do it now, that young Rossmore had more than
once hinted his desire to accompany them ; yet though
somewhat of a favourite with the whole party, except
Julius, who disliked him from an instinctive perception
of his superiority, somehow or another it so happened
that no one thought of giving him an invitation. He
however accompanied them to the boat ; and Minerva,
at parting, could not help saying, as she gave him a

hand as soft and white as the fleecy snow before it becomes contaminated by touching the dirty earth, accompanied by a smile like that of Aurora, when, in the charming month of June, she leads the rosy hours over the high eastern hills, diffusing light, and warmth, and gladness over the face of nature,—

"I hope we shall meet you in the course of our journey."

The last bell rung—the cry of "Ashore! ashore!" was heard fore and aft the vessel, which lay champing the bit, as it were, like an impatient race-horse; and heaving back and forth in a sort of convulsive effort to be free. Reuben jumped on the wharf—the word was given, the fasts let go, and as if by magic she glided off, first slowly, then swifter and swifter, until the wharves, the streets, the whole city seemed scampering behind and gradually disappearing like the shadows of a misty morning. For some reason or other, Minerva turned her head towards the receding city, and to the last saw Reuben standing at the end of the wharf, watching the progress of the enchanted barke that bore her away.

This was the first time our heroine had set forth to see the world, and of consequence, her imagination had never been blighted by the disappointment of those glowing anticipations with which the fancy of untried and inexperienced youth gilds the yet unexplored terra incognita. Her head was full of unknown beauties that were to spring up under her feet and greet her at every step; and of strange and novel scenes and adventures, of which as yet she could form no definite conception. The novelty of the steamboat, the swiftness of its motion, and the quick succession of beautiful scenery on either shore of the river, for awhile delighted her beyond expression; but she was mortified to find by degrees, that the monotony of motion, the heat of the weather, increased by the effusion of so much scalding steam and greasy vapour from the machinery, gradually produced an irksome and impatient feeling, a peevish wish to arrive at Albany. The confined air of the cabin, the crowd, the clattering of plates, knives, forks; the impatient bawlings of " waiter! boy !" from hungry passengers, all combined, took away her appetite, and gave her a headache, so that by the time they arrived at the hotel in Albany, she was glad to retire to her chamber, and seek that balmy rest she had hitherto enjoyed at her quiet home.   But in this she was sorely disappointed.   The hurly-burly of the house, which lasted till long after midnight—and the arrival and departure of stages just about the dawn of day ; together with that odd feeling which is experienced by persons who go from home for the first time, of occupying a strange bed, banished sleep from her pillow, and she arose languid and unrefreshed.   And thus ended the first lesson.

Childe Roeliff would gladly have sojourned a day or two in Albany.   It was the city of his ancestors, one of whom had emigrated to New-York, in high dudgeon at beholding the progress of that pestilent practice of building houses with the broadside in front, instead of the gable-end, as had been the custom from time immemorial.   He was moreover smitten with admiration of the noise and hurly-burly of the hotel, which reminded him of his old favourite place of resort, the tinman's shop.   But Mrs. Orendorf was impatient to reach the Springs, and Minerva, besides some little stimulus of the same kind, longed to get clear of the racket which surrounded her.   As to friend Julius, he had explored the larder of the hotel, and carried his researches into the kitchen ; there was nothing but commonplace materials in the one, and no French cook in the other.   He was therefore ready to turn his back upon Albany at a moment's warning.   Accordingly they departed immediately after dinner, and proceeded on their way to Saratoga.   The bill made Roeliff look rather blue, but he was too much of a man of spirit to demur, though there was a certain bottle of *chateaux margaux*, which squire Julius had called for, the price of which was above rubies.

The ostensible object of our travellers was to explore and admire the beauties of the country; but somehow or other they travelled so fast all day, and were so tired when night came, that they scarcely saw any thing except from the carriage, on their way to the Springs, which they reached rather late in the evening. A great piece of good fortune befell them on their arrival. A large party had left Congress Hall in the afternoon, and they were consequently enabled to obtain excellent rooms at that grand resort of beauty and fashion. That very evening they had a ball, and Minerva was dragged to it by her mother, though she would not have been able to keep herself awake, had it not been for her astonishment at seeing some of the elderly married ladies dance the waltz and gallopade. Julius was in his element, and created a sensation, by the exuberance of his small-talk and whiskers. Indeed, he was so much admired that Minerva was almost inclined to doubt her understanding, as well as her experience, both which had long since pronounced him a heartless, headless coxcomb. Two fashionable married ladies at once took him under their patronage, and Childe Roeliff was sometimes so much annoyed at his neglect of his daughter, that he said to himself, in the bitterness of his heart, " I wonder what business married women have with young beaux ? In my time it was considered very improper." Poor man, he forgot that he was but lately initiated into high life, and that the march of intellect had been like that of a comet since his time, as he called it.

Minerva was at first astonished, then amused, and then delighted with the noisy, easy system of flirtation at that time in vogue at Congress Hall. In the course
F   11

of a few days,—such is the influence of example on the
mind of a young inexperienced female,—she lost all
that feeling of delicate shyness, which is so apt to embarrass a timid, high-souled, intellectual girl, in her first
outset in life ; she could run across a room, bounce
into a chair, talk loud and long, and quiz people
nobody knew, just as well, and with as little of that
exploded vulgarism called, if I recollect aright, blushing, as either Mrs. Asheputtle or Mrs. Dowdykin, both
of whom had made the "*grand tower*," as their husbands took care to inform everybody ; and had learned
the true Parisian pronunciation, from a French fille-de-
chambre of the first pretensions. These two lady
patronesses of Congress Hall took our heroine under
their special protection, and Mrs. Orendorf affirmed she
could see a great improvement in her every day. " I
declare," said she to Roeliff, " I do think Minerva could
talk to six gentlemen all at once, and even dance the gallopade with a man she never saw before, without being in
the least frightened."—" So much the worse," said the
Childe. " In my time a young woman could not say
boo to a goose in a strange company, without your
hearing her heart beat all the while."—" So much the
worse," said Mrs. Roeliff, " what is a woman good for
if she can't talk, I wonder."—" I don't know," said the
Childe, " except it be to make puddings and mend
stockings."—" I wish to heaven you'd mend your
manners," cried Mrs. Roeliff; and thus the conference
ended, as it generally does in these cases, with a mutual
conviction in the mind of each that the other was a
most unreasonable person. Nothing, in fact, reconciled
Roeliff to the Springs, except the inspiring racket of the
drawing-room of Congress Hall, which he declared
put him always in mind of the tinman's shop. The
following letters were written by Minerva and her
cousin Julius, about a week after their arrival at Saratoga Springs.

" *To Miss Juliana Grantland, New-York.*

" My dear Juliana :—

" I am quite delighted with this place, now that I have got over that bad habit of blushing and trembling, which Mrs. Asheputtle assures me is highly indecent and unbecoming. She says it is a sign of a bad conscience and wicked thoughts, when the blood rushes into the face. I wish you knew Mrs. Asheputtle. She has been all over Europe, and seen several kings of the old dynasties, who, she says, were much more difficult to come at than the new ones, who are so much afraid of the *canaille*, that they are civil to everybody. Only think, how vulgar. Mrs. Asheputtle says, that she knew several men with titles ; and that she is sure, if she had not been unfortunately married before, she might have been the wife of the Marquis of *Tête de Veau.* The marquis was terribly disappointed when he found she had a husband already ; but they made amends by forming a Platonic attachment, which means —I don't know really what it means—for Mrs. Asheputtle, it seemed to me, could not tell herself. All I know is, that it must be a delightful thing, and I long to try it, when I am married—for Mrs. Asheputtle says it won't do for a single lady. What can it be, I wonder ?

" You can't think how delightful it is here. The company is so fashionable. I had almost said genteel. But fashion and gentility are quite opposite things, as I have learned since I came. At least, fashion is very opposite to what my ideas of genteel used to be at home. There it was thought genteel, among the humdrum people that visited at our house, to speak in a gentle subdued tone of voice ; to move, if one moved at all, without hurry or noise ; to refrain from talking with one's mouth full of sweetmeats ; to give the floor to others after dancing a cotillon ; not to interrupt any

F 2

one in speaking ; and above all not to talk all together,
and as loud as possible.   But here, my dear Juliana,
every thing is different.   Everybody talks at once, and
as loud as they can, which is very natural and proper,
you know, or how could they make themselves heard ?
Nothing is more common than to see them run from one
end of the long-room to the other, and flounce into a
chair, as in the game of puss in a corner.   And it does
seem to me that when the young ladies get a place in a
cotillon, or waltz, for cotillons are vulgar, they don't
know when to sit down.   I must tell you an odd thing
that made me laugh the other night.   Julius was dancing the waltz with Mrs. Asheputtle, and their faces
somehow came so close together that his whiskers
tickled her nose, and set her sneezing, so that she was
obliged to sit down.   We are so musical here, you
can't think ; and have private concerts, where the young
ladies sing before two or three hundred people.   I was
foolish enough to be persuaded one night to sing, or
rather attempt to sing, ' Thou art gone awa frae me,
Mary,' but my heart beat so I could not raise a note,
and I was obliged to leave the piano, mortified almost
to death, to think I had exposed myself before so many
people.   Mrs. Asheputtle lectured me finely, declaring
she was ashamed to see a young lady, who had been
under her tuition more than a week, blushing and panting like a miserable innocent.   My mother too was
very angry, and scolded me for my want of breeding.
But I was a little comforted by overhearing a gentleman, who is looked up to by everybody here, on account of his sense and learning, say to another, ' It
is quite a treat now-a-days to see any thing like feminine timidity.   The ladies of the present day have the
nerves of the Nemean lion, and are afraid of nothing
but spiders.   For my part, I had rather have seen that
pretty little girl shrink from this public exhibition, than
hear Pasta sing her best.   However, if I know the lady

who has taken her under her tuition, it will not be long
before she is able to sing at a theatre, or in a bear-
garden.'

"When I cóuld muster courage to look up, and round
about me, who should I see but Reuben Rossmore,
standing close at my side, and eying me with such a
look of affectionate kindness, that I could have fairly
cried, if I had not been ashamed. He spoke to me in
a voice, too, that went to my heart, and I should have
been happy again, if I had not seen Mrs. Asheputtle
looking at Reuben, and giggling. 'Lord, my dear,'
whispered she, coming up close to my ear, 'Lord, who is
that you shook hands with just now. I never saw such
a barbarian, to come here with such a coat as that;
why, I believe it was made before the flood. I'll tell
you what, my dear, if you don't cut that coat, which
was certainly cut by Noah's tailor, I shall cut you, and
so will all your fashionable acquaintance.' I could not
stand this, so I turned away from Reuben, and pretended not to notice he was near me, or to hear what
he said. In a little while he left me, and I saw him no
more that evening. I felt my heart sink at his leaving
me, though it was my own fault; and was standing by
myself, thinking whether he would come again, when I
was addressed by the gentleman who made the speech
about my singing, or rather my not singing. He beguiled me into a conversation, such as I have not heard
since I came; and that so charmingly, that in a little
while I forgot my mortified feelings, and chatted away
with him, with as little effort or timidity as if I had
been talking to my father. He spoke of the beauties
of a ride he had taken to Lake George, a day or two
before, by the way of Jesup's Landing; and described
it in such unaffected, yet rich language, that I was drawn
completely out of the scene before me, into rural shades,
among rugged rocks, and murmuring waters, and roaring cascades. He seemed pleased with my replies, or

11*

rather, I believe, with the deep attention I paid him;
and when called away by my mother, I heard him say
to his friend,—

"'A charming little girl: it is a great pity she has
fallen into such bad company.'

"'Bad company!' replied the other, 'is it not highly
fashionable?'

"'Doubtless, but not the less dangerous to a young
and inexperienced girl on that account. People who
aspire to lead the *ton* are not always the best bred;
and the union of fashion and vulgarity is not uncommon. A hoydenish familiarity is often mistaken for
graceful ease; loud talking and boisterous laughter for
wit and vivacity; a total disregard to the feelings of
supposed inferiors for a lofty sense of superiority;
affectation for grace, and swaggering impudence for the
air noble.'

"I have since had several conversations with Mr.
Seabright—that is his name,—who sometimes puts me
out of conceit with Mrs. Asheputtle and her set. He
seems to single me out; and though the other young
ladies affect to laugh at my conquest of the old bache-
lor, I can see very well they all consider his notice an
honour. Mr. Seabright and Reuben have formed an
acquaintance, and take long rides and walks together.

"'That is a young man of merit as well as talents,
Miss Orendorf,' said he, this morning, 'very different
from the common run.'

"I believe I blushed—I am sure I felt my heart
beat at this praise of Reuben. I wish to heaven he
would change his tailor.

"My father begins to get tired of this place; and
as for myself, notwithstanding the excitement of
talking, flirting, waltzing, gallopading, and dressing, I
sometimes catch myself getting tired too, and last
night yawned in the face of Mrs. Asheputtle as she
was describing a Platonic walk by moonlight on the

Lake of Geneva with the Marquis of *Tête de Veau.*
I fancy she is rather cool since.   Since talking with
Mr. Seabright I feel my taste for rural scenes re-
viving, and have persuaded my father to go to Lake
George to-morrow, by the way of Jesup's Landing.   Mamma seems rather inclined to stay a few
days longer, though I don't know why, for Mrs. Asheputtle laughs at her before my face ; and I blush to
tell you that I have almost lost the spirit to resent it.
Nay, I will confess to you, Juliana, that I have more
than once caught myself being ashamed of my kind
good parents, because they are ignorant of certain fac-
titious nothings, as Mr. Seabright calls them, which are
supposed to constitute good breeding.   My cousin Julius
don't seem much pleased with the idea of leaving Mrs.
Asheputtle, with whom he has formed a Platonic
attachment ; for you must know, though fashionable
women can have but one husband at a time, they may
have as many Platonics as they please.   However, he
is to accompany us, and seems to think we ought to be
grateful for the sacrifice.   For my part, I had just as
soon he would stay where he is ; for though I like to
be gallanted by him in public, between ourselves, Juliana, he is the most stupid man in private you ever
knew.   Adieu, I will write you again.

" Yours, ever,

" MINERVA ORENDORF.

" P.S.—I am so pleased !   You must know there
has been a little coolness between Reuben and me—
about—about his coat, I believe.   But it so happened,
that my father was in such a good humour at the pros-
pect of getting away from this place at last, that in the
fulness of his heart he has invited Reuben to be of the
party to Lake George.   Reuben pretended to make
some excuses, but I could see his eyes sparkle brighter
than ever, and he soon got over his scruples.   If I don't
fit him for this I'm no woman."

The same post carried the following letter from Mr. Julius Dibdill to his friend Count Rumpel Stiltskin, a distinguished foreigner, and *eléve* vice-cousul.

"My dear Count,

"One of the great disadvantages of foreign travel is, that it unfits one for the enjoyment of any thing in one's own country, particularly when that country is so every way inferior to the old world. It is truly a great misfortune for a man to have too much taste and refinement. I feel this truth every day of my life; and could almost find in my heart to regret the acquirement of habits and accomplishments that almost disqualify me for a citizen of this vulgar republic, which, I am sorry to perceive, seems in a fair way of debauching the whole world with her pernicious example of liberty and equality. If it were not for Delmonico and Palmo, the musical soirées, and a few other matters, I should be the most miserable man in the world. Would you believe it, my dear count, there is not a silver fork to be seen in all the hotels between New-York and Saratoga? And yet the people pretend to be civilized!

"I will acquaint you with my reasons for submitting to the martyrdom of beauing my cousin to this place. My uncle, whose wealth, and nothing else, redeems him from utter and irretrievable condemnation in my eyes, has hinted to me, that if I can make myself agreeable to the goddess Minerva, he will come down handsomely on the happy day, and leave us all he has in his will. I thought I might possibly make my courtship endurable by mixing it up with a little flirtation with the dames at the Springs. By-the-way, count, almost the only improvement I have observed in this country since I first left it, is in the well-bred married ladies, who begin to relish the European fashion of encouraging young gentlemen in a little harmless flirtation wonderfully. It is one of the highest proofs of the progress of refinement among these barbarians, that can be conceived.

"Travelling in the steamboat is detestable. The same vile system of equality which pervades all this horrible country, where no respect is paid to the aristocracy, reigns in all its glory in these abominable inventions of republican genius. At breakfast I sat next a fellow who actually put his knife in his mouth with a bushel of potatoes on it; loaded his plate with contributions from all parts of the table at once; bawled out ' boy !' to the waiters five hundred times, with his mouth full of the produce of the four quarters of the globe; and concluded his trencher feats by upsetting a cup of moderate hot coffee right into my lap. The gormandizing cyclop made me an apology, it is true; but I make a point now of understanding nothing but French and Italian, and looked at the monster with an air of perfect ignorance of what he was pleased to say. 'He is a foreigner, I believe,' said the cyclop to his friend. And I forgave him the coffee, on the score of a mistake so highly complimentary.

"At Albany, where we spent a night, it is sufficient to say that they affected great state at the hotel; with what success you may conjecture, when I tell you there was neither French cookery nor silver forks. Mine honoured uncle and predestined father-in-law was hugely delighted, however, with his entertainment; and he and the jolly landlord cracked jokes in a style of the most abominable republican equality; or rather, I should say, the landlord joked, and my uncle laughed, having never attempted a joke, I believe, since the old continental war.

"I find this place more tolerable, notwithstanding the absence of the *summum bonum*—an accomplished travelled cook. They are musical here; the amateurs officiate and keep time, like the two buckets of a well,—one up, the other down. But this is neither here nor

F 3

there—it is fashionable abroad—and whatever is fashionable is worthy the attention of fashionable people.
My intended was one night persuaded, or rather commanded, by her mother, to attempt a horrible ballad ;
and, awful to relate, such was her vulgar timidity that
she faltered, panted, and was obliged to give it up at
the conclusion of the first verse.   What under heaven
shall I do with such a woman ?   I shall positively take
her abroad and shut her up in a nunnery.

" We have also the waltz, the gallopade, and the
exquisite mazourka—each more delightful than the
other.   Nothing in the world is better calculated to
dissipate that vulgar awkwardness which is so apt to
subsist among strange men and women, accidentally
thrown together, than these highly sociable dances, which
break down all ceremony and introduce the greatest
strangers, as it were, into each other's arms.   The
first night of my arrival I singled out the most dashing
of the married ladies, a Mrs. Asheputtle, who has
travelled : we danced the gallopade, and were as inti-
mate as if we had been hatched in the same dovecot.
She is a charming, spirited being, who has travelled
to the greatest advantage ; is perfectly aware of the
innocence of flirtation ; admires young fellows of spirit ;
and has a sovereign contempt for her husband.   What
excellent materials for a Platonic arrangement are here
met together in one person.   I foresee we shall be
the best friends in the world ; or rather, we are already
so much so that some of the vulgar begin to look significantly and whisper knowingly on the matter.   This
is delightful, and gives such a zest to flirtation you
know.   For my part, I would not care for Venus herself, except we could conjure up a little wonder among
these republicans.

" Mine uncle, the execrable Roeliff Orendorf, has
just announced his determination to leave this to-morrow for Lake George, where the ladies are to banquet

on the picturesque, and the said Roeliff on black bass.
But I—I who have seen the Lago Maggiore, and the
Isola Bella—I who have sailed in a gondola on a Venetian canal—I who have eaten of maccaroni and Ver-
micelli soup, concocted by an Italian artist in the very
air of Italy—and I who have luxuriated at the Café
Hardy on *turbot à la crème et au gratin*—I to be bam-
boozled into admiration or ecstasy by Lake George
and its black bass !—forbid it, Hamel Frères ; forbid
it, immortal Corcellet ; and forbid it, heaven ! But
the fiat is gone forth, and we depart to-morrow by a
new route, which has been recommended by one Seabright, a quiz, who pretends to taste and all that, though,
so far as I can learn, he has never been outside Sandy
Hook in his life. He has talked a great deal to the
goddess Minerva, and, I dare say, persuaded her she
came full formed from the brain of Jove ; for though
she treats me with attention in public, I must confess
to thee, count, that in private it is exactly otherwise.
I sometimes suspect a horrid monster by the name of
Reuben Rossmore, who has made his appearance here,
and was a beau of hers in New-York. Could I conceive the possibility of a woman who has been accustomed to the cut of my coat for months past, enduring the abstract idea of a man wearing a garment like
that of Master Reuben, I should be inclined to a little
jealousy. But the thing is impossible. Why, count, the
coat was, beyond all doubt, contrived at least six months
ago, and must have been perpetrated by the tailor of
King Stephen, whose inexpressibles, you may chance
to recollect—for you sometimes pretend to read Shaks-
peare to please John Bull—coset xactly half a crown.
I am therefore compelled to believe that she entertains
this monstrous oddity for the truly feminine purpose of
spurring me on through the medium of a little jealousy
to a premature disclosure of my intentions, and a di-

rect offer of my hand.   Jealous !—I, that—but the
thing is too ridiculous.

" However this may be, I intend to propose shortly,
for I can't keep up the farce of courtship and attention
much longer.   When I am married, you know, it will
be in the highest degree vulgar to be civil to her.   I
shall be a free man then, and hey for Mrs. Asheputtle
and the gallopade.   I do therefore purpose to take the
first opportunity in the course of this diabolical tour,
when the moon shines, the stars twinkle, the zephyr
whispers, and the very leaves breathe soft aspirations
of love, to declare myself to the goddess Minerva,
who, if she refuses me, must be more or less than woman.   Then shall we be married—then shall I be free
—then will that detestable and vulgar old man, mine
uncle Roeliff, come down with the shiners—then shall
we, or rather I, Julius Dibdill, cut a sublime caper—
then will the wicked old man and woman, yclept my
father and mother-in-law, go the way of all flesh—and
then shall I be worth two plums at least.   Glorious
anticipation ! and certain as glorious.

" Thine assuredly and ever,

" JULIUS DIBDILL.

" P.S.—I have just learned that the man in the antediluvian coat is invited to join our party.   So much
the better ; I shall have somebody to take the goddess
Minerva off my hands and study the picturesque with
her.   But the divine Asheputtle is abroad—she looks
up at my window—she smiles—she beckons !   Away
goes my pen, and I bequeath mine inkstand to the
d—l : videlicet, the printer's devil."

The morning shone bright, and "all nature smiled in
dewy tears," as the great bard Whipsyllabub saith,
when our party set forth on their way to Lake George.
Following the advice of Seabright, who intimated a possibility of his joining them at the lake, they chose a

route not generally followed, and not laid down in any of the books. It led them through a fine fruitful and picturesque country, the inspiration of which affected the party in various ways. Minerva and Reuben pointed out with sympathetic delight the little clear rivulets that meandered through the meadows, crossing the road back and forth in their devious windings—the rich fields of golden grain in which the happy hus-bandman was now reaping the harvest of his autumn and spring labours; and the distant waving mountains that marked the vicinity of the beautiful Hudson—beautiful in all its course, from its departure from the little parent lake to its entrance into the boundless ocean.   Julius took no note of the country, except that when occa-sionally called upon to admire, he would lug in a com-parison with some scenery on the Rhine, the Lake of Geneva, or the like, intimating something like pity of those unlucky wights who never had an opportunity of seeing them, and who could admire the homely charms of an American landscape.   Mrs. Orendorf did nothing but talk about what a charming place they had just left, and what a charming woman was Mrs. Asheputtle; and Childe Roeliff, having made two or three desperate efforts to resist the inroads of the enemy, and keep his eyes open, fell fast asleep.   Happy is he who can thus at will shut out the world, evade the tediousness of time, and, as it were, annihilate that awful vacuum which intervenes between the great epochs of the day—to wit, breakfast, dinner, and supper.

About midday they came in sight of Jesup's Land-ing, as it is called, a little village close to the banks of the Hudson, which here presents a scene of exquisite beauty.   The river is scarcely half a quarter of a mile wide, and seems to sleep between its banks, one of which rises into irregular hills, bounded in the distance by lofty mountains, the other is a velvet carpet, just spread above the surface of the stream, and running

back to the foot of a range of round full-bosomed hills,
that are succeeded by a range of rugged cliffs.   Several
little streams abounding in trout, and as clear as crystal,
meander through these meadows, fringed with alders
and shrubs of various kinds, wild flowers, and vines;
and here and there a copse of lofty trees.   The little
village consisted of a few comfortable houses, scattered along the right bank of the river, and extending
perhaps a quarter of a mile.   At sight of this charming
scene Reuben and Minerva exchanged looks of mutual
pleasure, indicating that sympathy of taste and feeling
which forms one of those imperceptible ties which
finally bind two hearts together, and constitute the basis
of the purest species of youthful love.   There was
nobody present to call in question the orthodoxy of
Reuben's coat; no coterie of fashion to make Minerva
ashamed of so unfashionable a beau, and she resigned
herself gently into that respect and admiration which
his goodness of heart, his natural talents, and extensive
acquirements merited, and which nothing but the fear
of being laughed at could repress in her bosom.

It was decided that they should take dinner at a neat
comfortable inn, the names of whose owners we would
certainly immortalize in this our story, did we chance
to recollect them.   But as there is but one public house
in the village, the traveller, who we hope may be
tempted to visit this scene, when peradventure he shall
peruse the adventures of the good Childe Roeliff, cannot
well mistake the house.   While dinner was preparing
Minerva proposed a walk, for the purpose of viewing a
fall distant about half a mile, which Mr. Seabright had
excited her curiosity to see.   The old folks were too
tired; and Julius had seen the cascade of Lauterbrunn,
and a dozen besides, in foreign parts, so there was no
use in his going to visit one that by no possibility could
be supposed equal to these.   Minerva and Reuben
therefore set out together, after being enjoined by the

old gentleman not to keep them waiting dinner. Julius, in the mean time, meditated a scrutiny into the kitchen, to see into the flesh-pots of Egypt.

After proceeding over a high ridge which hid the river from their view, the road suddenly turned to the left down a steep hill, and they beheld the river raging in violent whirlpools, covered with foam, and darting through its narrow channel with noisy vehemence. A few houses, and a sawmill lay far beneath them, scattered among rocks and little gardens, where the sunflower paid its homage to the god of its idolatry, and the cabbage grew in luxuriant and chubby rotundity. Descending the hill, they began to notice the white spray rising above the tops of the pine-trees which crowned the perpendicular cliff on the opposite side of the river, and gradually the roar of the torrent strengthened into sublimity. At length they turned the corner of the mill, and beheld one of the finest scenes to be found in a state abounding in the beautiful and sublime of nature.

Minerva had taken the arm of the young man in descending the hill, and she continued to lean on it, with a more perceptible pressure, as they stood, in the silence of strong emotion, gazing at the scene before them. Perhaps we should have said Minerva stood gazing at the scene—for it is due to the strict accuracy we mean to preserve throughout our progress, to state that Reuben, after glancing at the fall, happened to cast his eye upon the damsel leaning on his arm, and pressing unconsciously against him in thrilling admiration, mixed with apprehension of the tremendous uproar of the waters, which shook the earth at their feet. He there beheld a countenance so beautiful, yet so apparently unconscious of beauty, so lighted up with feeling, intelligence, and delight, that for some moments he forgot the charms of inanimate nature in the contemplation of a rarer mas-

terpiece. As he stood thus gazing in her face, their eyes
happened to meet, and the rose was never in the dewy
spring morning decked with such a tint as spread,
like the Aurora Borealis, over the mild heaven of her
countenance.   We will not affirm that Reuben blushed
too, for that might bring him into disgrace with some
of our fashionable readers.   But we can affirm that his
pulse beat in such a style that if the doctor had been
called in, he would certainly have pronounced him in a
high fever.   Recovering herself in a few moments,
Minerva said, with the prettiest affectation of petulance
imaginable,—

"Pray, young gentleman, did you come here to see
the fall or not ?"

"I did," said Reuben, somewhat surprised.

"Then I wish you would take the trouble to look at
it a little.   I never before suspected you of being insensible to the beauties of nature."

He took out his pencil—it was a self-sharpening
one,—and wrote a few verses which he presented
her.   They turned upon the superiority of the charms
of woman, embellished with gentleness, beauty, intellect, tenderness, sympathy, and, above all, an immortal
soul, over all other triumphs of creative power.   We
would insert them here, but Minerva always declared
she threw the manuscript into the torrent.

"What nonsense !" exclaimed she, after reading it ;
and there is every reason to believe she was affronted
at being thus put in comparison with a waterfall.   But,
somehow or other, she still held his arm while they
staid at the foot of the torrent, and until they reached
the inn.   Nay, she held it while they mounted the
steps, and after they entered the dining-room, when Mrs.
Orendorf observed, rather significantly, "Minerva, can't
you stand alone ?"

Minerva started, let go the arm, and ran up-stairs ;

for what purpose is a mystery to this day : perhaps
it was because she wanted to convince the old lady she
could stand alone. Master Julius listened to the account of their excursion with astonishing apathy; but
was actually inspired to rub his hands in ecstasy, by
the sight of a fine dish of trout, which, for the time
being, banished the recollection of *turbot à la crème et
au gratin.*

Nothing on earth can exceed the beauty of the
scenery from Jesup's Landing to Hadley's Falls, of a
fine summer afternoon ; and the party, at least two of
them, enjoyed it with all the zest of youthful feeling
awakened into admiration of every thing delightful, by
the new-born excitement of that universal passion which
in its first dawnings communicates a charm to every
thing we hear, every thing we see, every thing we
enjoy.   The youthful lover, ere his hopes are poisoned
by jealousy and doubt, feels a glow about his heart, an
elasticity of spirit, a capacity for enjoyment he never
knew before.   Solitude acquires a new charm, for his
fancy has now an object of perpetual contemplation,
which is everywhere its associate, and with which his
spirit holds converse absent as well as present.   He
imagines every thing grateful and endearing to his
heart ; creates a thousand occasions of innocent gratification ; conjures up smiles, blushes, and glances more
eloquent than words ; the present is happiness, the
future enchanting ; and this fretful world the garden of
Eden, inhabited by one more blooming, beautiful, and
pure than the mother of mankind at the first moment
of her creation, ere the serpent whispered his first
temptations, and the first transgression stained the virgin
earth.   Such, or something like these, were the feelings
of Minerva and Reuben, as they stole a few minutes
to ramble along the river to the mouth of a little stream
that joined it out of the meadows about a quarter of a
mile from the inn.   12*

"Nothing is wanting to the beauty of this fairy scene," said the young man.

"Yes," replied Minerva, "you have named the very thing wanting. It is indeed a fairy scene, and could we only imagine it the occasional haunt of these charming little folks, it would derive additional interest and beauty from the association. I have been told that few, if any, of the rivers of the ancient world are to be compared with this; but they are ennobled by their nymphs, their river gods, and their connexion with poetry, romance, and religion, while our pure and beautiful streams have nothing but reality to recommend them. I sometimes wish I could believe in the fairies."

"And so do I," answered Reuben. "I confess I often look back with regret upon that happy period, before fancy became the slave of reason; when the youthful imagination was filled with the unseen glories of enchanted palaces; with spirits, fairies, and genii, guarding virtue, punishing vice; alluring us to the practice of all the moral duties by the most splendid rewards, and deterring us from the commission of crimes by the most awakening punishments. I sympathize with the French poet, when he complains that,

> ' The fays and all are gone,
> Reason, reason reigns alone ;
> Every grace and charm is fled,
> All by dulness banished.
> Thus we ponder slow and sad,
> After truth the world is mad ;
> Ah ! believe me, error too
> Hath its charms nor small nor few.' "

The carriage now overtook them, and they proceeded on their journey sitting side by side, now bowling along the level banks of the river, crowned with trees, whose velvet foliage was reflected in the still, pure water, with an inimitable softness and beauty; and now slowly ascending the round green hills, which every moment opened to their view new and distant landscapes—hills rising above hills, and ending at last in blue mountains seeming to mingle with the skies. Little was said by either, except in that language which all understand,— as an unknown poet says,—

> The Indian maid at home
> Who makes the crystal lake her looking-glass,
> As well as she that moves in courtly balls,
> And sees in full-length mirrors scores of angels.

They followed the direction of each other's eyes in search of nature's masterpieces, or looked into them and beheld them reflected as in the gliding river.

Master Julius Dibdill, having had the misfortune to be a great traveller, saw nothing in the scenery to merit his attention ; but he saw something in these glances which he did not at all like. They spoke a language which he comprehended perfectly, and he began to ponder within himself that it was high time to come to an explanation ; for, incredible as it might seem, the antediluvian coat seemed in a fair way to eclipse the whiskers, at least in these romantic solitudes.

" But I will wait till we arrive at Lake George, where I shall find an assemblage of fashionable people, and resume my empire," thought he.

In the mean time he bestirred himself to make the agreeable ; talked about the musical soirées, the fashions, the great people, the cookery, " and all that sort of thing." But these topics, it would seem, have no enchantment out of the sphere of the drawing-room and fancy ball. Within the magic circle of nature, among meadows, and streams, and rocks, and mountains, and in the deep solitudes of the touching melancholy woods, they hold no sway. The heart responds not to them, and even echo disdains to reply from her sequestered

hiding-place.   Minerva heard what he said, but she
looked at the distant cascade of Hadley, where the
Hudson and the dark rolling Sacondaga come forth
from their empire in the woods, unite their waters, and
quarrel away with angry vehemence, until, becoming as
it were reconciled to their enforced marriage, they jog
on quietly together like Darby and Joan, till they mingle
at last with that emblem of eternity, the vast, unfathom-
able, endless ocean, which swallows up the waters of
the universe at one mighty gulp.

Crossing the river at Hadley, by a bridge hanging
in the air directly over the falls, the scene changed by
degrees into a vast mountainous forest of gloomy pines,
destitute of cultivation, except that here and there, at
long intervals, the hand of man was indicated by a
little clear field, along some devious winding brook,
groping its way through the little valleys, and turning
a sawmill, sore enemy to the gigantic pines, and de-
structive to the primeval forests that have braved the
elements for ages past.   The road was rough and
rocky, and the people they passed were few and far
between ; wild in their looks, and wild in their attire.
Still there was a romantic feeling of novelty connected
with the scene ; it was a perfect contrast to that they
had just quitted ; and there was a solemn and desolate
wildness about it, which partook of sublimity.   Minerva
and Reuben enjoyed it, for they were studying the early
and enchanting rudiments of a first love together,—
the good lady-mother complained sorely of the bruises
she sustained,—Childe Roeliff grumbled, and bitterly
reviled the road because it would not let him sleep,—
while the accomplished Dibdill whiled away the tedious
hours, by every moment asking the driver how far it
was to Lake George, and expressing his impatience to
get there.

The night set in ere they had cleared this wild dis-
trict, and grew exceedingly dark in consequence of the

approach of a storm. The lightning and thunder became frequent and appalling, while the intervals were enveloped in tenfold darkness. The progress of the carriage became necessarily so slow that the excellent Roeliff was at length enabled to accommodate himself with a nap, from which not even the thunder could rouse him. The horses, as is common on such occasions, became dogged and obstinate, and at length came to a dead stand. In the mean time the distant roaring of the woods announced that the tempest was let loose, and approaching on the wings of the whirlwind.

The situation of the party became extremely unpleasant, and Minerva unconsciously pressed against Reuben, as if for protection. The expostulations of the driver with his team at length roused Childe Roeliff from his sleep, who, on being made to comprehend the situation of affairs, forthwith began to scold the unfortunate women, on whom he laid all the blame. In the first place, it was his wife who urged him on to travelling in foreign parts; and in the second, his daughter, who proposed this route through the wilderness, or desert of Moravia, as he termed it. What a capital thing it is to have some one to lay the blame upon in times of tribulation ! To be able to say to another, " It is all your fault," is better in the eyes of some people than all the consolations of philosophy.

The darkness, as we observed before, was intense in these gloomy woods, and it became impossible to distinguish objects through the void, except during the flashes of lightning. In this dilemma, they sat consulting what was to be done, without coming to a determination, occasionally appealing to the driver ; who at length threw them into despair by acknowledging that he feared he had deviated from the right road in the darkness of the night.

" Is there a house near ?" asked Reuben.

"If we are on the right track, there must be one somewhere hereabouts, sir," replied the driver. "But the people who live in it are not of the best character, they say."

A flash of lightning, that seemed to set the heavens and the earth in a blaze, and quivered among the lofty trees, followed by a fearful crash of thunder, interrupted this dialogue. As the explosion rolled away, grumbling at a distance, the silence was interrupted by two or three voices, exclaiming, close to the horses' heads,—

"Hollo! hollo! hollo! who are you?"

The ladies shrieked—Childe Roeliff was struck dumb, and Julius began to think about bandits and brigands. Poor Minerva, frightened out of all recollection of the dignity of the sex, actually seized Reuben's hand, and held it fast, as if she feared he was going to run away.

"Hollo! hollo!—I say, who are you?" repeated the same rough voices.

"Travellers benighted in the woods," replied Reuben.

"Where do you come from?"

"Saratoga."

"Where are you going?"

"To Lake George."

"You'll not get there to-night I reckon."

"Why, how far is it?"

"Five miles, through the worst road in all York state."

"Is there any house near?"

"I suspect I live just nigh hand yonder. You have just passed it.—We heard something queer like, and came out just to see what it was."

"Can you accommodate us for the night?"

"Can't I?—do you think I live in a hollow tree?"

"How far is it to your house?"

"Not a hundred yards yonder. There, you may see it now."

And by the flashes of lightning, they distinguished the house at a little distance.

" O don't let us go with these men !" whispered Minerva to Reuben.

" I dare say they are as rude and as wild as bears," mumbled Mrs. Orendorf.

" No doubt they are squatters," quoth the Childe.

"I can swear to them," said Julius, in an undertone of great apprehension. " They talk and look just like banditti—and this is a most capital place for murder. I wish I had brought my hair-triggers."

" Banditti !" screamed the old lady.

" Don't be alarmed," said Reuben. " There is no danger of banditti in a happy and well-governed country."

" Why, hollo! I say, mister—are you going to light or not ? We can't stand all night here. I felt a drop of rain on my nose just now, and hear the storm coming like fury down yonder. You are welcome to go or stay, only make up your minds at once, or I'm off like a shot."

" We had better go with them," said Reuben. "If they had any mischief in their heads, they could do it here better than anywhere else."

All finally assented to this proposition, warned by the increasing whispers of the woods and the pattering of the rain that no time was to be lost.

The horses, who seemed conscious they had been driven past a place of shelter, willingly suffered the night-walkers to take them by the reins and turn them round, and in less than a minute they drew up before a house, at the door of which stood a woman with a light.

" Quick ! quick ! jump like lamplighters," exclaimed the master of the house ; " or in less than no time you'll be as wet as drowned rats."

The increasing rain and uproar warned them to follow this advice, and the whole party, trunks, band-boxes, and all, were in a trice received into the solitary mansion, which, to their dismay and mortification, they found already occupied by a party of the most question-able figures they had ever seen. It consisted of five or six of what, in the common phrase of Brother Jonathan, are called " hard-looking characters," seated on benches made of slabs, and tippling whiskey in a pretty considera-ble fine style. They looked a little queer at our travellers as they entered, but offered no rudeness of speech or manner; and one of them, a native of the most gallant of all countries, offered Minerva his seat on the slab with great courtesy, considering he was dressed in a red flannel shirt, and had forgotten his shoes some-where or other.

The house in which accident had thus cast our travellers was entirely new, or rather, we may affirm it was not above half-finished. Of the vast superfluity of windows, only two were furnished with glass, and the rest boarded up to keep out the weather. Half the room they occupied was plastered, the other half lathed only, and every thing, in fact, squared with the distinguishing characteristic of honest Brother Jonathan, who of all people in the world excels in building big houses, which he never finishes. The furniture was ex-ceedingly " sparse," as the western members of Con-gress say of the population of the new states : there was a bed in one corner, in which lay ever so many little white-headed rogues, who ever and anon popped up their polls to take a sly look at the strangers. It was sufficiently clean, and the vanity of woman peeped forth even in these wild regions, in the form of a coarse cotton fringe, which hung like a fishing net from the ends of the pillow-cases. There were only two chairs visible, the seats composed of pieces of pine boards. Still nothing was slovenly, and every

thing about the place indicated, not the incurable poverty of an old country, which neither toil nor industry
can remedy, but that temporary absence of conve-
niences, which opportunity had not yet permitted them
to supply.

But to the ladies, and to Childe Roeliff, who for some
years past had been accustomed to the luxuries of a
splendid establishment, all this appeared the very quin-
tessence of poverty and misery combined. They
looked round them with dismay, and to their view all
seemed to indicate that species of want and wretched-
ness which impels mankind to the violation of social
duties, and the perpetration of the deepest crimes.
They trembled for their lives, especially when they
saw suspended above the mantelpiece, and standing
up in the corners, at least half a dozen guns. Squire
Julius, whose head was full of banditti, observed these
mortal weapons as well as the ladies, and gave himself up for lost that night.

"This comes of family parties, and rides in search
of the picturesque. I shall never dance the gallopade
again with the divine Asheputtle, that's certain," thought
he, as he glanced his eye upon the harsh features, athletic
forms, and above all, infamous costume, of the convivial
party.

Mine host was indeed of a face and figure most
alarming to behold. He was fast approaching to the
gigantic in height, and bony in the extreme—in short,
he seemed all bone and sinew. His features were
awfully strong; and of his nose it might be predicated,
that it was no wonder the first drop of rain which
came from the heavens that night fell upon that extensive promontory, for the chances were in its favour
a hundred to one. He was, however, not uncourteous
in his way; but to the eyes of the refined portion of
society, rusticity always conveys an idea of rudeness

and barbarity. It was plain that he was the master of the house, for the tone of his voice indicated as much. Mine hostess was rather a little woman—not deformed or ugly, but quite the contrary. She might have been handsome, had it not been for a garment of green baize, which threw friend Julius into a perspiration of horror.

Our travellers had scarcely entered the house when the storm commenced its career, and such a storm as carries with it all the sublime of nature. The wind howled, the thunder crashed, and the trees groaned, while the rain beat a tattoo upon the roof and sides of the building, as if it was determined to pepper some of those within.

"I've seen many a storm in ould Ireland," exclaimed one of the worshipful members, in a strong Irish accent; "but never any tunder like dis."

"Pooh!" replied a figure that seemed to have been made out of a shingle; "how should you when everybody knows neither the sky nor the earth is half as big in Ireland as in this country."

"Well, suppose and it isn't; what den?—is it any reason why the tunder and lightning wouldn't be as big? answer me dat, you Dutch Yankee."

"Why, I should guess so, arguing from analogy—"

"Ann what?—devil burn me if I know such a woman —and I don't care what she argufies."

"I say," continued the other with great gravity, "that, arguing from analogy, it is quite impossible, as I should partly guess, that the thunder should be as loud in such a small splice of a country, as it is in these United States of Amerrykey. You see now, Mister McKillicuddy—that's a queer name of yours—I wonder your daddy wasn't ashamed to give you such a snorter of a cognomen."

"Do you compare me to a cog-wheel, you shingle

faced monkey?" interrupted Mister McKillicuddy, who, like all his company, was a dealer in sawing boards in this region, where vast quantities are made and sent to New-York by way of the Hudson.

"I compare you?—I'll see you pickled first," said Jonathan; "I was only saying you had a tarnal droll name—I wouldn't have such a name for all the bogs of Ireland."

"Bogs!—you tief—none of your coming over me with bogs;—I've seen a bog in Ireland bigger than the whole State of New-York—yes, and if you come to dat, bigger dan your whole Untied States as you call 'em."

"Whew—w—w!" whistled Jonathan; "what a miserable country that Ireland of yours must be: I don't wonder the snakes and toads have all left it, of their own accord, long ago."

"Of their own accord!—no such ting I tell you.—St. Patrick driv 'em all out by preaching to the rascals."

"Whew!—why I spose maybe you calculate on that as a mighty slick piece of horsemanship. But for all that, he can't hold a candle to our Deacon Mabee. Let the deacon alone for driving a wedge— why, the other night, at a four-days meetin, I wish I may be shot if he didn't drive every cretur out of the schoolhouse exceptin old Granny Whimblebit, who is as deaf as an adder. St. Patrick can't hold a candle to Deacon Mabee, I'm considerably inclined to think."

"May be or may be not, Mister Longreach; nobody shall say any ting, or tink any ting, or dream any ting to the undervallying Saint Patrick."

"Ever in Bosting? I'm from Bosting or thereabouts, I guess, don't you?" replied Mr. Longreach.

"Bosting!—none of your coming over me with your Bosting—Dublin for ever for me, honey!"

"Dubling—I've heard say by one of the slickest fellers within a hundred miles of Bosting—that the city

of Dubling was so leetle you might kiver it all over
with the peeling of a potato."

"By the holy poker, but I'd like to come over that
slick feller.—The peel of a peraty !—By St. Patrick's
blue eyes !"

"Was his eyes blue?" asked Mr. Longreach, with
great apparent earnestness.   "I always heard your
Irish people were great dealers in black eyes, maybe."

"Yes, by the hokey, and I'll give you a short specimen off-hand if you go to make fun upon me, Mister
Longreach."

"I make fun of you !—I'd see your neck stretched
first."

"You wouldn't now, would you," cried Mr. McKillicuddy, rising in great wrath, and making immediate
demonstrations of hostility.   But the rest of the company, who understood the dry humour of Jonathan, and
were enjoying the colloquy, interfered, and insisted
they should drink friends, assuring Mr. McKillicuddy
no harm was meant.   Peace was accordingly restored,
and a short silence ensued.   This, however, was soon
interrupted by the vespers of Childe Roeliff, who, being
tired with his ride and of waiting for supper, had fallen
asleep in one of the two chairs we have commemorated.

"Hush," cried McKillicuddy ; "we will disturb the
ould New-Yorker there.   And, now I think of it, 'tis time
to be going home to the ould woman.   The storm is
over in one-half the time it would have been in swate
Ireland, for all dat tundering Yankee says."

Accordingly, seeing that the moon was peeping forth
from her recesses in the clouds, they made their
homely compliments to the strangers, and quietly sought
their burrows among the rocks and hills.   Julius, who
watched them narrowly, overheard, with the quick ear
of apprehension, one of them say to the landlord, in an
under-tone, "What time shall we be here?"   "About
an hour before day," replied he.

During the preceding dialogue, the mistress of the
mansion had been preparing supper for the travellers,
and Minerva and Reuben had listened with amusing
interest to this homely display of national character.
But Squire Dibdill could not divest himself of the impression that these ill-dressed people were first-rate
banditti, and that they only retired to throw the party
off their guard, and induce them to spend the night in
this dangerous abode. After supper, which was of
the most plentiful kind—for however our people may
lodge, they all feed well—he hinted pretty strongly
about going on to the lake that night. But it was now
ten o'clock, the clouds had again obscured the moon,
and the driver, who heard the proposal from his corner,
declared that neither he nor his horses were in a humour
to undertake such a road at such an hour, in such a
night as this. The road, always bad, must be now
almost impassable, with the torrent of rain which had
just fallen; and he could not answer to his master or
the party for running the risk of a midnight journey.
Julius gave up the point unwillingly, and it was settled
to remain where they were till morning.

No small difficulty occurred in arranging accommo-
dations, as mine host was not accustomed to entertain
strangers of distinction, or indeed any strangers at all.
Seldom did a traveller pass that way, and still more
rarely did they tarry there for the night. We profess
not to know what became of the rest of the party; but
it hath come to our knowledge that Master Julius slept,
or was supposed to sleep, in a little excrescence of a
building that projected from the rear of the house,
usually occupied by the owner of the mansion himself, who resigned it on this occasion to his guest.
About eleven the party retired to rest, and soon a
deathlike silence reigned everywhere, interrupted only
at intervals by the whooping of the owl or the barking
of the dogs about the house, occasionally disturbed by

13*

those "varmints" which still infest the more obscure
recesses of our mountains.   All save Julius were soon
fast asleep, or,—to speak more in accordance with the
"big" style of describing small things now-a-days,—
soon all were locked in the arms of Morpheus ; and it
hath been asserted on good authority, that the last
thoughts of Reuben and the pretty little Minerva were
of each other.

Julius examined his sleeping-room with great attention, but saw nothing to excite his suspicions save a few
spots on the floor, which looked very much like recent
stains of blood.   He went to bed ; but he was nervous,
and could not sleep for thinking of banditti.   He lay
listening for hours after all was quiet as the grave around
him, and the dread silence increased his apprehensions,
insomuch that he wished he had permitted Reuben to
sleep in the room with him, notwithstanding the horror
with which travelled gentlemen, and more especially
English travellers, look upon such a republican enor-
mity.   The state of his mind aggravated every little
sound that met his ear ; the stir of a mouse made his
heart beat double ; the hooting of the solitary owl
sounded like a prophetic foreboding of danger ; and
the barking of the dogs announced to his exaggerated
apprehensions, the approach of the robbers.

After a long probation of tantalizing fears, he at length
worried himself into a sleep, from which he was roused
by a cautious and ominous tap at his window, which
had no shutter, and was but a few feet from the
ground.   All was dark within and without, and there
reigned all around that deathlike stillness which may
be called the empire of fear, since to the excited fancy
it is far more appalling than the uproar and confusion
of the elements.   After an interval of a moment, during
which he lay without drawing his breath, some one
said, in an under-tone,

  "Knock louder."

" We shall disturb the ladies."

" 'That's true, I guess, but then how shall we get at him?"

" By de hokey, he sleeps as dough he knowed it was his last."

Julius recognised the voices of Longreach and McKillicuddy, and his apprehensions now ripened into certainty. His forehead became cold with the dews of fear, and every feeling, every function of life resolved itself into one horrible apprehension as he heard them cautiously trying first at the door, then at the window, and uttering low curses of disappointment at finding them fastened.

" By J—s, we shall be too late, for I see de day coming over de top of de mountain yonder."

" Well, then, I'll be darn'd if I don't go without him."

" By de holy poker, but I won't; he shall go wid us, dead or alive. So here goes."

Mr. McKillicuddy hereupon essayed himself more vigorously to open the door, and the apprehensions of Julius being now wrought up to the highest pitch, he roared out,—

" Murder! murder!" as loud as he could bawl.

" Och, murder!" shouted McKillicuddy in astonishment and dismay, as he heard the voice of the stranger.

Julius continued to vociferate the awful cry until he roused Reuben and mine host, and waked the ladies, who began to echo him with all the might of female lungs. Dressing themselves with great expedition, our hero and the landlord proceeded to the place where Julius was so sorely beset by the banditti, and beheld by the slight tint of the gray morning, the figures of McKillicuddy and his companion standing under the window. Mine host hailed them, and was answered by a well-known voice.

" A pretty kettle of fish you have made of it."

" Yes, I guess if he'd studied nine years and a half

for a blunder, he wouldn't have made a better. Darna-
tion, whý did you direct us to the wrong place?"

"By jingo," replied the landlord, "that's true, I forgot, or rather I didn't know, the strange gentleman was
to sleep in my room."

All this while the valiant Dibdill was vociferating
"Murder, murder!" in his best style, and Reuben, per-
ceiving there was no danger of such a catastrophe at
present, managed, by the assistance of the landlord, to
force the door. Their attempts redoubled the horrors
of poor Julius, who for some time withstood all the assur-
ances of Reuben that there was not the least danger of
being murdered this time. He stood in a perfect abstraction of horror, with but one single impression on his
memory, and that was of banditti; repeating, as it were
unconsciously, the awful cry of murder, murder! as fast
as his tongue could utter it, until it gradually died away
in a whisper.

Having tried what shaking, and pushing, and arguments would do, in vain, the landlord at length brought
him to his recollections by dashing a basin of water in
his face. For a minute or two he stood congealed and
astounded, then rubbing his eyes, and looking round
with a most ludicrous stare, exclaimed,

"Bless my soul, what is the matter?"

"By de soul of ould Ireland," cried McKillicuddy,
bursting into a roar of laughter, "by de soul of ould
Ireland, I believe de squire took us for robbers."

The whole scene changed at once, and shouts of
laughter echoed in these solitudes which had just been
alarmed with the cry of murder. Reuben could not
forbear joining in the chorus, as he looked at Julius,
who stood in his nightcap and oriental gown, shaking
with the cold ablution he had received, aided by the remains of his fears, and exhibiting a ludicrous combination of shame and apprehension.

The mystery was soon unravelled.   Master McKillicuddy had, a week or two before, got, as it were,
into a row on occasion of some anniversary,—we believe it was that of the famous battle of the Boyne,—with
some of his dear countrymen, and a lawsuit, which was
to be tried that day, was the natural consequence.   The
landlord and Mr. Jonathan Longreach were his principal witnesses, and the place of holding court being
somewhat distant, it had been arranged to set out before
daylight, and that the other two were to awaken mine
host on their way.

The story came to the ears of Minerva, by some
means or other.   We will not affirm that Reuben did
not tell her, for it was very natural she should ask the
reason of the great noise that had frightened her, and
it would have been impolite for him to keep it to himself.   All mankind, and most especially all womankind,
love courage.   It is in itself so noble a quality,—and
then it is so indispensable to the protection of the weaker
sex, that we do not wonder they admire a soldier, because his profession indispensably leads him at some
time or other into dangers, which he could not encounter
without disgrace, if he lacked courage.   The conduct
of Julius on this awful night most sensibly diminished
the influence of his coat, his whiskers, and travelled
accomplishments, over Minerva.   Her imagination gradually got the better of her senses, and instead of the
perfect dandy arrayed from top to toe in the very quin-
tessence of fashionable adornment,—with chains, and
ribands, and diamonds bright, charming all eyes, and
taking captive every ear ; he ever after appeared to
her, yclad in satin cap, and oriental nightgown, crying
" Murder ! murder !" while the water trickled down his
cheeks like floods of tears.   Still, however, he continued to be the admiration of Mrs. Orendorf, who had
the authority of Mrs. Asheputtle that he was perfect ,
and as for Childe Roeliff, the marriage of his daughter

and nephew was the favourite project of his declining
years; and who ever knew an elderly gentleman abandon such a thing on the score of want of merit, want
of affection, incompatibility of temper, or prior attachment? Had Roeliff done this, he would have
been the most remarkable old man ever recorded in
tradition, history, or romance; and if in the course of
this his Progress, he should chance to present such an
extraordinary example, we shall do all in our power to
transmit his fame to future ages.

Nothing ruins a man in this age of improvement so
effectually as being ashamed of himself or his conduct.
So long as he puts a good brazen face on the matter,
let it be what it will, he gets along tolerably well; but
it is all over with him if he gives the slightest reason
for believing that he is himself conscious of having
committed a wrong or ridiculous action.   Julius was a
man of the world, and had crossed Mount St. Gothard;
of course he was aware of these truths, and appeared
in due time full dressed for travel, with an air so unconscious, a self-possession so perfect, that one might
have believed the whole of the night's adventure nothing but a dream.

"You were disturbed I hear, last night?" said Minerva,
with as mischievous a look and smile as ever decked
the lip and eye of an angel.

"Y-e-e-s," replied Julius, adjusting his stock, and
twisting his whiskers—"Y-e-s—I believe I got the
nightmare—eating that confounded supper. I dreamed
I was in Italy and about being murdered by robbers. In
fact, 'pon my honour, I was in a complete trance, and
nothing but a basin of cold water brought me to myself."

Minerva was ready to die at this ingenious turn; and
not a day passed after this that she did not annoy his
vanity by some sly allusion to the nightmare.   Being
roused so early, they determined to proceed to Lake

George to breakfast, where they arrived, and found lodgings at the pretty village of Caldwell, so called after the founder and proprietor, now gone down to his grave, but still living in the recollection of hundreds, yea, thousands, who have shared his liberal hospitality and banqueted on his sparkling wit, his rich humour, and his generous wines.

Everybody worth writing for has seen this pleasant village and delightful lake, and therefore we shall not describe it here. Else would we envelop it in the impenetrable fog of some " powerful writing," and give such a picture of its pure waters, enchanting scenery, and fairy isles, as might, peradventure, confound the reader, and cause him to mistake perplexity and confusion for lofty sublimity. A party was arranged the next morning for a voyage to the Diamond Isle; and Julius determined in his own mind to lure the fair goddess Minerva into some romantic recess, and there devote to her his coat, his accomplishments, and his whiskers. They embarked in a gondola, one of the most leaky and unmanageable inconveniences ever seen, and rowed by two of the laziest rogues that ever swung upon a gate, or sunned themselves on a sand-beach.

It had rained in the night, and the freshness of the morn was delightful to the soul, as all nature was beautiful to the eye. There may be other lakes equally lovely in every thing but the transparency of its water. You look down into the air, and see the fish sporting about the bottom of the pure element. Julius had prepared himself for conquest—he was armed at all points, from head to toe—from his whiskers to his pumps and spatterdashes. As he contemplated, first himself, and next the rustic Reuben—he whispered, or rather he was whispered in the ear by a certain well-dressed dandy, " It is all over with him, poor fellow—this day I shall do his business to a dead certainty."

The gondola, as we said before, was rowed by two

of the very laziest fellows that every plied oars.   They
were perfect lazaroni, and the vessel was almost half
filled with water ere they reached the enchanted shores
of Diamond Island.   While the rest of the party were
stumbling over the ground, broken up in search of the
crystals with which it abounds, and whence it derives
its name, Julius—having, by a masterly manœuvre,
fastened good Mrs. Orendorf to the arm of Reuben,
and led the Childe into a jeopardy, where he broke his
shin, and becoming disgusted with every species of
locomotion, sat himself down quietly to wait the motions
of the party—drew Minerva, by degrees, along the shore
until they reached the opposite extremity to that where
they landed.   Whether she, with the true instinct of
the sex, anticipated that " the hour and the man was
come," and wilfully afforded this opportunity for the
purpose of putting an end for ever to his expectations ;
or whether beguiled into forgetfulness by the beauties
of the scene, we cannot say ; but Minerva accompanied
him without hesitation, and thus afforded a favourable
opportunity to speak his mind.   He did speak his mind,
but he might just as well have held his tongue.   We
grieve to defraud our fair readers of a love scene in
such a romantic spot; but time presses, and we have
yet a long space to travel over before Childe Roeliff
finishes his progress.   Suffice it to say, Julius was
rejected irrevocably, in spite of his coat, his whiskers,
and his spatterdashes ; and thus Minerva established
her title to be either more or less than woman.   They
rejoined the party, and Reuben, who studied their
countenances with the jealous scrutiny of a lover,
detected in that of Julius deep mortification, under the
disguise of careless levity ; in that of the young lady a
red tint, indicating something like the remains of angry
emotion.

On their return from the island, Julius took the

earliest opportunity of announcing to Childe Roeliff his intention to depart for the Springs that very day.

" What !" exclaimed the astonished old gentleman— " leave us in the middle of our journey ! why, what will Minerva say to it, hey ?"

" She has no right to say any thing ; she has this day given me a walking ticket," answered Julius, forcing himself into an explanation so mortifying to his vanity.

" A walking ticket ! and what the d—l is that ?"

" She has rejected me."

" Plump, positive ?"

" Irrevocably, split me !"

" Pooh ! Julius, don't be in such a hurry ; try again : she'll be in a different humour to-morrow, or next day ; now don't go—don't ;" and the Childe was quite over-come.

" I must go, sir ; it would be too excruciating to my feelings to remain any longer."

" But what did the girl say ?"

" She said she could never love me, sir."

" Pshaw ! that's all in my eye, Julius—never is a long day. Her mother, I remember, told me just the same thing, until I made my great speculation, when she all at once found out it was a mistake."

" But it is not likely I shall ever make a great specu-lation, uncle. Besides, I suspect, from appearances, that she begins to be fond of Reuben Rossmore. It is quite impossible that I should ever bring myself to enter the lists with him ;" and Julius drew himself up with great dignity, at the same time scanning himself in the glass.

" Fond of Reuben Rossmore ! what makes you think so, eh ?"

" I'm not certain, uncle, but I believe some such absurd preference induced her to reject me."

" If I was certain of that, I'd leave all my estate to
Vol. I.—14

you, Julius, and cut her off with a shilling." And he swore a great oath, that if Minerva married against his wishes, she was no daughter of his from that moment.

" Hum !" thought Julius ; " that would be the very thing itself. The money without the girl—delightful ! I must change my tack, and persuade her to marry this rustic Corydon instead of myself. I will gain his confidence, and forward their wishes in all possible ways. If I can only bring about a runaway match—hum"— and he mused on this scheme, until it almost amounted to a presentiment.

" Now don't go, Julius—do stay with us till we get back to New-York.   I want you to take care of Minerva, and keep her out of the hands of Reuben, whom I like very much, except in the character of son-in-law. Now do stay and take care of her, till I get rid of Reuben.   I wonder what possessed me to invite him to join our party ?"

" By no means, uncle ; don't let them suspect that you know or believe any thing of this matter.   If you send him away, you must give a reason for so doing, and without doubt they will ascribe your suspicions to malice on my part at having been rejected.   No, no, sir, let him remain where he is ; and in the mean time, at your request, I will renew my addresses, or rather try what silent attentions can do towards conciliating Minerva's favour.   If I should fail, I can, at all events, be on the watch, and interfere in various ways to thwart the views of this ungrateful and interested young man."

Childe Roeliff accorded his consent to the plan, at the same time informing Julius that he should take the first opportunity of apprizing Minerva of his unalterable intentions towards him, and of his determination to punish her if she dared to oppose them, by adopting his nephew, and making him his heir.   Julius thought he knew enough of the pompous, self-willed Childe to be certain that he would fulfil his threats to the letter ;

and departed from his presence with the design of
immediately commencing operations.

The next morning, before daylight, they embarked
in a steamboat for the foot of the lake, on their way
to foreign parts.   There was a large party of fashion-
ables on board, and Julius was in his element again.
The Childe, who hated being disturbed so early in the
morning most mortally, retired into the cabin to take a
nap ; and Mrs. Orendorf was delighted with meeting
some of her Saratoga acquaintance.   Julius taking
advantage of the absence of his uncle, devoted himself
to entertain them ; and Minerva and Reuben were for a
while left to the undisturbed society of each other.   Fortunately, the boat did not go above five or six miles an
hour, and thus they had an opportunity of almost studying the beautiful scenery of the lake, which, narrowing
at the lower end, bears on its pure bosom a hundred
little verdant isles.   Some with a single tree, others
tufted with blossomed shrubbery, and all, as it were,
imitating the motion of the vessel, and dancing like
corks on the surface of the waters.   It was a rare and
beautiful scene, such as seldom presents itself to travellers in any region of the peopled earth, and such as
always awakens in hearts disposed to love, thoughts,
feelings, and associations which cannot fail to attract and bind them to each other in the ties of mutual
sympathy and admiration.   Much was not said by
either, except in that language which sparkles in the
lucid eye, glows in the gradually warming cheek, and
lurks in the meaning smile.

" How slow the boat goes !" exclaimed a fashionable
lover of the picturesque, associated with the party
before mentioned.   " I'm tired to death.   I wish
we were at Ticonderoga."   And the sentiment was
echoed by the rest of the picturesque hunters, who all
declared they never were so tired in their lives, and
that they wished to heaven they were at Ticonderoga.

How often people mistake being tired of themselves for being tired of every thing else?

Minerva and Reuben exchanged a look, which said, as plain as day, that *they* did not wish themselves at Ticonderoga, and were not above half tired to death.

In good time they were landed at the foot of the lake, which they quitted to enter a stage coach waiting to carry them across to Lake Champlain, a distance of five or six miles. The ride was interesting to Reuben especially, whose grandfather had fought and fallen in the bloody wars that raged at intervals for a century or more between the French and English during their struggles for the possession of North America. Lake Champlain and Lake George furnished the only practicable route by which armies, and the necessary supplies of armament and provisions could be transported by the rival candidates for the empire of half a world, and the famous pass of Ticonderoga was the theatre of a series of battles which have made it both traditionally and historically renowned.

The fashionable party of picturesque hunters, in their haste to get on they did not know themselves whither, passed Ticonderoga at full trot, although they had been in such a hurry to get there; crossed the lake to the little village of that name, in Vermont, and remained at the tavern, wishing and wishing the steamboat Franklin would come along, and lengthening every passing hour by fidgetty impatience. By the persuasion of Minerva, the Childe Roeliff was wrought upon reluctantly to visit the ruins of the famous old fortress of Ticonderoga.

Just at the point of junction, where the outlet of Lake George enters Lake Champlain, a high, rocky, round promontory projects boldly into the latter, covered with the walls of massive stone barracks, the remains of which are still standing; cut and indented by deep ditches, breasted with walls, and cased on the

outer sides towards the south and east with a facing
of rocks, from which you look down with dizzy head
upon the waters of the sister lakes. Across the outlet
of Lake George is Mount Independence towering to a
great height ; to the east and south-east, Lake Champlain appears entering the mountains on the other side
by a narrow strait; while to the north it gradually
expands itself from a river to a lake, until it makes a
sudden turn at Crown Point, and disappears. The
whole promontory is one vast fortress, and even the
bosom of the earth appears to have been consecrated
to the purposes of defence,—for ever and anon our travellers were startled at coming upon an opening, the
deep, dark recesses of which they could not penetrate.

There are few more grand and interesting scenes in
the wide regions of the western world than old Ticonderoga. Ennobled by nature, it receives new claims
and a new interest from history and tradition; it is
connected with the early events of the brief but glorious career of this new country ; and independently of
all other claims, it presents in its extensive, massy,
picturesque ruins a scene not to be paralleled in a
region where every thing is new, and in whose wide
circumference scarce a ruined building or desolate village is to be found.

In pursuance of his deep-laid plan, Julius attached
himself to Mrs. Orendorf, to whom he was so particularly attentive in the ramble, that Childe Roeliff was
not a little astonished.

" What the devil can that fellow see in the old lady
to admire, I wonder ?" quoth he. " Hum, I suppose
these are what the blockhead calls his silent attentions
to my daughter, and be hanged to him."

While engaged in these cogitations he neglected to
look which way he was going, and tumbled inconti-
nently to the bottom of an old half-filled ditch, where

14*

he lay in a featherbed of Canada thistles. Fortunately he was extracted with no injury except a little scratching ; but the accident occasioned such a decided disgust towards Ticonderoga and its antiquities, that he peremptorily commanded a retreat to the carriage, which, by a somewhat circuitous route, conveyed them to the shores of Lake Champlain. Here they found a ferry-boat of the genuine primitive construction, being a scow with a great clumsy sail, steered with a mighty oar by a gentleman of colour, and rowed, in default of wind, by two other gentlemen of similar complexion. By the aid of all these advantages they managed to cross the lake, which is here, perhaps, a mile wide, in about the time it takes one of our steam ferry-boats to cross the bay from New-York to the quarantine. Blessings on the man that first invented steamboats, for the time he has saved to people who don't know what to do with it is incalculable ! On arriving at the hotel in the little village of Ticonderoga, they found the fashionable, picturesque-hunting party whiling away the tedious hours until the Franklin should come from Whitehall, with that delightful recreation yclept sleep, the inventor of which deserves an equal blessing with him of the steamboat.

The Franklin at length made her appearance ; all the fashionable picturesque party waked up as by magic, and hastened on board, in as great a hurry as if she had been Noah's ark and the deluge approaching. About two o'clock they became exceedingly impatient for dinner. After dinner they retired to their berths—waked up, and became exceedingly impatient for tea. After tea they began to be tired to death of the steamboat, the lake, and of every thing, and longed with exceeding impatience to get to St. John's. Enjoying nothing of the present, they seemed always to depend on something in perspective ; and their whole lives appeared to be spent in wishing they were somewhere else. The day was of a charming temperature ; the

sweet south wind gently curled the surface of the lake,
which gradually expanded to a noble breadth, and all
nature invited them to share in her banquet. But they
turned from it with indifference, and were continually
yawning and complaining of being "tired to death."

The other party, whose progress is more peculiarly
the subject of our tale, were somewhat differently con-
stituted and differently employed. The sage Roeliff
was telling a worthy alderman with whom he had
entered into a confabulation, the history of his speculation, and how he made his fortune by a blunder. The
worthy alderman had got rich simply by the growth of
the city of New-York, which had by degrees overspread
his potato patch, and turned the potatoes into dollars.
Neither of them could in conscience ascribe their success in life to any merits of their own, and they agreed
perfectly well in their estimate of the worthlessness of
calculation, and forethought, and sagacity, " and such
kind of nonsense," as the Childe was pleased to say.
Roeliff declared it was the most pleasant day he had
spent since he left home. That excellent woman Mrs.
Orendorf, with her now inseparable attendant Julius
Dibdill, was enjoying upon sufferance the society of
the picturesque hunters, and echoing their complaints
of being tired to death; while Minerva and Reuben,
sitting apart on an elevated seat, which commanded a
view of the lake and both its shores, were enjoying
with the keen relish of taste and simplicity the noble
scene before them.

They were delighted as well as astonished at the
magnificent features of this fine lake, and exchanged
many a glance that spoke their feelings. The tourists
and compilers of Travellers' Guides, had not prepared them on this occasion for disappointment; and
they enjoyed the scenery a thousand times more,
for not having been cheated by exaggerated anticipations.   They expected nothing after Lake George,
which had been hitherto the exclusive theme of admi-

ration with poets and descriptive writers of all classes ;
but they found here something far more extensive and
magnificent.   As they approached the beautiful town of
Burlington, the lake gradually expanded, and its shores
became more strikingly beautiful.   On either side lay
a tract of cultivated country diversified with hill and
dale, and gradually rising and rising until it mingled
with the lofty Alleghanies on the west, and the still more
lofty mountains of Vermont on the east, some of them
so distant they looked almost like visions of mountains,
the creation of the imagination.   Everywhere visible,
they range along, following the course of the lake, now
approaching nearer, and anon receding to a great distance, and presenting in the evening of the day, on one
side, the last splendours of the setting sun, on the other
the soft gentle tints of the summer twilight gradually
fading away into the deep hues of night.

If an author, like unto an actor, might peradventure
be tolerated in making his bow before his readers, and
blundering out a speech which no one hears or comprehends, we might here bear witness that nowhere in
all our sojournings among the matchless beauties of this
our favoured country have we beheld a scene more
splendidly magnificent, more touching to the heart and
the imagination, than the bay of Burlington presents,
just as the summer sun sheds his last lustres on its
spacious bosom, and retires from his throne of many-
coloured clouds, glowing in the ever-changing radiance
of his departing beams, behind the distant Alleghanies.
The charming town of Burlington, basking on the hill-
side towards the west ; the rich farms which environ it;
the noble expanse of waters studded with pine-crowned
isles, and stretching in one direction to the beautiful
village and county of Essex, in the other towards
Plattsburg ; the vast range of mountains rising tier over
tier, and presenting every varied tint of distance,—all
form a combination, which to hearts that throb at the touch
of nature is, beyond expression, touching and sublime.

The temple of Jehovah is his glorious works.   The
soul imbued with the pure spirit of piety, unadulterated
and unobscured by the subtilties of ingenious refinement
or fanatical inspiration, sees, feels, and comprehends in
the woods, the waters, the mountains, and the skies, the
hand of a Being as far above it in intelligence as in
power, and is struck with an impression of awful
humility.   In the words of a nameless and obscure
bard, it

> Hears the still voice of *Him* in the mild breeze,
> The murmuring brook, the silent, solemn night,
> The merry morning, and the glorious noon.
> Sees him in darkness when no eye can see ;
> In the green foliage of the fruitful earth ;
> The mirror of the waters, in the clouds
> Of the high heavens, and in the speechless stars,
> That sparkle of his glory.

It was just at the witching hour of sunset, in a calm
luxurious evening, such as the most orthodox writers
of fiction describe with enthusiasm, when they are
about making their hero or heroine do something
naughty, that the noble steamboat Franklin (of which
and her excellent commander we beg to make most
honourable mention) entered the bay of which we
have just given a sketch, and stopped a few minutes at
the wharf to land her passengers at Burlington.   The
fashionable party of picturesque-hunters still continued
almost tired to death, and longed more than ever to
get to St. John's.   But I need not say that the souls of
Minerva and Reuben were wide awake to the scene
before them.   Abstracted from the hurry and bustle of
the moment, they turned their eyes towards the glowing
west, and their spirits communed together in the luxury
of silence.   They followed each other's looks, from the
floating isles that lay like halcyons on the bosom of
the lake, to the shores beyond, softened by distance
into the most beautiful purple tints, and thence their
eyes rested together on the vast sea of hills rising
above hills beyond.   One feeling animated them, and

though not a word was said, the electricity of looks communicated that feeling to the hearts of both.

That evening a melancholy partaking of sweet and bitter anticipations stole over the two young people. Hitherto they had been satisfied to be together, and partake in the enjoyments of each other. But the progress of true love ends but at one single point all over the universe. From being satisfied with the present, we begin to explore the future, and the delight of associating with one being alone carries us at length to the desire and necessity of possessing that being for ever. To this point were the hearts of Minerva and Reuben at length brought by the sweet communions we have described. A mutual consciousness of approaching troubles, of certain disappointments in store for each, came suddenly over them. Minerva suspected the views of her father in favour of Julius, and long experience had taught her that when he had once got hold of a notion he stuck to it as a fowl does to a crumb. Reuben also had his presentiments; he was neither rich nor fashionable; it was therefore clear to his mind that he was not likely to be particularly distinguished either by Childe Roeliff or his aspiring dame, who was in great hopes of catching one of the seignors of Montreal for her daughter. It was observed by Julius, who kept an eye upon them, although he never interrupted their intercourse, that, after tea, Minerva joined the fashionable picturesque-hunting party, who by this time were tired to death for the hundredth time; and that Reuben retired from her side, and stood apart leaning over the railing of a distant part of the vessel. Julius thought this a favourable opportunity to open his masked battery.

Accordingly, he sauntered towards him, apparently without design, and entered into conversation on some trifling subject. Reuben never at any time liked his society, and still less at the present moment, when he was deep in the perplexities of love. He answered

Julius neglectingly, and in a voice that partook in the depression of his feelings.

"You seem out of spirits, Rossmore," at length said Julius, gayly; "come, tell me what has come over you of late, and especially this evening?"

Reuben felt indignant; he had never invited or encouraged any thing like this familiarity, and replied, with a cool indifference,—

"Nothing in particular; and if there were, I do not wish to trouble any but my friends with my thoughts or feelings."

"Well, and am I not your friend?"

"Not that I know of."

"You will know it soon. Now listen to me, Rossmore; I see what is going forward, not being exactly blind, as I believe you think me. I know what is going forward."

"Know what is going forward, sir! well, and what is going forward?" answered Reuben, whose heart whispered at once what Julius meant.

"Will you suffer me to speak, and listen coolly to what I am going to say?"

"Mr. Dibdill, there are certain subjects on which none but a confidential friend ought to take the liberty of questioning another. Allow me to say, that nothing in our intercourse has entitled you to that privilege."

"Pooh, pshaw now, Rossmore, don't be so stiff and awful. I know what is going on between my cousin and you, as well as—"

"Stop, Mr. Dibdill," cried Reuben, vehemently, "the subject is one on which *you* have no right to speak to me, nor will I permit it, sir."

"Rossmore," said Julius, with a deep and serious air, which riveted the attention of Reuben, in spite of himself,—"Rossmore, I know your thoughts at this moment as well as you do yourself. You think me your rival, of course your enemy—on my soul, I am neither one nor the other."

" No !" exclaimed the other, turning full upon him.

" No—that I have been, I acknowledge, but it was more to please my uncle than myself. The fact is, Minerva, though a very good girl, is not to my taste." And he said this with a mighty supercilious air.

" The d—l she isn't," cried Reuben, in a fury ; " and pray, sir, what have you to say against her ? I insist on your admiring her, or, by my soul, you shall take the consequences."

Julius laughed. " Well, if I must, I must. Then I presume you insist upon my paying my addresses to Minerva ?"

" No-o-o, not exactly that either. But you will oblige me by condescending to give your reasons for not admiring Miss Orendorf."

" Why, in the first place, she talks English better than French ; in the second place, she likes a ballad better than a bravura ; in the third place, she exhibits a most ludicrous unwillingness to dance the waltz and the gallopade ; in the fourth place, she is no judge of a coat; in the fifth place, she can't sing before five or six hundred people without losing her voice ; and in the last place, she blushes in the most unbecoming style. That last objection is decisive. What under the sun should I do with such a woman ?"

Reuben was so pleased with the assurance of his having renounced Minerva, that he neglected to knock Julius down for this blasphemy. He only replied,

" Well, sir ?"

" Well, to come to the point at once, you love my cousin Minerva—"

" By what right, sir ?—"

" Be quiet, Rossmore, till I have done, and then blow my brains out if you will. I am your friend, at least in this business. My uncle, I know, will give me no rest about this ridiculous plan of his for bringing us together, until Minerva is fairly disposed of; I have, therefore, an interest in this business of yours, and you may command all my services."

"What a heartless coxcomb!" thought **Reuben**, "to be insensible to the charms of such an angel." However, he forgave him on the score of having a rival out of the way.

"I cannot but feel obliged to you, whatever may be your motives," said he, addressing Julius ; "but I see no benefit I can derive from your services, and therefore beg leave to decline them."

"But let me tell you, Rossmore, you ought to see it. I have influence with old Roeliff and his wife, the latter especially, which, if properly exerted, may smooth the way to the gratification of your wishes, and, say what you will, I mean to do all I can for you. Though I admire not my cousin, as I said before, because, in the first place—"

"Pray, Mr. Dibdill, to the point. You need not repeat your reasons," interrupted Reuben, rather pettishly.

"To the point, then. My uncle is determined to make a match between his daughter and **myself**; but that is out of the question, as I said before ; because, in the first place—"

"Pray spare me any more of your reasons."

"Well—it is quite out of the question, because— you must hear another reason, Rossmore—because Minerva don't like me, and does like you." Reuben smiled in spite of himself. He thought this last reason worth all the rest. Julius continued :

"Now, whatever you may think of me, my dear friend—for I mean to prove I hold you such—I am not the man to marry any woman unless sure of her affections, however wealthy she may be in possession or reversion."

"Nor I," said Reuben ; "I despise Miss Orendorf's fortune as much as I admire her person, and love her good qualities."

Vol. I.—15

" No doubt, no doubt, my dear friend; but, as I said before, I wish Minerva married, that my uncle may see the impossibility of his wishes being fulfilled in relation to me. My ridiculous aunt differs in her views for her daughter with my ridiculous uncle. She has heard of the seignors and seignories at Montreal, and has good hopes of making her daughter a baroness some how or other, Heaven knows how—for, as I said before, there is no chance of my cousin being distinguished in fashionable society, because, in the first place—"

" D—n it, sir, do stick to the point, can't you? Your reasons can be of no consequence to me," cried Reuben, chafing.

" Well, well, I will. Now, my plan is this—but are you sure of the affections of Minerva?"

"I have never said a single word to her on the subject."

" No! not in all the romantic walks and *tête-à-têtes* you have had together?"

" No, on my honour. I felt a presentiment that her parents would never consent to our union, and therefore scorned to engage her affections."

" O, marry come up!" cried Julius, laughing. " You scorned to engage her affections, did you? You never spoke a word to her on the subject, you say? I suppose you never said any thing with your eyes, hey? and you never received an answer, hey? in a language no man in his senses can mistake? You have behaved in the most honourable manner, without doubt, and I can't help admiring your high notions! Pooh! pooh! Rossmore! you know my cousin likes you; everybody on board this boat might see it, if they had not something else to attend to, and you know it too, for all your confounded hypocrisy."

Reuben could not deny this, for the soul of him. The fact is, the consciousness was too delicious to admit of denial.

" You must be married at Montreal," said Julius, abruptly.

"Her parents will never consent."

"Then you must marry without it."

"Her father will never forgive her."

"Don't believe it.   She is his only child; he dotes on her, and in a little while, finding he could not live without her, he will recall her home, and dote on her more than ever.   I know him from top to toe, and I know the influence I have over him, which I will exert in your behalf.   I am, besides, pretty certain I can command the services of mine excellent aunt, if it be only from the pure spirit of opposition."

"I cannot but feel obliged to you; but my course shall be different.   I mean first to procure the consent of Minerva, and then plainly, directly, and honestly lay my proposal before her father."

Julius was startled at this declaration.   It upset all his plans.   Recovering himself in a few moments, he resumed:

"Then take my word, you will never see her after that exhibition of candour and honesty, as you call it. I know my uncle rather better than you do, and I know that so long as he can prevent a thing he never gives up; but the moment it is out of his power, he gradually relinquishes all his former hostility and reconciles himself at last to what is inevitable.   He hates vexation so much, that he never voluntarily indulges it long.   If you ask his consent he will never give it—nay, he will bind himself by some foolish oath, that will prevent his forgiving her after it is done."

"I can't help it; I shall pursue the straight-forward course."

"Fool!—but I beg pardon.   You see the anxiety I feel for your success by its making me ill-mannered. But if you pursue this course, I pledge myself you will never be the husband of Minerva Orendorf."

"Time and perseverance, or chance and good fortune, may bring it about at last."

" One word, then," replied Julius, earnestly and precipitately, as he saw Childe Roeliff approaching. " One word more.   Promise me you will not take any decisive steps until we arrive at Montreal."

" I do."

" Upon your honour ?"

" Upon my honour."

Here the presence of Mr. Orendorf put an end to the conversation, which had attracted the notice of Minerva, who wondered what they could have been talking about so warmly and earnestly.   Her heart fluttered as Reuben approached her, but whether with apprehension that the two young men had quarrelled, or any other more occult feeling, has never come to our knowledge.

By this time the evening had set in, but it was moonlight—the full of the moon—and such is the bland and balmy and innocent air that floats upon the bosom of the lake, its purity, dryness, and elasticity, that there is not the least danger in being exposed to it during the whole of a clear evening.   They entered the Bay of Saranac, scarcely less distinguished for its beauty, and far more renowned in history, than that of Burlington. It was here that the gallant McDonough, now, with his famous contemporaries Decatur and Perry, gone to immortality, won laurels that will never fade while the grass is green on the bank that overlooks the bay, or the water runs in the Saranac River.   Reuben and Minerva had both been known, the former intimately, to these distinguished men, and the scene recalled them to mind as if they had perished yesterday.

They remembered the simplicity which marked the characters of the two young sailors, who were united in glory, and might be said to be united in death, in the flower of their age.

" What a striking figure was McDonough !" cried Minerva.

" And what a sweet, mild, yet manly expression was in the blue eye of Perry !" replied Reuben.   " Both

were of a high class of men, but they neither of them
equalled Decatur.   I knew him well, and have studied
his character.   He was one of the few—the very, very
few great men I ever met with.   There are plenty of
great men in this world, my dear Minerva"—Dear
Minerva ! thought our heroine—" of a certain kind.
Some are great by virtue of high station, some by
high birth, some by chance, and some by necessity.
Nature makes these by dozens ; but a truly great man
is a rare production.   Such was Decatur: he was
not merely a brave man—I might almost say the bravest
of men—but he was a man of most extraordinary intellect, a statesman as well as a warrior ; one who, like
David Porter, could negotiate a treaty as well as gain
a victory ; one who could influence the most capacious
minds by his eloquence and reasoning, as easily as he
quelled the more weak and ignorant by his authority
and example.   His influence over others was that of
strength over weakness, and had he run the career of
civil life, he would have been equally, if not more, distinguished than he became in that of active warfare.
He has been blamed for the manner of his death ; but
his inflexible maxim in life was, that the man whom
he considered not sufficiently beneath his notice to
escape insult or injury was fairly entitled to reparation.
He did not, as many men do, put himself on a par with
another in bandying abuse and exchanging mutual impu-
tations, and then take refuge at last in the cowardly
pretext that his adversary was beneath his notice !
Peace to his ashes, and honour to his memory, say I ;
and may he find many to emulate his example !"
    Minerva listened with enthusiasm to this eulogium
on one of her favourite heroes, and watched with delighted interest the glow which gradually mantled the
cheek, the fire that lightened in the eye of the young
man as he dwelt on a theme so animating.   A silence
of some minutes followed, which was suddenly interrupted by Minerva—

                        15*

" Pray, what were you and my cousin talking about so long ?"

It was well that the moon was just then obscured by a cloud, else Reuben would inevitably have been detected in the absurd act of blushing up to the eyes, not only by Minerva, but by the fashionable picturesque-hunting party—but now we think of it, these last were gone to bed " tired to death."

Minerva, however, perceived a hesitation in his speech and an embarrassment of manner which excited her apprehensions.

" I entreat you, Reuben, to answer me one question. Have you and my cousin quarrelled ?"

" No, on my honour."

" You seemed deeply interested in the conversation you had this evening."

" True, it was on a most interesting subject."   Minerva looked curious.   " Did it concern only myself, I would tell you what it was about.

" Whom else did it concern ?"

" You."

" Then I *must* know what it was about.   I have a right to know, as a party concerned," cried the young lady, with one of her sweetest smiles.

Reuben looked confused and doubtful, and Minerva's curiosity became very troublesome to her.   It was highly indelicate and improper, certainly ; but the fact is, she felt a most unaccountable interest in the particulars of this conversation.   She became a little offended at his silence, and Reuben remained in a most painful embarrassment.

" Well," said she at length, " if I am not thought worthy of knowing what you say so nearly concerns myself, I will bid you good-night.   It is time, indeed, for the passengers, I see, have quitted the deck some time," and she was retiring.

" For Heaven's, dear Mi—for Heaven's sake, Miss Orendorf, don't leave me !"

" Why should I stay ? You won't tell me any thing I wish to know."

" But only stay, and I will tell you."

" What ?" replied Minerva archly.

" That I—that you—that your father, I mean—that your cousin Julius—that is to say—that it would be folly, nay, it would be dishonourable in me to tell— what I wish to tell"—here poor Reuben, as they say, got into a snarl, and could not utter another word of sense or nonsense.

Women, though ever so young and inexperienced, have a mighty quick instinct in love matters, and Minerva at once began to comprehend the nature of the subject on which Reuben had just spoken so eloquently and with such wonderful clearness. She became still more embarrassed than he, and, hardly knowing what she said, asked, in a trembling voice—

" What *can* be the matter with you, Reuben ?"

" I love you, dearest Minerva !"

" Good-night !" replied Minerva, and disappeared in an instant from his sight.

That night Reuben could not sleep, and we don't much wonder at it, for, sooth to say, what with the hissing, and puffing, and jarring, and diabolical noises of all kinds, commend us to a fulling-mill, a cotton manufactory, or even Childe Roeliff's favourite resource, a tinman's shop, for a sound nap, rather than to a steam boat. And yet we have often lain awake in all the horrors of sleepless misery, and heard villains snore as lustily as if they reposed themselves on a bed of down in the cave of Morpheus. How we did hate the monsters !

But our hero had other matters to keep him awake It would have puzzled the most perfect adept in the science of woman's heart, to decide whether Minerva had left him in a good or a bad humour ; whether she resented his abrupt declaration, or ran away to hide her confusion. No wonder, then, it puzzled honest Reu-

ben Rossmore, who had scarcely studied the A B C
of a woman's mind, much less investigated its hidden
mysteries.

At the dawn of the morning the party awoke and
found themselves in a new world. It seemed that they
had been transported during the night, like some of the
heroes of the Arabian tales, from one distant country
to another. The houses, the fields, the cattle, the
sheep, the pigs, dogs, cats, hens and chickens, men,
women, and children, all seemed to belong to a different species. They neither looked, dressed, nor talked
like the people they had left the night before, for the
women wore men's hats, and the men red night-caps,
and they all spoke in a tongue which Squire Julius
pronounced to be a most execrable patois. Nothing
was ever equal to the metamorphosis produced by a sail
of a few miles, between two grassy banks almost level
with the surface of the lake, and destitute alike of
stream or mountain to mark the division between the
domains of two powerful empires.

"As I live," exclaimed Mrs. Orendorf, as she
emerged from the ladies' cabin, " I believe we have got
into a foreign country at last. If there isn't a woman
with a man's hat !"

" Mercy upon us !" ejaculated Childe Roeliff; " if
there isn't an oven on the top of a pig-sty !"

" Good Heavens ! what can these people be talking
about so fast ? Come here, Minerva, and tell me what
they are saying."

" They are discussing the price of a cabbage," said
Minerva.

" Well, who'd have thought it ? I was afraid they
were just going to fight with each other. I never saw
such strange people."

" We are in Canada, madam," observed Reuben,
who had ventured to join them on the invitation of a
smile and a blush from Minerva ; " we are in Canada,

or rather in the old world, for I have heard it observed by travellers, that this portion of the province of Canada exhibits an exact picture of the interior of France, or rather of what France was nearly three centuries ago, in dress, language, manners, and rural economy."

" Is it possible !" exclaimed Mrs. Orendorf ; " then I can't think what people go to France for. I'm sure I see nothing here worth the trouble of crossing a lake, much less the sea. Do they wear such caps in France ?"

" In some of the old fashioned towns, I am told they do, madam," said Reuben.

" And such dirty garments and faces ? and are they shaped like these queer people ? and have the men such long beards ?"

" On week-days, I believe."

" Well," exclaimed Mrs. Orendorf, " if that's the case, I thank my stars I did not go to France."

" No thanks to you or your stars," quoth Childe Roeliff ; " if it hadn't been for me you'd have gone fast enough."

It is thus that husbands ruin the tempers of their wives, who are naturally the best creatures in the world, by taking all the merit of their discretion and good works to themselves. The spirit of contradiction came over the good lady.

" I deny it," said she sharply ; " I gave up the point voluntarily."

" Yes, when you couldn't have your own way."

" Well, then, if you come to that, I wish I had gone."

" That is exactly what I said ; you wanted to go then, and so you do now."

We don't know what the plague came over Childe Roeliff to get into such a bad humour this morning, except it might be that he was hungry, than which there is no greater foe to that dulcet composure and sweet submissive meekness, so becoming in a husband when confabulating, as it were, with his helpmate. All

the Childe got by this effervescence of ill-humour was
a determination on the part of Mrs. Orendorf to have
her own way for the next twelvemonth at least.

By this time the arrangements for landing were com-
pleted, and the passengers, almost as numerous and
various as those of Noah's ark, descended upon terra
firma.   Among them was observed the fashionable
picturesque-hunting party, who were as usual " tired to
death," and who, after breakfasting at St. John's, were
again " tired to death," and whirled away towards
Montreal as fast as horses could carry them.

The road from St. John's to La Prairie, a distance
of about eighteen miles, is over a dead level, which
soon becomes tiresome from its monotony. Yet still
to one accustomed only to the scenery, dress, manners
and modes of the United States, it is not devoid of
interest.   Many, indeed all their customs, carry us
back to old times.   Nearly all the property is held
under the seigneurs, by ancient tenures which restrict
the occupants of the land to one single inflexible rou-
tine of cultivation ; a circumstance which places a
barrier in the way of all improvements.   Most of the
farms consist of one field, bordering on the high road,
extending on a dead level back as far as the eye can
reach, and separated from the adjoining ones by a
ditch.   Half the distance between St. John's and
La Prairie is almost one continued village of houses,
built entirely on the same plan, with here and there
a Gothic-fronted church, whose steeple, covered
with tin, shines gorgeously at a distance in the sun.
Women are seen at work in the fields almost as commonly as men, dressed in straw hats, and scarcely to
be distinguished from them. The sickle is still the
only implement in cutting down the harvest ; no cattle
graze in the fields, except in large droves on the commons ; and the houses are either of mud or wood,
small in size, with a single door right in the centre.
Plain and contracted as they are, they still exhibit dis

tinctive marks of that national characteristic of Frenchmen, in all situations and countries.   There is always
some little attempt at ornament,—such as the shingles
of the roof being scalloped at the edges, along the
eaves, or at the pinnacle of the roof; and poor, miserably poor must be that habitation which does not present
some little indication of a superfluity of labour and expense.   The little gardens, though often overrun with
that atrocious and diabolical production of nature in
her extremest spleen, called the Canada thistle, abound
in flowers, and look gay in the midst of neglect and
desolation ; and of a Sunday evening it is surprising to
see the metamorphosis which takes place among the
inhabitants.   Neither rags, nor dirt, nor long beards,
nor old straw hats are visible.   The young girls are
tight, and neat, and gay ; and you see them gathering
in groups at some appropria house, in the little vil-
lages, to spend the evening in their favourite amusement of dancing.   The Longobards, or long beards,—
the same, we presume, mentioned by Tacitus,—appear
in chins as smooth as the new-mown meadow ; and
here and there a red sash figures among them, the
relic and memento of a former age.   A few years ago
this was the universal dress of the men ; but the Yan-
kees have come among them, and, sad to relate, our
party saw but two red sashes in all their sojournings in Canada.   One of these they met on the road to
La Prairie, on horseback, and saluted.   The ancient
remnant of French chivalrous courtesy, stopped his
horse, which he was obliged to do to pull off his cap,
and bowed profoundly, about the time the party had
reached a distance of half a mile.   The other was telling his beads with great devotion in the magnificent
cathedral of Montreal.   Had we time and space we
would dwell at more length on these matters, for we
confess we delight in old times, old customs, and old
oddities of all kinds, not so much because they are

better than new ones, but because there is something
about them which, like old wine, smacks tastefully on
the palate, and produces an agreeable excitement.
But we must hasten on our Progress, lest peradventure the committee appointed by that munificent patron
and goodly pattern of literature, Mr. Francis Herbert,
to pass judgment on our respective contributions, should
fall asleep over our story, which, to say truth, lacketh
much of that delectable mystification and bloodshed
which rendereth romances so piquant and acceptable
to the gentle reader, who, judging from appearances,
sitteth down to peruse them, animated by the same
vehement feeling of curiosity which impelleth so many
of the tender sex to run after an execution.   Suffice it
then to say, that Childe Roeliff and his party reached
the ancient village of La Prairie, which belongs to the
old world and not to the new, after a ride of three or
four hours over one of the worst roads in the universe ;
a circumstance somewhat remarkable, seeing that there
was neither hill or stone in all the long way.   Some
interloping " *Varmounters*" talked of a railroad here ;
but the old Frenchmen threw up their caps, and cried
" Diable !"

From La Prairie our travellers were delighted with
the noble view which presented itself.   The St. Lawrence makes a bend, and expands into a lake-like sheet
of water of the most magnificent dimensions, and
greatest purity.   Above, it is all quiet and repose ;
below, it tapers off in a series of rapids approaching to
sublimity.   Beyond these lies Montreal, basking at the
foot of the mountain which gives its name to the city
and island, and stretching along the side of the abruptly
rising shores of the river.   It exhibited a most imposing appearance, with its tin steeples towering into the
air, and glittering in the noonday beam of a glorious
summer day.   In addition to the steeples, nearly all
the houses and public edifices are covered with tin,

which, such is the dryness of the atmosphere, never rusts; and certainly, in a clear day, and across the noble St. Lawrence, the appearance of Montreal is that of one of the creations of the Arabian Nights. Of all places in the world to look down upon from the sky, this ancient city is the finest. Childe Roeliff was not the least delighted of the party, for he thought to himself, " There is no danger but there are plenty of tinmen's shops, to prevent one from being *onnewed* by silence, and I shall enjoy myself wonderfully." One of the finest steam ferry-boats in the world carried them like thought through the roaring rapids, and between the jutting rocks; and it seemed scarcely a moment from their embarking at La Prairie to their landing at Montreal,—the city of tin roofs, iron window-shutters, and stone walls. Minerva actually saw a great stone wall on the very pinnacle of a roof; such is their inveterate propensity to heaping up masses of granite and limestone.

On landing at the end of a long wooden bridge jutting out into the river,—for there are few or no wharves here, —they were struck with a most enormous din of voices, a vociferous confusion of individual tongues, that made Childe Roeliff think the whole universe was about falling together by the ears. Such an effusion of bad French never before was heard in any other spot of this new world, as we verily believe. All the draymen, with their long-queued drays, seemed to have approximated to this chosen spot, to meet the steamboat, this being the trip in which she generally brought the travellers from the " States," as they are called at Montreal, I presume on the score of some lingering doubt whether they are really "united" or not. The consequence of collecting together in a small space was, that these long-tailed inconveniences got entangled with each other in a perfect Gordian knot. But though the vehicles were tied, the tongues of the drivers were not.

We nave heard " pretty considerable" of scolding and
vociferation ; but, by the account received from Reuben
Rossmore, it was the trickling of a rill to the roaring
of ¹a cataract, the chirping of a flock of snow-birds to
the sonorous gabble of a rencounter of two flocks of
turkeys.   We are credibly informed, on the same authority, that the gesticulation was equal to the vociferation, and altogether it seemed that every moment would
produce a battle royal.   By degrees, however, the long-
tailed vehicles got disentangled, the little Canadians
gradually cooled down, and, in one minute after the
vociferation subsided, were as merry and good-humoured as crickets in a warm winter's hearth.   Our
travellers put up at the British American Hotel, on the
score of patriotism,—the sign of this establishment being
so happily disposed, by accident probably, towards the
river, that in approaching from La Prairie you see
only the words " American Hotel."   Here Julius and
Mrs. Orendorf were delighted to meet again the fashionable picturesque-hunting party, who declared they
had been tired to death riding across the Prairie, tired
to death of waiting a full hour for the ferry-boat at La
Prairie, tired to death of the ferry-boat, and lastly, that
they were now tired to death of Montreal, and were
going that very afternoon to embark in the steamboat
for Quebec.   Childe Roeliff, who sometimes accidentally blundered out a spice of common sense, observed,
after listening to all this,—

" I wonder, if you are so tired of every thing, you
don't go home and stay there."

" *Quel bête !*" whispered Mrs. Dowdykin, the head
matron of the picturesque party, to Count Capo d'Oca,
her Platonic.

The soft, gentle, quiet kindness of Minerva towards
Reuben since the declaration which caused such a pre-
cipitate flight on the part of that young lady, had assured him that the offence was not unpardonable ; and,

though nothing more had been said on the subject, there existed a perfect understanding of the sentiments of each other.　Julius, who watched them closely, though he appeared to take little interest in their movements, and seldom intruded upon their *tête-à-têtes*, determined to let the affair float along on the current of events for the present, foreseeing that it would ere long come to a crisis either one way or other.　In the mean time the party visited the parade ground, where they were astonished at the triumph of discipline in converting men into machines ; the vast and magnificent cathedral, the most majestic erection of the kind in all North America, and the nunneries, where Minerva, who had pictured nuns as the most ethereal and spiritual of all flesh, was astonished to find them, in the language of Childe Roeliff, " as fat as butter."

It was in one of these excursions that the Childe was struck all at once with a conviction that Julius paid no more attention to his daughter than if they had been married ten years.　It occurred to him that he left Minerva entirely to the care of Reuben, affected to lag behind in the most negligent manner, and whistle Lillebullero, or some other tune, in a sort of under-tone, as if to indicate his utter indifference to what was going forward.　He forthwith determined to speak to the young man on the subject the first opportunity, which luckily occurred that very afternoon.　Minerva and Reuben had strolled out on the bank of the river ; Mrs. Orendorf was napping ; and Julius was left alone with Childe Roeliff to finish a bottle of hock and discuss fruit and nuts at leisure.　Roeliff had lighted his segar and taken a whiff or two, when the spirit moved him, and, gathering himself together, he spoke as follows :

" Nephew, somehow or other—I may be mistaken —but it seems to me you have given up all thoughts of Minerva.　I don't see any of those silent attentions you talked about, or any attentions at all. You leave her entirely to Reuben, so far as I can see."

"But, my dear uncle, you don't see every thing; there are times and seasons, when nobody sees or hears us, when I flatter myself I am making slow and sure progress in her heart."

"Slow enough, I believe; but whether sure or not is more than I will say. On the contrary, it appears to me that she likes Reuben much better than you."

"My dear sir, don't you know that this is one of the best reasons in the world for believing she likes me the best?"

"Not I,—I don't know any such thing; and I'll tell you what, Julius, I mean to leave this place—though I confess I am delighted with the perpetual ringing of the bells—to-morrow morning, after having signified to master Reuben Rossmore that his room is better than his company."

"By no means, sir; this will derange my whole system, and lose me the young lady to a certainty. Only wait a little longer, sir."

"Shilly shally, tilly vally.—I'll tell you what, Julius, I can see as far into a millstone as you, I suspect, and I tell you that Reuben is gaining more in one day than you do in ten."

"But, my dear uncle,—"

"Tut, tut! I tell you to-morrow morning we dissolve partnership with master Reuben, as sure as to-morrow comes. You need not say any more—I am determined not to listen to another word on the subject." And so it seemed, for in half a minute Childe Roeliff, who had a great alacrity in falling asleep extempore, was seen leaning back in his chair, with his nose elevated at an angle of forty-five degrees, and the stump of a segar in his mouth, as fast as a church.

Julius was taken somewhat unaware by this sudden determination of Childe Roeliff; his plans were not

quite matured, and he was obliged to vary them a little
to suit the present crisis. That evening he invited
Reuben into the sitting parlour occupied by the party,
but now dark and deserted, the ladies having retired
to their chamber to rest after the fatigues of a sultry
day spent in rambling about the city. Here he communicated to him the determination of Roeliff to dismiss him on the morrow, and urged him, by every motive he could conceive, to arrange a clandestine match
with Minerva immediately.

"What!" cried Reuben, "before I have done the
old gentleman the honour of first asking his consent?"

"I tell you, Rossmore, it is useless for you to ask
it. You have heard of his determination in my favour,
and a more obstinate old fool does not live than mine
honoured uncle. You will be insulted by his rough
vulgarity, and driven from the sight of Minerva, who, I
can see, will break her heart to lose you."

"I am resolved to try, at any rate. You may say
what you will of Mr. Orendoff, but to me he appears
a person of a good heart, excellent principles, and correct understanding of what is right and proper. He
has treated me kindly; at his fireside I have been always
received with unaffected welcome, and he has displayed
on all occasions a generous confidence. I am determined to try the appeal."

"And if it fails, then I presume your ticklish conscience will not stand in the way of an elopement.
The old blockhead will forgive you in a month afterward."

"I will never give him an opportunity. I love Miss
Orendorf with an affection as warm, sincere, and last-
ing as ever impelled a hero of romance to betray the
happiness of his mistress by making her an exile from
the home and the hearts of her parents. But I will
never ask her—and if I did, I am sure she would
spurn me—I will never, by a look or a hint, a word

or an action, tempt her to forget her duty and the re
gard which every virtuous female owes to her own
honour. If I cannot gain her by honourable, open
means, I will bear her loss like a man."

Julius burst into a long, loud laugh.

" One need not go to church to hear a sermon, I
find," at length he said, wiping his eyes. " Then I
presume you have no objection to my prosecuting my
views upon the young lady ?"

This was rather a sore question, but Reuben rallied
himself to meet it.

" It is the will of her parent, and I have no right to
oppose him any more than you have."

" Her parent !—you don't—you can't look upon him
in any other light than as the wolf that suckled Romu-
lus and Remus, or the bear that nurtured his great pro-
totype Orson. Pooh, pooh ! Rossmore, I beseech thee
once again to get over this unmanly squeamishness.
If you cheat this old dotard out of his daughter, it is
no more than he has done to every man, woman, or
child with whom he ever had any dealings."

" You lie like a rascal !" exclaimed an appalling voice
from a distant and dark corner of the room, and presently the veritable Childe Roeliff advanced upon the
astonished young men. Julius was stricken dumb with
guilt, and Reuben with astonishment. The Childe had
quietly ensconced himself in a corner to take his evening nap, and was awakened by the earnest voices of
the young men, early in the discussion. The interest
of the subject caused him, we presume, to forget he was
enacting the questionable part of a listener.

" So, sir !" cried the wrathful Childe Roeliffe ; " so
master Julius Dibdill, I am an obstinate old blockhead
it seems ; a rough ignorant bear, a she-wolf that suckles
young men—a man that deserves to be cheated out of
his only daughter, because he has cheated every man,

woman, and child he ever had any dealings with. Do I quote you right, sir?"

"I—I—I believe, sir, I might have said some such thing in jest, sir."

"In jest was it, sir? Now hear what I have got to say to you in earnest. You are an ungrateful hypocrite;—you have abused my confidence, and returned my kindness with insult and falsehood. I say falsehood, sir, for, however ignorant and vulgar I may be, I never wronged man, woman, or child, nor dog, nor cat, nor any of God's creatures wilfully or wantonly. Thou art a base slanderer, if thou sayest that. I would— that is to say, I *might* have forgiven the only son of my only sister, now gone to her place of rest, had he but said I was vulgar and ignorant. It may be I am so, sir, for I never had an opportunity in early youth of gaining that knowledge of the world and of books which others had ; but a villain or a rogue I am not—I never have been—and with God's help I never will be. Quit my sight, liar and hypocrite, and never come into it again."

Julius had nothing to say—he was dumbfounded. He saw that all was over, and that nothing was left him but a creditable retreat. So he mustered all the ready cash of brass he had about him, and walked out of the room whistling " Di tanti palpiti."

Childe Roeliff now turned to Reuben. The dense appeared to be in the old son of a tinman, who all at once seemed transmuted to sterling gold ; anger had made him eloquent. He turned to Reuben—

" As for you, young man—"

" Ah ! now comes my turn !" thought Reuben.

" As for you, sir, I heard what you said, too ; and— and"—here the old man's eyes almost overflowed,— " and you may be assured that I will not lose the good opinion you have of me if I can help it. You said, when I am sure you could not have the least expecta-

tion I should ever know it, that I appeared to you a
man of a good heart, excellent principles, and a correct
understanding of what was right and proper. You
also said—and every word went to my heart, seeing I
was about to treat you otherwise to-morrow—you said
I had treated you kindly, welcomed you at my fireside,
and bestowed my confidence on you. I remember all
this, and I will never forget it while I live. You said,
too, you would not abuse that confidence, but appeal to
me, and abide by the result. Now hear me—or rather
hear this young woman ;"—for just at this moment the
light step of Minerva was heard, and her dim shadow
seen entering the door ;—" hear what she has to say,
and take this with you, that whatever she says, I will
sanction, as sure as my name is Roeliff Orendorf ;"
saying which, he marched out of the room before Reuben could reply.

What passed between Minerva and Reuben we cannot disclose ; we were not near enough to overhear
what they said, and it was too dark to see what they
did ; but the waiting-maid, who happened to approach
the room in which they were, privately declared she
distinguished something that sounded for all the world
like a kiss, and the next morning not the bright sun
himself arose more bright and glorious than did the fair
goddess Minerva. Youth revelled in her limbs, hope
sparkled in her rosy cheek and speaking eye ; the
past was forgotten, the present Elysium, the future heaven. So beautiful did she look that morning, that the
waiter who brought in breakfast forgot the tea-tray,
and letting it fall plump on the floor, stood stock still
with eyes and mouth wide open, just as if he had
seen a ghost.

Julius was no longer visible. He had hastened
down to the wharf, after the oration of Childe Roeliff,
where he found the steamboat just departing for Quebec, and joined the party of Mrs. Dowdykin, the Count

Capo d'Oca, and the picturesque hunters, who were " tired to death," as usual.

Of the condescending assent of Mrs. Orendorf to the marriage of Minerva and Reuben, to which she was partly induced by a secret belief that Childe Roeliff was in his heart opposed to the match ; partly by having learned that all the seignors of Montreal were either married, or forbidden to marry, or dead ; and partly by the solemn promise of Reuben Rossmore to employ in future a more fashionable tailor ;—how she, all her life, talked of her travels into foreign parts—how the young couple married, and did, in good time, become, as it were, the parents of a goodly race ;—and concerning the final catastrophe of the Platonics of Mrs. Asheputtle and Julius, behold ! will they not, peradventure, be found in the second part of Childe Roeliff's Pilgrimage, provided that erudite and liberal patron and pattern of literature, Mr. Francis Herbert, shall think proper to propound another prize to be contested and tilted for, with gray-goose lance in rest, by all comers of honourable descent and degree ?

THE SKELETON'S CAVE.

THE SKELETON'S CAVE.

CHAPTER I.

Qual è quella ruina che, nel fianco
  Di quà da Trento, l'Adige percosse.
O per tremuoto, o per sostegno manco,
  Che, da cima del monte onde si mosse,
Al piano è si la rocca discoscesa,
  Ch' alcuna via darebbe a chi su fosse—
Cotal di quel burrato era la scesa.
                    DANTE, *Infern.*

WE hold our existence at the mercy of the elements; the life of man is a state of continual vigilance against their warfare. The heats of noon would wither him like the severed herb; the chills and dews of night would fill his bones with pain; the winter frost would extinguish life in an hour; the hail would smite him to death, did he not seek shelter and protection against them. His clothing is the perpetual armour he wears for his defence, and his dwelling the fortress to which he retreats for safety. Yet, even there the elements attack him; the winds overthrow his habitation; the waters sweep it away. The fire, that warmed and brightened it within, seizes upon its walls and consumes it, with his wretched family. The earth, where she seems to spread a paradise for his abode, sends up death in exhalations from her bosom; and the heavens dart down lightnings to destroy him. The drought consumes the harvests on which he relied for sustenance;

or the rains cause the green corn to " rot ere its youth
attains a beard." A sudden blast ingulfs him in the
waters of the lake or bay from which he seeks his
food ; a false step, or a broken twig, precipitates him
from the tree which he had climbed for its fruit; oaks
falling in the storm, rocks toppling down from the precipices are so many dangers which beset his life.
Even his erect attitude is a continual affront to the great
law of gravitation, which is sometimes fatally avenged
when he loses the balance preserved by constant care,
and falls on a hard surface. The very arts on which
he relies for protection from the unkindness of the elements betray him to the fate he would avoid, in some
moment of negligence, or by some misdirection of skill,
and he perishes miserably by his own inventions. Amid
these various causes of accidental death, which thus
surround us at every moment, it is only wonderful that
their proper effect is not oftener produced—so admi-
rably has the Framer of the universe adapted the facul-
ties by which man provides for his safety, to the perils
of the condition in which he is placed. Yet there are
situations in which all his skill and strength are vain to
protect him from a violent death, by some unexpected chance which executes upon him a sentence as
severe and inflexible as the most pitiless tyranny of
human despotism. But I began with the intention of
relating a story, and I will not by my reflections anti-
cipate the catastrophe of my narrative.

One pleasant summer morning a party of three persons set out from a French settlement in the western
region of the United States, to visit a remarkable cavern in its vicinity. They had already proceeded for
the distance of about three miles, through the tall original forest, along a path so rarely trodden that it required all their attention to keep its track. They now
perceived through the trees the sunshine at a distance,
and as they drew nearer they saw that it came down

into a kind of natural opening, at the foot of a steep precipice. At every step the vast wall seemed to rise higher and higher; its seams and fissures, and inequalities became more and more distinct; and far up, nearly midway from the bottom, appeared a dark opening, under an impending crag. The precipice seemed between two and three hundred feet in height, and quite perpendicular. At its base, the earth for several rods around was heaped with loose fragments of rock, which had evidently been detached from the principal mass, and shivered to pieces in the fall. A few trees, among which were the black walnut and the slippery-elm, and here and there an oak, grew scattered among the rocks, and attested by their dwarfish stature the ungrateful soil in which they had taken root. But the wild grape vines which trailed along the ground, and sent out their branches to overrun the trees around them, showed by their immense size how much they delighted in the warmth of the rocks and the sunshine. The celastrus also here and there had wound its strong rings round and round the trunks and the boughs, till they died in its embrace, and then clothed the leafless branches in a thick drapery of its own foliage. Into this open space the party at length emerged from the forest, and for a moment stopped.

" Yonder is the Skeleton's Cave," said one of them, who stood a little in front of the rest. As he spoke he raised his arm, and pointed to the dark opening in the precipice already mentioned.

The speaker was an aged man, of spare figure, and a mild, subdued expression of countenance. Whoever looked at his thin gray hairs, his stooping form, and the emaciated hand which he extended, might have taken him for one who had passed the Scripture limit of threescore years and ten; but a glance at his clear and bright hazel eye would have induced the observer to set him down at some five years younger. A broad-brimmed

palmetto hat shaded his venerable features from the
sun, and his black gown and rosary denoted him to be
an ecclesiastic of the Romish faith.

The two persons whom he addressed were much
younger. One of them was in the prime of manhood
and personal strength, rather tall, and of a vigorous
make. He wore a hunting-cap, from the lower edge
of which curled a profusion of strong dark hair, rather
too long for the usual mode in the Atlantic States, shad-
ing a fresh-coloured countenance, lighted by a pair of
full black eyes, the expression of which was com-
pounded of boldness and good-humour. His dress
was a blue frock-coat trimmed with yellow fringe, and
bound by a sash at the waist, deer-skin pantaloons,
and deer-skin mocasins. He carried a short rifle on his
left shoulder ; and wore on his left side a leathern bag
of rather ample dimensions, and on his right a powder-
flask. It was evident that he was either a hunter by
occupation, or at least one who made hunting his principal amusement ; and there was something in his air
and the neatness of his garb and equipments that be-
spoke the latter.

On the arm of this person leaned the third individual
of the party, a young woman apparently about nineteen
or twenty years of age, slender and graceful as a
youthful student of the classic poets might imagine a
wood-nymph. She was plainly attired in a straw hat
and a dress of russet-colour, fitted for a ramble through
that wild forest. The faces of her two companions
were decidedly French in their physiognomy ; hers was
as decidedly Anglo-American. Her brown hair was
parted away from a forehead of exceeding fairness,
more compressed on the sides than is usual with
the natives of England ; and showing in the pro-
file that approach to the Grecian outline which is remarked among their descendants in America. To complete the picture, imagine a quiet blue eye, features

delicately moulded, and just colour enough on her cheek to make it interesting to watch its changes, as it deepened or grew paler with the varying and flitting emotions which slight cause will call up in a youthful maiden's bosom.

Notwithstanding this difference of national physiognomy, there was nothing peculiar in her accent, as she answered the old man who had just spoken.

"I see the mouth of the cave, but how are we to reach it, Father Ambrose? I perceive no way of getting to it without wings, either from the bottom or the top of the precipice."

"Look a few rods to the right, Emily. Do you see that pile of broken rocks reaching up to the middle of the precipice, looking as if a huge column of that mighty wall had been shivered into a pyramid of fragments? Our path lies that way."

"I see it, father," returned the fair questioner; "but when we arrive at the top, it appears to me we shall be no nearer the cave than we now are."

"From the top of that pile you may perceive a horizontal seam in the precipice extending to the mouth of the cave. Along that line, though you cannot discern it from the place where we stand, is a safe and broad footing, leading to our place of destination. Do you see, Le Maire," continued Father Ambrose, addressing himself to his other companion, "do you see that eagle sitting so composedly on a bough of that leafless tree, which seems a mere shrub on the brow of the precipice directly over the cavern? Nay, never lift your rifle, my good friend; the bird is beyond your reach, and you will only waste your powder. The superfluous rains which fall on the highlands beyond are collected in the hollow over which hangs the tree I showed you, and pour down the face of the rock directly over the entrance of the cave. Generally, you will see the bed of that hollow perfectly dry, as it is at present, but

17*

during a violent shower, or after several days' rain, there descends from that spot a sheet of water, white as snow, deafening with its noise the quiet solitudes around us, and rivalling in beauty some of the cascades that tumble from the cliffs of the Alps. But let us proceed."

The old man led the party to the pile of rocks which he had pointed out to their notice, and began to ascend from one huge block to another with an agility scarcely impaired by age. They could now perceive that human steps had trodden that rough path before them; in some places the ancient moss was effaced from the stones, and in others their surfaces had been worn smooth. Emily was about to follow her venerable conductor, when Le Maire offered to assist her.

"Nay, uncle," said she, "I know you are the politest of men, but I think your rifle will give you trouble enough. I have often heard you call it your wife; so I beg you will wait on Madame Le Maire, and leave me to make the best of my way by myself. I am not now to take my first lesson in climbing rocks, as you well know."

"Well, if this rifle be my spouse," rejoined the hunter, "I will say that it is not every wife who has so devoted a husband, nor every husband who is fortunate enough to possess so true a wife. She has another good quality—she never speaks but when she is bid, and then always to the point. I only wish for your sake, since I am not permitted to assist you, that Henry Danville were here. I think we should see the wildness of the paces that carry you so lightly over these rocks, a little chastised, while the young gentleman tenderly and respectfully handed you up this rude staircase, too rude for such delicate feet. Ah, I beg pardon, I forgot that you had quarrelled. Well, it is only a lover's quarrel, and the reconciliation will be the happier for being delayed so long. Henry is a worthy lad and an excellent marksman."

A heroine in a modern novel would have turned back this raillery with a smart or proud reply, but Emily was of too sincere and ingenuous a nature to answer a jest on a subject in which her heart was so deeply interested. Her cheek burned with a blush of the deepest crimson, as she turned away without speaking, and fled up the rocks. But though she spoke not, a tumult of images and feelings passed rapidly through her mind. One vivid picture of the past after another came before her recollection, and one well-known form and face were present in them all. She saw Henry Danville as when she first beheld, and was struck with his frank, intelligent aspect and graceful manners,—respectful, attentive, eager to attract her notice, and fearing to displease,—then again as the accepted and delighted lover,—and finally, as he was now, offended, cold, and estranged. A rustic ball rose before her imagination—a young stranger from the Atlantic States appears among the revellers—the phrases of the gay and animated conversation she held with him again vibrate on her ear—and again she sees Henry standing aloof, and looking gloomy and unhappy. She remembered how she had undertaken to discipline him for this unreasonable jealousy, by appearing charmed with her new acquaintance, and accepting his civilities with affected pleasure ; how he had taken fire at this—had withdrawn himself from her society, and transferred his attentions to others. It was but the simple history of what is common enough among youthful lovers ; but it was not of the less moment to her whose heart now throbbed with mingled pride and anguish, as these incidents came thronging back upon her memory. She regretted her own folly, but her thoughts severely blamed Henry for making so trifling a matter a ground of serious offence, and she sought consolation in reflecting how unhappy she must have been had she been united for life to one of so jealous a temper. " I am

confident," said she to herself, " that his present indifference is all a pretence ; he will soon sue for a reconciliation, and I shall then show him that I can be as
indifferent as himself."

Occupied with these reflections, Emily, before she
was aware, found herself at the summit of that pile of
broken rocks, and midway up the precipice.

CHAPTER II.

———————I'll look no more,
Lest my brain turn.—*King Lear.*

THE ecclesiastic was the first of the party who arrived at the summit.   He had seated himself on one
of the blocks of stone which composed the pile, with
his back against the wall of the precipice, and had
taken the hat from his brow that he might enjoy the
breeze which played lightly about the cliffs ; and the
coolness of which was doubly grateful after the toil of
the ascent.   In doing this he uncovered a high and
ample forehead, such as artists love to couple with the
features of old age, when they would represent a countenance at once noble and venerable.   This is the only
feature of the human face which Time spares : he dims
the lustre of the eye ; he shrivels the cheek ; he de-
stroys the firm or sweet expression of the mouth ; he
thins and whitens the hairs ; but the forehead, that temple of thought, is beyond his reach, or rather, it shows
more grand and lofty for the ravages which surround it.

The spot on which they now stood commanded a
view of a wide extent of uncultivated and uninhabited
country.   An eminence interposed to hide from sight

the village they had left; and on every side were
the summits of the boundless forest, here and there
diversified with a hollow of softer and richer verdure,
where the hurricane, a short time before, had descended
to lay prostrate the gigantic trees, and a young growth
had shot up in their stead. Solitary savannas opened
in the depth of the woods, and far off a lonely stream
was flowing away in silence, sometimes among venerable trees, and sometimes through natural meadows,
crimson with blossoms. All around them was the
might, the majesty of vegetable life, untamed by the
hand of man, and pampered by the genial elements
into boundless luxuriance. The ecclesiastic pointed
out to his companions the peculiarities of the scenery;
he expatiated on the flowery beauty of those unshorn
lawns; and on the lofty growth, and the magnificence
and variety of foliage which distinguish the American
forests, so much the admiration of those who have seen
only the groves of Europe.

The conversation was interrupted by a harsh stridu-
lous cry, and looking up, the party beheld the eagle who
had left his perch on the top of the precipice, and having
passed over their heads, was winging his way towards
the stream in the distance.

"Ah," exclaimed Le Maire, "that is a hungry note,
and the bird is a shrewd one, for he is steering to a
place where there is plenty of game to my certain
knowledge. It is the golden eagle; the war eagle, as
the Indians call him, and no chicken either, as you may
understand from the dark colour of his plumage. I
warrant he has gorged many a rabbit and prairie hen
on these old cliffs. At all events, he has made me think
of my dinner: unless we make haste, good Father Ambrose, I am positive that we shall be late to our venison
and claret."

"We must endeavour to prevent so great a misfortune," said Father Ambrose, rising from the rock where

I 3

he sat, and proceeding on the path towards the cavern.
It was a kind of narrow terrace, varying in width from
four to ten feet, running westwardly along the face of
the steep solid rock, and apparently formed by the
breaking away of the upper part of one of the perpendicular strata of which the precipice was composed.
That event must have happened at a very remote
period, for in some places the earth had accumulated on
the path to a considerable depth, and here and there
grew a hardy and dwarfish shrub, or a tuft of wild-
flowers hanging over the edge.   As they proceeded, the
great height at which they stood, and the steepness of
the rocky wall above and below them, made Emily
often tremble and grow pale as she looked down.   A
few rods brought the party to a turn in the rock, where
the path was narrower than elsewhere, and precisely
in the angle a portion of the terrace on which they
walked had fallen, leaving a chasm of about two feet
in width, through which their distance from the base
was fearfully apparent.   Le Maire had already passed
it, but Emily, when she arrived at the spot, shrunk back
and leaned against the rock.

"I fear I shall not be able to cross the chasm," said
she, in a tone of alarm.   "My poor head grows giddy
from a single look at it."

"Le Maire will assist you, my child," said the old
man, who walked behind her.

"With the greatest pleasure in ·life," answered Le
Maire; "though I confess I little expected that the
daughter of a clear-headed Yankee would complain of
being giddy in any situation.   But this comes of having
a French mother I suppose.   Let me provide a convenient station for Madame le Maire, as you call her, and
I will help you over."   He then placed his rifle against
the rock, where the path immediately beyond him grew
wider, and advancing to the edge of the chasm, held
forth both hands to Emily, taking hold of her arms near

the elbow. In doing this he perceived that she
trembled.

"You are as safe here as when you were in the
woods below," said Le Maire, "if you would but think
so. Step forward now, firmly, and look neither to the
right nor left."

She took the step, but at that moment the strange
inclination which we sometimes feel when standing on
a dizzy height, to cast ourselves to the ground, came
powerfully over her, and she leaned involuntarily and
heavily towards the verge of the precipice. Le Maire
was instantly aware of the movement, and bracing himself firmly, strove with all his might to counteract it.
Had his grasp been less steady, or his self-possession
less perfect, they would both inevitably have been pre-
cipitated from where they stood; but Le Maire was
familiar with all the perilous situations of the wilderness, and the presence of mind he had learned in
such a school did not now desert him. His countenance bore witness to the intense exertion he was
making; it was flushed, and its muscles were working
powerfully; his lips were closely compressed; the
veins on his brow swelled, and his arms quivered with
the strong tension given to their sinews. For an instant
the fate of the two seemed in suspense, but the strength
of the hunter prevailed, and he placed the damsel beside him on the rock, fainting and pallid as a corpse.

"God be praised," said the priest, drawing heavily
the breath which he had involuntarily held during that
fearful moment, while he had watched the scene, unable
to render the least assistance.

CHAPTER III.

————————A hollow cave,
Far underneath a craggy cliff ypight,
Dark, doleful, dreary, like a greedy grave.
SPENSER.

——·——Beneath whose sable roof,
————————————ghostly shapes
Might meet at noontide,—Fear and trembling Hope—
Silence and Foresight,—Death the Skeleton,
And Time the Shadow.—WORDSWORTH.

SOME moments of repose were necessary before Emily was sufficiently recovered from her agitation to be able to proceed. The tears filled her eyes as she briefly but warmly thanked Le Maire for his generous exertions to save her, and begged his pardon for the foolish and awkward timidity, as she termed it, which had put his life as well as her own in such extreme peril.

" I confess," answered he, good-naturedly, " that had you been of as solid a composition as some ladies with whom I have the honour of an acquaintance, Madame Le Maire here would most certainly have been a widow. I understood my own strength, however," added he, for on this point he was somewhat vain, " and if I had not, I should still have been willing to risk something rather than to lose you. But I will take care, Emily, that you do not lead me into another scrape of the kind. When we return I shall, by your leave, take you in my arms and carry you over the chasm, and you may shut your eyes while I do it, if you please."

They now again set out, and in a few moments arrived at the mouth of the cavern they had come to visit. A

projecting mass of rock impended over it, so low as not
to allow in front an entrance to a person standing upright, but on each side it receded upwards in such a
manner as to leave two high narrow openings, giving
it the appearance of being suspended from the cavern
roof.　Beneath it the floor, which was a continuation of
the terrace leading to the spot, was covered, in places,
to a considerable depth, with soil formed by the disinte-
gration of the neighbouring rocks, and traversed by
several fissures nearly filled with earth.　As they entered by one of the narrow side openings, Emily looked
up to the crag with a slight shudder.　" If it should
fall !" thought she to herself ; but a feeling of shame at
the idle fear she had lately manifested restrained her
from giving utterance to the thought.　The good ecclesiastic perceived what was passing in her mind, and
said, with a smile—

" There is no danger, my child ; that rock has been
suspended over the entrance for centuries, for thousands of years perhaps, and is not likely to fall to-
day.　Ages must have elapsed before the crags could
have crumbled to form the soil now under our feet.
It is true that there is no place sacred from the intrusion of accident ;　everywhere may unforeseen events
surprise and crush us, as the foot of man surprises and
crushes the insect in his path ; but to suppose peculiar
danger in a place which has known no change for hundreds of years is to distrust Providence.　Come, Le
Maire," said Father Ambrose, " will you oblige us by
striking a light ?　Our eyes have been too much in the
sunshine to distinguish objects in this dark place."

Le Maire produced from his hunting bag a roll of
tinder, and lighting it with a spark from his rifle, kindled
in a few moments a large pitch-pine torch.　The circumstance which first struck the attention of the party
was the profound and solemn stillness of the place.
The most quiet day has under the open sky its multi-

tude of sounds—the lapse of waters, the subtle motions
of the apparently slumbering air among forests, grasses,
and rocks, the flight and note of insects, the voices of
animals, the rising of exhalations, the mighty process
of change, of perpetual growth and decay, going on all
over the earth, produce a chorus of noises which the
hearing cannot analyze—which, though it may seem to
you silence, is not so; and when from such a scene
you pass directly into one of the rocky chambers of the
earth, you perceive your error by the contrast.   As the
three went forward they passed through a heap of dry
leaves lightly piled, which the winds of the last autumn
had blown into the cave from the summit of the surrounding forest, and the rustling made by their steps
sounded strangely loud amid that death-like silence.
A spacious cavern presented itself to their sight, the
roof of which near the entrance was low, but several
paces beyond it rose to a great height, where the smoke
of the torch ascending, mingled with the darkness, but
the flame did not reveal the face of the vault.

They soon came to where, as Father Ambrose informed them, the cave divided into two branches.
"That on the left," said he, "soon becomes a low and
narrow passage among the rocks; this on the right
leads to a large chamber, in which lie the bones from
which the cavern takes its name."

He now took the torch from the hand of Le Maire,
and turning to the right guided his companions to a
lofty and wide apartment of the cave, in one corner of
which he showed them a human skeleton lying extended on the rocky floor.   Some decayed fragments,
apparently of the skins of animals, lay under it in places,
and one small remnant passed over the thighs, but
the bones, though they had acquired from the atmosphere of the cave a greenish yellow hue, were seemingly unmouldered.   They still retained their original
relative position, and appeared as never disturbed since
the sleep of death came over the frame to which they

once belonged. Emily gazed on the spectacle with that natural horror which the remains of the dead inspire. Even Le Maire, with all his vivacity and garrulity, was silent for a moment.

"Is any thing known of the manner in which this poor wretch came to his end?" he at length inquired.

"Nothing. The name of Skeleton's Cave was given to this place by the aborigines; but I believe they have no tradition concerning these remains. If you look at the right leg you will perceive that the bone is fractured: it is most likely the man was wounded on these very cliffs either by accident or by some enemy, and that he crawled to this retreat, where he perished from want of attendance and from famine."

"What a death!" murmured Emily.

The ecclesiastic then directed their attention to another part of the same chamber, where he said it was formerly not uncommon for persons benighted in these parts, particularly hunters, to pass the night. "You perceive," added he, "that this spot is higher than the rest of the cavern, and drier also; indeed no part of the cavern is much subject to moisture. A bed of leaves on this rock with a good blanket, is no bad accommodation for a night's rest, as I can assure you, having once made the experiment myself many years since, when I came hither from Europe. Ah, what have we here? coals, brands, splinters of pitch-pine! The cave must have been occupied very lately for the purpose I mentioned, and by people too who, I dare say, from the preparations they seem to have made, passed the night very comfortably."

"I dare say they did so, though they had an ugly bedfellow yonder," answered Le Maire; "but I hope you do not think of following their example. As you have shown us, I presume, the principal curiosities of the cave, I take the liberty of suggesting the propriety of getting as fast as we can out of this melancholy

place, which has already put me out of spirits.   That
poor wretch who died of famine !—I shall never get
him out of my head till I am fairly set down to dinner.
Not that I care more for my dinner than any other man
when there is any thing of importance in the way, as,
for example, a buffalo, or a fat buck, or a bear to be
killed; but you will allow, Father Ambrose, that a
saddle of venison, or a hump of buffalo and a sober
bottle of claret are a prettier spectacle, particularly at
this time of day, than that mouldy skeleton yonder.   I
had intended to shoot something in my way back just
to keep my hand and eye in practice, but it is quite too
late to think of that.   Besides, here is Emily, poor
thing, whom we have contrived to get up to this place,
and whom we must manage to get down again as well
as we can."

The good priest, though by no means participating
in Le Maire's haste to be gone, mildly yielded to his
instances, particularly as they were seconded by Emily,
and they accordingly prepared to return.   On reaching
the mouth of the cave, they were struck with the change
in the aspect of the heavens.   Dark heavy clouds, the
round summits of which were seen one beyond the
other, were rapidly rising in the west; and through
the grayish blue haze which suffused the sky before
them, the sun appeared already shorn of his beams.
A sound was heard afar of mighty winds contending
with the forest, and the thunder rolled at a distance.

" We must stay at least until the storm is over," said
Father Ambrose; " it would be upon us before we
could descend these cliffs.   Let us watch it from where
we stand above the tops of these old woods : I can
promise you it will be a magnificent spectacle."

Emily, though she would gladly have left the cave,
could say nothing against the propriety of this advice ;
and even Le Maire, notwithstanding that he declared
he had rather see a well-loaded table at that moment

than all the storms that ever blew, preferred remaining
to the manifest inconvenience of attempting a descent.
In a few moments the dark array of clouds swept over
the face of the sun, and a tumult in the woods announced the coming of the blast.   The summits of the
forest waved and stooped before it, like a field of young
flax in the summer breeze,—another and fiercer gust
descended,—another and stronger convulsion of the
forest ensued.   The trees rocked backward and forward, leaned and rose, and tossed and swung their
branches in every direction, and the whirling air above
them was filled with their leafy spoils.   The roar was
tremendous,—the noise of the ocean in a tempest is
not louder,—it seemed as if that innumerable multi-
tude of giants of the wood, raised a universal voice of
wailing under the fury that smote and tormented them.
At length the rain began to fall, first in large and rare
drops, and then the thunder burst over head, and the
waters of the firmament poured down in torrents, and
the blast that howled in the woods fled before them as
if from an element that it feared.   The trees again
stood erect, and nothing was heard but the rain beating
heavily on the immense canopy of leaves around, and
the occasional crashings of the thunder, accompanied
by flashes of lightning, that threw a vivid light upon
the walls of the cavern.   The priest and his companions
stood contemplating this scene in silence, when a rush-
ing of water close at hand was heard.   Father Ambrose showed the others where a stream, formed from
the rains collected on the highlands above, descended
on the crag that overhung the mouth of the cavern,
and shooting clear of the rocks on which they stood,
fell in spray to the broken fragments at the base of the
precipice.

   A gust of wind drove the rain into the opening where
they stood, and obliged them to retire farther within.
The priest suggested that they should take this opportu-

18*

nity to examine that part of the cave which in going to the skeleton's chamber they had passed on their left, observing, however, that he believed it was no otherwise remarkable than for its narrowness and its length. Le Maire and Emily assented, and the former taking up the torch which he had stuck in the ground, they went back into the interior. They had just reached the spot where the two passages diverged from each other, when a hideous and intense glare of light filled the cavern, showing for an instant the walls, the roof, the floor, and every crag and recess, with the distinctness of the broadest sunshine. A frightful crash accompanied it, consisting of several sharp and deafening explosions, as if the very heart of the mountain was rent asunder by the lightning, and immediately after a body of immense weight seemed to fall at their very feet with a heavy sound, and a shock that caused the place where they stood to tremble as if shaken by an earthquake. A strong blast of air rushed by them, and a suffocating odour filled the cavern.

Father Ambrose had fallen upon his knees in mental prayer, at the explosion; but the blast from the mouth of the cavern threw him to the earth. He raised himself, however, immediately, and found himself in utter silence and darkness, save that a livid image of that insufferable glare floated yet before his eyeballs. He called first upon Emily, who did not answer, then upon Le Maire, who replied from the ground a few paces nearer the entrance of the cave. He also had been thrown prostrate, and the torch he carried was extinguished. It was but the work of an instant to kindle it again, and they then discovered Emily extended near them in a swoon.

"Let us bear her to the mouth of the cavern," said Le Maire; "the fresh air from without will revive her." He took her in his arms, but on arriving at the spot he placed her suddenly on the ground, and raising both

hands, exclaimed, with an accent of despair, " The rock
is fallen !—the entrance is closed !"

It was but too evident,—Father Ambrose needed but
a single look to convince him of its truth,—the huge
rock which impended over the entrance had been loos-
ened by the thunderbolt, and had fallen upon the floor
of the cave, closing all return to the outer world.

CHAPTER IV.

Had one been there, with spirit strong and high,
Who could observe as he prepared to die ;
He might have seen of hearts the varying kind,
And traced the movements of each different mind ;
He might have seen that not the gentle maid
Was more than stern and haughty man afraid.
CRABBE.

BEFORE inquiring further into the extent of the disaster, an office of humanity was to be performed.
Emily was yet lying on the floor of the cave in a
swoon, and the old man, stooping down and placing her
head in his lap, began to use the ordinary means of
recovery, and called on Le Maire to assist him.   The
hunter, after being spoken to several times, started
from his gloomy revery, and kneeling down by the side
of the priest, aided him in chafing her temples and
hands, and fanned her cheek with his cap until consciousness was restored, when the priest communicated
the terrible intelligence of what had happened.

Presence of mind and fortitude do not always dwell
together.   Those who are most easily overcome by the
appearance of danger often support the calamity after
it has fallen with the most composure.   Le Maire had
presence of mind, but he had not learned to submit

with patience to irremediable misfortune ; Emily could
not command her nerves in sudden peril, but she could
suffer with a firmness which left her mind at liberty to
employ its resources. The very disaster which had
happened seemed to inspire both her mind and her
frame with new strength. The vague apprehensions
which had haunted her were now reduced to certainty ;
she saw the extent of the calamity, and felt the duties
it imposed. She rose from the ground without aid and
with a composed countenance, and began to confer with
Father Ambrose on the probabilities and means of
escape from their present situation.

In the mean time, Le Maire, who had left them as
soon as Emily came to herself, was eagerly employed
in examining the entrance where the rock had fallen.
On one side it lay close against the wall of the cavern ;
on the other was an opening of about a hand's breadth,
which appeared, so far as he could distinguish, to com-
municate with the outer atmosphere. He looked above,
but there the low roof, which met the wavering flame
of his torch, showed a collection of large blocks firmly
wedged together ; he cast his eyes downwards, but there
the lower edge of the vast mass which had fallen lay
imbedded in the soil ; he placed his shoulder against it
and exerted his utmost strength to discover if it were
moveable, but it yielded no more than the rock on which
it rested.

" It is all over with us," said he, at length, dashing
to the ground the torch, which the priest, approaching,
prudently took up before it was extinguished ; " it is all
over with us ; and we must perish in this horrid place
like wild beasts in a trap. There is no opening, no
possible way for escape, and not a soul on the wide
earth knows where we are, or what is our situation."
Then turning fiercely to the priest, and losing his
habitual respect for his person and office in the bitterness of his despair, he said, " This is all your doing.—

it was you who decoyed us hither to lay our bones beside those of that savage yonder "

" My son—" said the old man.

" Call me not son,—this is no time for cant. You take my life, and when I reproach you, you give me fine words. You call yourself a man of God,—can you pray us out of this horrible dungeon into which you have enticed us to bury us alive ?"

" Say not that I take your life," said Father Ambrose mildly, without otherwise noticing his reproaches; " there is no reason as yet to suppose our case hopeless. Though we informed no person of the place to which we were going, it does not follow that we shall not be missed, or that no inquiry will be made for us. With to-morrow morning the whole settlement will doubtless be out to search for us, and as it is probable that some of them will pass this way, we may make ourselves heard by them from the mouth of the cavern. Besides, as Emily has just suggested, it is not impossible that the cave may have some other outlet, and that the part we were about to examine may afford a passage to the daylight."

Le Maire caught eagerly at the hope thus presented. " I beg your pardon, father," said he, " I was hasty— I was furious—but it is terrible, you will allow, to be shut up in this sepulchre, with the stone rolled to its mouth, and left to die. It is no light trial of patience merely to pass the night here, particularly," said he, with a smile, " when you know that dinner is waiting for you at home. Well, if the cave is to be explored, let us set about it immediately ; if there is any way of getting out, let us discover it as soon as possible."

They again went to the passage which diverged from the path leading to the skeleton's chamber. It was a low, irregular passage, sometimes so narrow that they were obliged to walk one behind the other, and sometimes wide enough to permit them to walk abreast.

After proceeding a few rods it became so low that they were obliged to stoop.

"Remain here," said Le Maire, "and give me the torch. If there be any way of reaching daylight by this part of the cavern, I will give an account of it in due time."

Father Ambrose and Emily then seated themselves on a low bench of stone in the side of the cavern, while he went forward. The gleam of his torch appearing and disappearing showed the windings of the passage he was treading, and sometimes the sound of measured steps on the rock announced that he was walking upright, and sometimes a confused and struggling noise denoted that he was making his way on his elbows and knees. At length the sound was heard no longer, and the gleam of the torch ceased altogether to be descried in the passage.

"Father Ambrose!" said Emily, after a long interval. These words, though in the lowest key of her voice, were uttered in such a tone of awe, and sounded, moreover, with such an unnatural distinctness in the midst of that perfect stillness, that the good father started.

"What would you, my daughter?"

"This darkness and this silence are frightful, and I spoke that you might reassure me by the sound of your voice. My uncle is long in returning."

"The passage is a long and intricate one."

"But is there no danger? I have heard of death-damps in pits and deep caverns, by the mere breathing of which a man dies silently and without a struggle. If my poor uncle should never return!"

"Let us not afflict ourselves with supposable evils, while a real calamity is impending over us. The cavern has been explored to a considerable distance without any such consequence as you mention to those who undertook it."

" God grant that he may discover a passage out of the cave ! But I am afraid of the effect of a disappointment, he is so impatient—so impetuous."

" God grant us all grace to submit to his good pleasure," rejoined the priest ; " but I think I hear him on the return. Listen, my child, you can distinguish sounds inaudible to my dull ears."

Emily listened, but in vain. At length, after another long interval, a sound of steps was heard, seemingly at a vast distance. In a little while a faint light showed itself in the passage, and after some minutes Le Maire appeared, panting with exertion, his face covered with perspiration, and his clothes soiled with the dust and slime of the rocks. He was about to throw himself on the rocky seat beside them without speaking.

" I fear your search has been unsuccessful," said Father Ambrose.

" There is no outlet in that quarter," rejoined Le Maire sullenly. " I have explored every winding and every cranny of the passage, and have been brought up at last, in every instance, against the solid rock."

" There is no alternative, then," said the ecclesiastic, " but to make ourselves as tranquil and comfortable as we can for the night. I shall have the honour of installing you in my old bed-chamber, where, if you sleep as soundly as I did once, you will acknowledge to-morrow morning that you might have passed a worse night. It is true, Emily, that one corner of it is occupied by an ill-looking inmate, but I can promise you from my own experience that he will do you no harm. So let us adjourn to the skeleton's chamber, and leave to Providence the events of the morrow."

To the skeleton's chamber they went accordingly, taking the precaution to remove thither a quantity of the dry leaves which lay heaped not far from the mouth of the cave, to form couches for their night's repose. A log of wood of considerable size was found in this

part of the cavern, apparently left there by those who
had lately occupied it for the night ; and on collecting
the brands and bits of wood which lay scattered about
they found themselves in possession of a respectable
stock of fuel.   A fire was kindled, and the warmth, the
light, the crackling brands, and the ever-moving flames,
with the dancing shadows they threw on the walls, and the
waving trains of smoke that mounted like winged ser-
pents to the roof and glided away to the larger and
loftier apartment of the cave, gave to that recess lately so
still, dark, and damp, a kind of wild cheerfulness and
animation, which, under other circumstances, could not
have failed to raise the spirits of the party.   They
placed themselves around that rude hearth, Emily taking care to turn her back to the corner where lay the
skeleton.   Father Ambrose had been educated in Europe ; he had seen much of men and manners, and he
now exerted himself to entertain his companions by the
narrative of what had fallen under his observation in
that ancient abode of civilized man.   He was successful, and the little circle forgot for a while in the charm
of his conversation their misfortune and their danger.
Even Le Maire was enticed into relating one or two
of his hunting exploits, and Emily suffered a few of
the arch sallies that distinguished her in more cheerful
moments to escape her.   At length Le Maire's hunting
watch pointed to the hour of ten, and the good priest
counselled them to seek repose.   He gave them his
blessing, recommending them to the great Preserver of
men, and then laying themselves down on their beds
of leaves around the fire, they endeavoured to compose
themselves to rest.

But now that each was left to the companionship of
his own thoughts, the idea of their situation intruded
upon their minds with a sense of pain and anxiety
which repulsed the blessing of sleep.   The reflections
of each on the events of the day and the prospects of

the morrow were different ; those of Emily were the most cheerful, as her hopes of deliverance were the most sanguine. Her imagination had formed a picture of the incidents of her rescue from the fate that threatened her, a little romance in anticipation, which she would not for the world have revealed to living ear, but which she dwelt upon fondly and perpetually in the secrecy of her own meditations. She thought what must be the effect of her mysterious absence from the village upon Henry Danville, whose very jealousy, causeless as it was, demonstrated the sincerity and depth of his affection. She represented him to herself as the leader in the search that would be set on foot for the lost ones, as the most adventurous of the band, the most persevering, the most inventive, and the most successful.

" He will pass by this precipice to-morrow," thought she ; " like others, he has heard of this cave ; he will see that the fall of the rock has closed the entrance, his quick apprehension will divine the place of our imprisonment, he will call upon those who are engaged in the search, he will climb the precipice, he will deliver us, and I shall forgive him. But should it be my fate to perish ; should none ever know the manner and place of my death ; there will be one at least who will remember and regret me. He will bitterly repent the wrong he has done me, and the tears will start into his eyes at the mention of my name." A tear gushed out from between the closed lids of the fair girl as this thought passed through her mind, but it was such a tear as maidens love to shed, and it did not delay the slumber that already began to steal over her.

Sleep was later in visiting the eyes of Le Maire. The impatience which a bold and adventurous man, accustomed to rely on his own activity and address for escape in perilous emergencies, feels under the pressure of a calamity which no exertion of his own can remedy,

had chafed and almost maddened his spirit. His heart
sank within him at the thought of the lingering death
he must die if not liberated from his living tomb.   Long
and uneasily he tossed on his bed of leaves, but he too
had his hopes of deliverance by the people of the village, who would unquestionably assemble in the morning to search for their lost neighbours, and who might
discover their situation.   These thoughts at length prevailed over those of a gloomier kind ; and the fatigues of
the day overcoming his eyes with drowsiness, he fell
into a slumber, profound, as it seemed from his hard-
drawn breath, but uneasy and filled with unpleasant
dreams, as was evident from frequent starts and mut-
tered exclamations.

When it was certain that both were asleep, Father
Ambrose raised himself from his place and regarded
them sorrowfully and attentively.   He had not slept,
though from his motionless posture and closed eyes, an
observer might have thought him buried in a deep slumber.   His own apprehensions, notwithstanding that he
had endeavoured to prevent his companions from yielding themselves up to despair, were more painful than
he had permitted himself to utter.   That there was a
possibility of their deliverance was true, but it was
hardly to be expected that those who sought for them
would think of looking for them in the cavern, nor was
it likely that any cry they could utter would be heard
below.   The old man's thoughts gradually formed
themselves into a kind of soliloquy, uttered, as is often
the case with men much given to solitary meditation
and prayer, in a low but articulate voice.   "For myself," said he, "my life is near its close, and the day
of decrepitude may be even yet nearer than the day of
death.   I repine not, if it be the will of God that my
existence on earth, already mercifully protracted to the
ordinary limits of usefulness, should end here.   But
my heart bleeds to think that this maiden, in the blos-

som of her beauty and in the spring-time of her hopes,
and that he who slumbers near me, in the pride and
strength of manhood, should be thus violently divorced
from a life which nature perhaps intended for as long
a date as mine. I little thought, when the mother of
that fair young creature in dying committed her to my
charge, that I should be her guide to a place where she
should meet with a frightful and unnatural death. Accustomed as I am to protracted fastings, it is not impossible that I may outlive them both, and after having
closed their eyes, who should have closed mine, I may
be delivered and go forth in my uselessness from the
sepulchre of those who should have been the delight
and support of their friends. Let it not displease thee,
O, my Maker! if, like the patriarch of old, I venture
to expostulate with thee." And the old man placed
himself in an attitude of supplication, clasping his hands
and raising them towards heaven. Long did he remain
in that posture motionless, and at length lowering his
hands, he cast a look upon the sleepers near him, and
laying himself down upon his bed of leaves, was soon
asleep also.

K 2

CHAPTER V.

A dull imprisoned ray,
A sunbeam that hath lost its way,
And through the crevice and the cleft
Of the thick wall is fallen and left.
Prisoners of Chillon.

Of course the slumbers of none of the party were long protracted. They were early dispersed by the idea of their imprisonment in that mountain dungeon, which now and then showed itself painfully in the imagery of their dreams. When Emily awoke she found herself alone in the skeleton's chamber. Her eyes, accustomed to the darkness, could now distinguish most of the objects around her by the help of a gleam of light, which appeared to come in from the larger apartment. The fire, kindled the night previous, was now a mass of ashes and blackened brands ; and the couches of her two companions yet showed the pressure of their forms. She rose, and not without casting a look at the grim inmate of the place, whose discoloured bones were just distinguishable in that dim twilight, passed into the outer chamber. Here she found the priest and Le Maire standing near the mouth of the cavern, where a strong light, at least so it seemed to her eyes, streamed in through the opening between the well and the fallen rock, showing that the short night of summer was already past.

"We are watching the increasing light of the morning," said the priest.

"And waiting for the friends whom it will bring to deliver us," added Le Maire.

" You will admit me to share in the occupation, I
hope," answered Emily. " I am fit for nothing else,
as you know, but to watch and wait, and I will endeavour to do that patiently."

It was not long before a brighter and a steady light,
through the aperture, informed the prisoners that the
sun had risen over the forest tops ; and that the perfect
day now shone upon the earth. To those, who could
look upon the woods and savannas, the hills and the
waters around, that morning was one of the most beautiful of the beautiful season to which it belonged. The
aspect of nature, like one of those human countenances
we sometimes meet with, so radiant with cheerfulness
that it seems as if they had never known the expression of sorrow, showed, in the gladness it now put on,
no traces of the tempest of the preceding day. The
intensity of the sun's light was tempered by the white
clouds that now and then floated over it, trailing through
a soft blue sky ; and the light and fresh breezes seemed
to hover in the air, to rise and descend, with a motion
like the irregular and capricious course of the butter-
fly ; now stooping to wrinkle the surface of the stream,
now rising to murmur in the leaves of the forest, and
again descending to shake the dew from the cups of
the opening flowers in the natural meadows. The re-
plenished brooks had a livelier warble, and the notes
of innumerable birds rang more cheerfully through the
clear atmosphere. The prisoners of the cavern, however,
could only distinguish the beauty of the morning by
slight tokens,—now and then a sweep of the winds
over the forest tops—sometimes the note of the wood-
thrush, or of the cardinal bird as he flew by the face
of the rocks ; and occasionally a breath of the
perfumed atmosphere flowing through the aperture.
These intimations of liberty and enjoyment from the
world without only heightened their impatience at the
imprisonment to which they were doomed.

19*

" Listen !" said Emily ; " I think I hear a human voice."

" There is certainly a distant call in the woods," said Le Maire, after a moment's silence. " Let us all shout together for assistance."

They shouted accordingly, Le Maire exerting his clear and powerful voice to the utmost, and the others aiding him as well as they were able, with their feebler and less practised organs. A shrill discordant cry replied, apparently from the cliffs close to the cave.

" A parrokeet," exclaimed Le Maire. " The noisy pest ! I wish the painted rascal were within reach of my rifle. You see, Father Ambrose, we are forgotten by mankind ; and the very birds of the wilderness mock our cries for assistance."

" You have a quick fancy, my son," answered the priest ; " but it is yet quite too soon to give over. It is now the very hour when we may expect our neighbours to be looking for us in these parts."

They continued therefore to remain by the opening ; and from time to time to raise that shout for assistance. Hour after hour passed, and no answer was returned to their cries, which indeed could have been but feebly heard, if heard at all, at the foot of the precipice ; hour after hour passed, and no foot climbed the rocky stair that led to their prison. The pangs of hunger in the mean time began to assail them, and, more intolerable than these, a feverish and tormenting thirst.

" You have practised fasting," said Le Maire to Father Ambrose ; " and so have I when I could get nothing to eat. In my hunting excursions I have sometimes gone without tasting food from morning till the night of the next day. I found relief from an expedient which I learned of the old hunters, but which I presume you churchmen are not acquainted with. Here it is."

Saying this, he passed the sash he wore once more round his body, drawing it tightly, and securing it by a firm knot. Father Ambrose declined adopting, for the present, a similar expedient, alleging that as yet he had suffered little inconvenience from want of food, except a considerable degree of thirst; but Emily, already weak from fasting, allowed her slender waist to be wrapped tightly in the folds of a silk shawl which she had brought with her. The importunities of hunger were thus rendered less painful, and a new tension was given to the enervated frame; but the burning thirst was not at all allayed. The cave was then explored for water; every corner was examined, and holes were dug in the soil which in some places covered the rocky floor, but in vain. Le Maire again ventured into the long narrow passage which he had followed to its termination the day previous, in the hope of now discovering some concealed spring, or some place where the much desired element fell in drops from the roof, but he returned fatigued and unsuccessful. As he came forth into the larger apartment a light fluttering sound, as of the waving of a thin garment, attracted the attention of the party. On listening attentively it appeared to be within the cavern; but what most excited their surprise was, that it passed suddenly and mysteriously from place to place, while the agent continued invisible, in spite of all their endeavours to discover it. Sometimes it was heard on the one side, sometimes on the other, now from the roof, and now from the floor, near, and at a distance. At length it passed directly over their heads.

" It is precisely the sound of a light robe agitated by the wind, or by a swift motion of the person wearing it," said Emily.

" It is no sound of this earth, I will depose in a court of justice," said Le Maire, who was naturally of a superstitious turn ; " or we should see the thing that makes it."

" All we can say at present," answered the priest, " is, that we cannot discover the cause ; but it does

20*

not therefore follow that it is any thing supernatural. What is perceived by one of our senses only does not necessarily belong to the other world. I have no doubt however, that we shall discover the cause before we leave the cavern."

"Nor I either," rejoined Le Maire, with a look and tone which showed the awe that had mastered him ; "I am satisfied of the cause already. It is a warning of approaching death. We must perish in this cavern."

Emily, much as she was accustomed to rely on the opinions of the priest, felt in spite of herself the infection of that feeling of superstitious terror which had seized upon her uncle, and her heart had begun to beat thick, when a weak chirp was heard.

"The mystery is resolved," exclaimed Father Ambrose, "and your ghost, my good friend, is only a harmless fellow-prisoner, a poor bird, which the storm doubtless drove into the cave, and which has been confined here ever since." As he spoke, Emily, who had looked to the quarter whence the sound proceeded, pointed out the bird sitting on a projection of rock at no great distance.

"A godsend !" cried Le Maire ; "the bird is ours, though his little carcass will hardly furnish a mouthful for each of us." Saying this, he took up his rifle, which stood leaning against the wall of the cavern, and raised the piece to his eye. Another instant and the bird would have fallen, but Emily laid her hand on his arm.

"Cannot we take him alive," asked she ; "and make him the agent of our deliverance ?"

"How will you do that?" said Le Maire, without lowering his rifle.

"Send him out at the opening yonder with a letter tied to his wing to inform our friends of our situation. It will at least increase the chances of our escape."

"It is well thought of," answered Le Maire ; "and

now, Emily, you shall see how an experienced hunter
takes a bird without harming a single feather of his
wings."

Saying this, he went to the mouth of the cave, and
began to turn up, with a splinter of wood, the fresh
earth.   After considerable examination he drew forth a
beetle, and producing from his hunting-bag a quantity
of packthread, he tied the insect to one end of it, and
having placed it on the point of a crag, retired to a little
distance with the other end of the packthread in his hand.
By frequently changing his place, he caused the bird to
approach the spot where he had laid the insect.   It was
a tedious process; but when at length the bird perceived his prey, he flew to it and snapped it up in an
instant, with the eagerness of famine.   By a similar
piece of management he contrived to get the thread
wound several times about one of the legs of the little
creature ; and when this was effected, he suddenly
drew it in, bringing him fluttering and struggling to
his hand.   It proved to be of the species commonly
called the cedar bird.

"Ah, Father Ambrose," cried Le Maire, whose
vivacity returned with whatever revived his hopes, " we
have caught you a brother ecclesiastic, a *recollet*, as we
call him from the gray hood he wears.   No wonder we
did not see him before, for his plumage is exactly of
the colour of the rocks.   But he is the very bird for a
letter ; look at the sealing-wax he carries on his wings."
As he spoke he displayed the glossy brown pinions,
the larger feathers of which were ornamented at their
tops with little appendages of a vermilion colour, like
drops of delicate red sealing-wax.

" And now let us think," continued he, " of writing the
letter which this dapper little monk is to carry for us."
A piece of charcoal was brought from the skeleton's
chamber, and Le Maire having produced some paper
from his hunting-bag, the priest wrote upon it a few

lines, giving a brief account of their situation. The
letter, being folded, and properly addressed, was next
perforated with holes, through which a string was in-
serted, and tied under the wing of the bird. Emily
then carried him to the opening, through which he
darted forth in apparent joy at regaining his liberty.
" Would that we could pass out," said she, with a sigh,
" as easily as the little creature which we have just
set free. But the *recollet* is a lover of gardens, and he
will soon be found seeking his food in those of the
village."

The hopes to which this little expedient gave birth
in the bosoms of all contributed somewhat to cheer
the gloom of their confinement. But night came at
length, to close that long and weary day ; a night still
more long and weary. The light which came in at
the aperture began to wane, and Emily watched it as it
faded, with a sickness of the heart which grew almost
to agony, when finally it ceased to shine altogether.
She had continued during the day to cherish the dream
of deliverance by the sagacity and exertions of her
lover ; and had scarcely allowed herself to contem-
plate the possibility of remaining in the cavern another
night. It was therefore in unspeakable bitterness of
spirit that she accompanied the priest and Le Maire to
the skeleton's chamber, where they collected the brands
which remained of the fire of the preceding night, and
kindled them into a dull and meager flame. That evening was a silent one—the day had been passed in various speculations on the probability of their release, in
searching the cave for water, and in shouting at the
entrance for assistance. But the hour of darkness,—
the hour which carried their neighbours of the village to
their quiet and easy beds, in their homes, overflowing
with abundance, filled with the sweet air of heaven,
and watched by its kindly constellations—that hour
brought to the unhappy prisoners of the rock a peculiar

sense of desolation and fear, for it was a token that they were, for the time at least, forgotten ; that those whom they knew and loved slumbered, and thought not of them. They laid themselves down upon their beds of leaves, but the horrible thirst, which consumed them like an inward fire, grew fiercer with the endeavour to court repose ; and the blood that crept slowly through their veins seemed to have become a current of liquid flame. Sleep came not to their eyes, or came attended with dreams of running waters, which they were not permitted to taste ; of tempests and earthquakes, and breathless confinement among the clods of earth and various shapes of strange peril, while their friends seemed to stand aloof, and to look coldly and unconcernedly on, without showing even a desire to render them assistance.

CHAPTER VI.

My brother's soul was of the mould
Which in a palace had grown cold,
Had his free breathing been denied
The range of the steep mountain side.
Prisoners of Chillon.

Shall Nature, swerving from her earliest dictate,
Self-preservation, fall by her own act ?
Forbid it Heaven ! let not, upon disgust,
The shameless hand be foully crimsoned o'er
With blood of its own lord.
Blair's Grave

On the third day the cavern presented a more gloomy
spectacle than it had done at any time since the fall of
the rock took place. It was now about eleven o'clock in
the morning, and the shrill singing of the wind about
the cliffs, and through the crevice, which now admitted
a dimmer light than on the day previous, announced
the approach of a storm from the south. The hope of
relief from without was growing fainter and fainter as
the time passed on ; and the sufferings of the prisoners
became more poignant. The approach of the storm,
too, could only be regarded as an additional misfortune,
since it would probably prevent or obstruct for that day
the search which was making for them. They were
all three in the outer and larger apartment of the cave.
Emily was at a considerable distance from the entrance
reclining on a kind of seat formed of large loose stones,
and overspread with a covering of withered leaves.
There was enough of light to show that she was exceedingly pale ; that her eyes were closed, and that

the breath came thick and pantingly through her parted lips, which alone of all her features retained the colour of life.   Faint with watching, with want of sustenance, and with anxiety, she had lain herself down on this rude couch, which the care of her companions had provided for her, and had sunk into a temporary slumber. The priest stood close to the mouth of the cave leaning against the wall, with his arms folded, himself scarcely changed in appearance, except that his cheek seemed somewhat more emaciated, and his eyes were lighted up with a kind of solemn and preternatural brightness. Le Maire, with a spot of fiery red on each cheek,— his hair staring wildly in every direction, and his eyes bloodshot, was pacing the cavern floor to and fro, carrying his rifle, occasionally stopping to examine the priming, or to peck the flint ; and sometimes standing still for a moment, as if lost in thought.   At length he approached the priest, and said to him, in a hollow voice,

" Have you never heard of seamen on a wreck, destitute of provisions, casting lots to see which of their number should die, that the rest might live ?"

" I have so."

" Were they right in so doing ?"

" I cannot say that they were not.   It is a horrid alternative in which they were placed.   It might be lawful—it might be expedient, that one should perish for the salvation of the rest."

" Have you never seen an insect or an animal writhing with torture, and have you not shortened its sufferings by putting an end to its life ?"

" I have—but what mean these questions ?"

" I will tell you.   Here is my rifle."   As he spoke, Le Maire placed the piece in the hands of Father Ambrose, who took it mechanically.   " I ask you to do for me what you would do for the meanest worm.   **You** understand me ?"

" Are you mad ?" demanded the priest, regarding

him with a look in which the expression of unaffected
astonishment was mingled with that of solemn reproof.

"Mad! indeed I am mad, if you will have it so—
you will feel less scruple at putting an end to the existence of a madman. I cannot linger in this horrid
place, neglected and forgotten by those who should
have come to deliver me, suffering the slow approaches
of death—the pain—the fire in the veins—and, worst
of all, this fire in the brain," said Le Maire, striking his
forehead. "They think,—if they think of me at all,—
that I am dying by slow tortures; I will disappoint
them. Listen, father," continued he; "would it not
be better for you and Emily that I were dead?—is
there no way?—look at my veins, they are full yet,
and the muscles have not shrunk away from my limbs;
would you not both live the longer, if I were to die?"

The priest recoiled at the horrid idea presented to
his mind. "We are not cannibals," said he, "thanks
be to Divine Providence." An instant's reflection,
however, convinced Father Ambrose that the style of
rebuke which he had adopted was not proper for the
occasion. The unwonted fierceness and wildness of
Le Maire's manner, and the strange proposal he had
made, denoted that alienation of mind which is no uncommon effect of long abstinence from food. He
thought it better, therefore, to attempt by mild and sooth-
ing language to divert him from his horrid design.

"My good friend," said he, "you forget what
grounds of hope yet remain to us; indeed, the probability of our escape is scarcely less to-day than it was
yesterday. The letter sent out of the cave may be
found, and if so, it will most certainly effect our deliverance; or the fall of the rock may be discovered by
some one passing this way, and he may understand
that it is possible we are confined here. While our
existence is prolonged there is no occasion for despair.
You should endeavour, my son, to compose yourself,

and to rely on the goodness of that Power who has never forsaken you."

"Compose myself!" answered Le Maire, who had listened impatiently to this exhortation; "compose myself! Do you not know that there are those here who will not suffer me to be tranquil for a moment? Last night I was twice awakened, just as I had fallen asleep, by a voice pronouncing my name, as audibly as I heard your own just now; and the second time, I looked to where the skeleton lies, and the foul thing had half-raised itself from the rock, and was beckoning me to come and place myself by its side. Can you wonder if I slept no more after that?"

"My son, these are but the dreams of a fever."

"And then, whenever I go by myself, I hear low voices and titterings of laughter from the recesses of the rocks. They mock me, that I, a free hunter, a denizen of the woods and prairies, a man whose liberty was never restrained for a moment, should be entrapped in this manner, and made to die like a buffalo in a pit, or like a criminal in the dungeons of the old world,—that I should consume with thirst in a land bright with innumerable rivers and springs,—that I should wither away with famine, while the woods are full of game and the prairies covered with buffaloes. I could face famine if I had my liberty. I could meet death without shrinking in the sight of the sun and the earth, and in the fresh open air. I should strive to reach some habitation of my fellow-creatures; I should be sustained by hope; I should travel on till I sank down with weakness and fatigue, and died on the spot. But famine made more frightful by imprisonment and inactivity, and these dreams, as you call them, that dog me asleep and awake, they are more than I can bear.— Hark!" he exclaimed, after a short pause, and throwing quick and wild glances around him; "do you hear them yonder—do you hear how they mock me!—you will not, then, do what I ask?—give me the rifle."

"No," said the priest, who instantly comprehended his purpose : "I must keep the piece till you are more composed."

Le Maire seemed not to hear the answer, but laying his grasp on the rifle, was about to pluck it from the old man's hands. Father Ambrose saw that the attempt to retain possession of it against his superior strength, would be vain ; he therefore slipped down his right hand to the lock, and cocking it, touched the trigger, and discharged it in an instant. The report awoke Emily, who came trembling and breathless to the spot.

"What is the matter?" she asked.

"There is no harm done, my child," answered the priest, assuming an aspect of the most perfect composure. "I discharged the rifle, but it was not aimed at any thing, and I beg pardon for interrupting your repose at a time when you so much need it. Suffer me to conduct you back to the place you have left. Le Maire, will you assist?"

Supported by Le Maire on one side, and by the priest on the other, Emily, scarcely able to walk from weakness, was led back to her place of repose. Returning with Le Maire, Father Ambrose entreated him to consider how much his niece stood in need of his assistance and protection. He bade him recollect that his mad haste to quit the world before called by his Maker would leave her, should she ever be released from the cavern, alone and defenceless, or at least with only an old man for her friend, who was himself hourly expecting the summons of death. He exhorted him to reflect how much, even now, in her present condition of weakness and peril, she stood in need of his aid, and conjured him not to be guilty of a pusillanimous and cowardly desertion of one so lovely, so innocent, and so dependent upon him.

Le Maire felt the force of this appeal. A look of human pity passed across the wild expression of his countenance. He put the rifle into the hands of Father Ambrose. "You are right," said he; "I am a fool, and I have been, I suspect, very near becoming a madman. You will keep this until you are entirely willing to trust me with it. I will endeavour to combat these fancies a little longer."

CHAPTER VII.

A burst of rain
Swept from the black horizon, broad descends
In one continuous flood.   Still overhead
The mingling tempest weaves its gloom, and still
The deluge deepens.—THOMSON.

IN the mean time the light from the aperture grew dimmer and dimmer, and the eyes of the prisoners, though accustomed to the twilight of the cavern, became at length unable to distinguish objects at a few paces from the entrance. The priest and Le Maire had placed themselves by the couch of Emily, but rather, as it seemed, from that instinct of our race which leads us to seek each other's presence, than for any purpose of conversation, for each of the party preserved a gloomy silence. The topics of speculation on their condition had been discussed to weariness, and no others had now any interest for their minds. It was no unwelcome interruption to that melancholy silence, when they heard the sound of a mighty rain pouring down upon the leafy summits of the woods, and beating against the naked walls and shelves of the precipice. The roar grew more and more distinct, and at length it

seemed that they could distinguish a sort of shuddering of the earth above them, as if a mighty host was
marching heavily over it. The sense of suffering was
for a moment suspended in a feeling of awe and curiosity.

" That, likewise, is the rain," said Father Ambrose,
after listening for a moment. " 'The clouds must pour
down a perfect cataract, when the weight of its fall is
thus felt in the heart of the rock."

" Do you hear that noise of running water ?" asked
Emily, whose quick ear had distinguished the rush of
the stream formed by the collected rains over the
rocks without at the mouth of the cave.

" Would that its channel were through this cavern,"
exclaimed Le Maire, starting up. " Ah ! here we have
it—we have it !—listen to the dropping of water from
the roof near the entrance. And here at the aperture !"
He sprang thither in an instant. A little stream detached from the main current, which descended over
rocks that closed the mouth of the cave, fell in a thread
of silver amid the faint light that streamed through
the opening ; he knelt for a moment, received it between his burning lips, and then hastily returning, bore
Emily to the spot. She held out her hollowed palm,
white, thin, and semi-transparent, like a pearly shell,
used for dipping up the waters from one of those sweet
fountains that rise by the very edge of the sea—
and as fast as it filled with the cool, bright element,
imbibed it with an eagerness and delight inexpressible.
The priest followed her example ; Le Maire also drank
from the little stream as it fell, bathed in it his feverish
brow, and suffered it to fall upon his sinewy neck.

" It has given me a new hold on life," said Le Maire,
his chest distending with several full and long breath-
ings. " It has not only quenched that hellish thirst,
but it has made my head less light, and my heart lighter.
I will never speak ill of this element again—the choicest

grapes of France never distilled any thing so delicious, so grateful, so life-giving. Take notice, Father Ambrose, I retract all I have ever said against water and water-drinkers. I am a sincere penitent, and shall demand absolution."

Father Ambrose had begun gently to reprove Le Maire for his unseasonable levity, when Emily cried out—"The rock moves!—the rock moves! Come back—come further into the cavern!" Looking up to the vast mass that closed the entrance, he saw plainly that it was in motion, and he had just time to draw Le Maire from the spot where he had stooped down to take another draught of the stream, when a large block, which had been wedged in overhead, gave way, and fell in the very place where he left the prints of his feet. Had he remained there another instant, it must have crushed him to atoms. The prisoners, retreating within the cavern far enough to avoid the danger, but not too far for observation, stood watching the event with mingled apprehension and hope. The floor of the cave just at the edge, on which rested the fallen rock, yawned at the fissures, where the earth with which they were filled had become saturated and swelled with water, and unable any longer to support the immense weight, settled away, at first slowly, under it, and finally, along with its incumbent load, fell suddenly and with a tremendous crash, to the base of the precipice, letting the light of day and the air of heaven into the cavern. The thunder of that disruption was succeeded by the fall of a few large fragments of rock on the right and left, after which the priest and his companions heard only the fall of the rain and the heavy sighing of the wind in the forest.

Father Ambrose and Emily knelt involuntarily in thanksgiving at their unexpected deliverance. Le Maire, although unused to the devotional mood, observing their attitude, had bent his knee to imitate it, when a glance at the outer world now laid open to his sight, made him start again to his feet with an exclamation of delight. The other two arose, also, and turned to the broad opening which now looked out from the cave over the forest. On one side of this opening rushed the torrent whose friendly waters had undermined the rock at the entrance, and now dashed themselves against its shivered fragments below. It is not for me to attempt to describe how beautiful appeared to their eyes that world which they feared never again to see, or how grateful to their senses was that fresh and fragrant air of the forests which they thought never to breathe again. The light, although the sky was thick with clouds and rain, was almost too intense for their vision, and they shaded their brows with their hands as they looked forth upon that scene of woods and meadows and waters, fairer to their view than it had ever appeared in the most glorious sunshine.

" That world is ours again," said Le Maire, with a tone of exultation. " We are released at last, and now let us see in what manner we can descend."

As he spoke, he approached the verge of the rock from which the severed mass had lately fallen, and saw to his dismay that the terrace which had served as a path to the cavern, was carried away for a considerable distance to the right and left of where they stood, leaving the face of the precipice smooth and sheer from top to bottom. No footing appeared, no projection by which the boldest and the most agile could scale or descend it. Le Maire threw himself sullenly on the ground.

" We must pass another night in this dungeon," said he, " and perhaps starve to death after all. It is clear enough that we shall have to remain here until somebody comes to take us down, and the devil himself would not be caught abroad in the woods in the midst of such a storm as this."

The priest and Emily came up at this moment ;—

" This is a sad disappointment," said the former, " but we have this advantage, that we can now make ourselves both seen and heard. Let us try the effect of our voices. It is not impossible that there may be some person within hearing."

Accordingly they shouted together, and though nothing answered but the echo of the forest, yet there was even in that reply of the inanimate creation something cheering and hope-inspiring, to those who for nearly three days had perceived that all their cries for succour were smothered in the depths of the earth. Again they raised their voices, and listened for an answering shout,—a third time, and they were answered. The halloo of a full-toned, manly voice arose from the woods below.

" Thank heaven, we are heard at last," said Emily.

" Let us see if the cry was in answer to ours," said the priest, and again they called, and again a shout was returned from the woods. " We are heard—that is certain," continued he, " and the voice is nearer than at first,—we shall be released."

At length the sound of quick footsteps on the crackling boughs was heard in the forest, and a young man of graceful proportions, dressed, like Le Maire, in a hunting-cap and frock, emerged into the open space at the foot of the precipice. As he saw the party standing in the cavity of the rock, he clapped his hands with an exclamation of surprise and delight. " Thank heaven, they are discovered at last ! Are you all safe—all well ?"

" All safe," answered Le Maire, " but hungry as wolves, and in a confounded hurry to get out of this horrid den."

The young man regarded the precipice attentively for a moment, and then called out, " Have patience a moment, and I will bring you the means of deliverance." He then disappeared in the forest.

Emily's waking dream was, in fact, not wholly un-
fulfilled. That young man was Henry Danville; she
knew him by his air and figure as soon as he emerged
from the forest, and before she heard his voice. He had
been engaged, with many others belonging to the settlement, in the pursuit of their lost curate and his companions, from the morning after their absence, and fortunately happened to be at no great distance when the
disruption of the rock took place. Struck with astonishment at the tremendous concussion, he was hastening
to discover the cause, when he heard the shout to which
he answered.

It was not long before voices and steps were again
heard in the wood, and a crowd of the good villagers
soon appeared advancing through the trees, one bearing a basket of provisions, some dragging ladders, some
carrying ropes and other appliances for getting down
their friends from their perilous elevation. Several of
the ladders being spliced together, and secured by
strong cords, were made to reach from the broken rocks
below to the mouth of the cavern, and Henry ascended.

My readers will have no difficulty in imagining the
conclusion. The emotions of the lovers at meeting
under such circumstances are of course not to be described, and the dialogue that took place on that occasion would not, I fear, bear to be repeated. The joy
expressed by the villagers at recovering their worthy
pastor brought tears into the good man's eyes; and
words are inadequate to do justice to the delight of Le
Maire at seeing his old companions and their basket of
provisions. My readers may also, if they please, imagine another little incident, without which some of them
might think the narrative imperfect, namely, a certain
marriage ceremony, which actually took place before
the next Christmas, and at which the venerable Father
Ambrose officiated. Le Maire, when I last saw him,
was living with one of Emily's children, a hale old man

of eighty, with a few gray hairs scattered among his raven locks, full of stories of his youthful adventures, among which he reckoned that of his imprisonment in the cave as decidedly the best. He had, however, no disposition to become the hero of another tale of the kind, since he never ventured into another cave, or under another rock, as long as he lived ; and was wont to accompany his narrative with a friendly admonition to his youthful and inexperienced hearers, against thoughtlessly indulging in so dangerous a practice.

MEDFIELD.

MEDFIELD.

—————————Obey !
Thy nerves are in their infancy again,
And have no vigour in them.—*Tempest*.

Two or three years ago I passed a few weeks,
about the end of summer and beginning of autumn, at
a pleasant village, within a few days' journey from the
city of New-York. Here I became acquainted with a
gentleman residing in the place, of the name of Medfield, one of the most interesting men I have known.
He lived on a beautiful and well-cultivated farm, and
was said by his neighbours to be in the possession of
an easy fortune. I, for my own part, found him possessed of leisure, knowledge, and courteous manners.
He showed me many civilities ; he introduced me to
all the pleasant walks and drives for miles round ; he
led me to all the picturesque spots in the neighbourhood, both those sheltered and retired places whose
beauty is in themselves, and those which are beautiful
from the scenery they command ; he made me acquainted with the vegetable and mineral riches of the
region, rare plants and curious fossils ; he related the
local traditions, and told me something of the state of
society, with which, however, as I gathered from his
conversation and from the account given me by others,
he mingled little, except in occasional acts of kindness.

Even now, while I write, I think I see him standing

L 2

before me, a man who with little license of speech
might be called handsome, rather tall of stature, and
somewhat slenderly but elegantly shaped ; his garb,
though negligent, adjusting itself to his person with a
natural and unavoidable grace—an oval countenance,
a complexion fair and somewhat pale, a finely arched
forehead, on the upper edge of which the lapse of
thirty-five years had somewhat thinned the light brown
hair that curled over it, a clear gray eye, and the remaining features moulded with more than usual regu-
larity.   There was, however, an unsettled and often
unpleasant expression, which almost neutralized the
agreeable effect of this symmetry of features.   In the
midst of an animated conversation you would all at
once perceive that his thoughts were wandering ; a
shade of alarm would pass over his countenance, and
a shudder over his frame, and he would shrink as if
from contact with some object which he wished to avoid.
From these peculiarities of manner I was prepared to
expect some eccentricities, not to call them by a worse
name, in his way of thinking.   Nothing of the kind
however appeared ; although he discoursed freely on
all subjects, and our conversation took in a large variety.   On questions of politics and religion, his
opinions were as rational as those of most men.   He
was a philanthropist after the fashion of the age, but
he was no more an enthusiast in his plans of benevolence than some hundreds of worthy persons of my acquaintance.   Of foreign and ancient literature he knew
as much as most well-educated men in this country ;
and of old English literature something more ; and his
remarks on the authors he had read were those of a
man of taste and judgment.   Many of the fine old
ballads in our language he knew by heart, as well as
the imitations of them produced by modern authors ;
and he would repeat to me, as we sat together in the
twilight, the ballad of Thomas the Rhymer with the

additions by Scott, and Coleridge's Ancient Mariner, in a fine impressive manner that even now vibrates on my nerves whenever I recall it to mind.

Among his neighbours Medfield had the reputation of great judgment and equity, as well as benevolence. He had formerly acted as a magistrate, but since the death of his wife, which happened a few years before I knew him, he had ceased to employ himself in that capacity, though his neighbours still referred their disputes to his friendly decision. Since that event his manners, formerly cheerful, and sometimes, when earnestly bent on gaining a favourite point, imperious to a fault, had, as I was told, undergone a change. Always kind and generous, he was now more so than ever; all sternness was gone from his temper, which was now marked by a uniform grave tenderness. Some even acknowledged to me that " the squire had some strange ways with him lately," a specimen or two of which I was shortly to witness.

I have no great passion either for angling or shooting; the former is a dull inactive sport, the latter a fatiguing one, and I am exceedingly awkward at both; but at the time I mention I was seized with the ambition of acquiring some skill in their exercise. I had therefore provided myself, before I left town, with an excellent fowling-piece, chosen for me by a good judge of such matters, and an ample and neatly-assorted store of hooks, lines, flies, and other implements for angling. With this apparatus I frequently went out, and sometimes solicited Medfield to accompany me, but without success. He pleaded sometimes an engagement, and always an aversion to these sports, and once or twice he ridiculed them so effectually that I was half-persuaded to throw my flies into the fire, and make a present of my fowling-piece to a ragged boy with a crownless hat, who looked at it most wishfully whenever I met him, and whom I once saw, when I

21*

had placed it against a tree, walking round it and contemplating it with an appearance of intense interest.
I could not, however, yet give up a favourite project I
had formed of performing some exploits in this line
worth telling of when I should return to the city.

I well remember the first and only time that I walked
out in company with Medfield, with my gun on my
shoulder. I was to visit a spot of much picturesque
beauty, to which he undertook to be my guide. We
set out from his house, and on our way passed by my
lodgings. Begging him to wait at the door for a moment in order to give me an opportunity of drawing on
a pair of boots, I entered the house, and when I
came out I had my fowling-piece on my arm.

" Let me beg of you," said Medfield, " if you value
your own comfort, to leave that unwieldy thing at home.
You will be fatigued enough, I assure you, before you
return, without encumbering yourself with any unnecessary burden."

" What !" I answered, " would you have us to go
scrambling over stiles and fences, and traversing fields
without any apparent purpose, like a couple of boys
looking for birds' nests? Or do you mean to alarm
the worthy farmers by leading them to suppose that we
are going to rob their orchards or cornfields? Or
would you have us pass for a lawyer and sheriff, coming
with a still more unwelcome design upon somebody's
real estate? This fowling-piece assures them of the
contrary, and clears up the mystery. I dare say I
shall have no occasion to use it—at all events I shall
not look out for any."

Medfield desisted from any further objection, though
somewhat reluctantly, as I could see by his subsequent
gravity and silence. Our path at length brought us to
the place of which he spoke. It was a long level
passage, three or four rods in width, between two parallel rows of steep precipices, while from the rich

mould on the shelves, and in the interstices, grew gigantic butternut and hickory trees, throwing their broad rough coated arms across the path, and forming a verdant canopy overhead. Below, the ground was carpeted with grass, and squirrels were leaping and chirping among the boughs above. One of these, a fine little animal, was very busily employed in shelling a half-ripe nut which he had gathered from one of the trees, stopping occasionally to utter a short sharp bark of defiance and scorn. The temptation was irresistible; I raised my piece and fired with better fortune than usual, for the creature fell dead at my feet. On turning to look for my friend, I perceived he had left me, and casting my eye down the embowered avenue, I caught a glimpse of him hurrying out of sight. I followed, however, walking as fast as I was able, and sometimes running a little, and in a few minutes had overtaken him. My game was in my hand, and I swung it about with an air of some ostentation.

" Well," said he, " you have killed a squirrel, I see; may I ask what you are going to do with it ?"

" A good shot, was it not? a part of the charge went through the head. Why, I may throw it away, or give it, perhaps, to my landlord's dog."

This answer drew upon me a rebuke, mild in its terms but somewhat severe in its import, for taking the life of a happy, harmless creature, from mere wantonness. I defended myself as well as I was able, but came to the conclusion that whatever might be my friend's other accomplishments, he was certainly, as I had heard him before acknowledge, no sportsman.

It was not long after this that I had engaged a black fellow to procure me a box of earth-worms, or " angle-dogs," as he called them. They were brought me in the morning; I put them in my pocket along with my fishing-tackle, and going out I met with Medfield, who asked me to accompany him, and look at some im-

provements he was making on his estate.   After a walk
of some length about his grounds, we sat down under
the shade of a large buttonwood-tree which stretched
its long arms over a brook pent in a narrow channel,
full of little cascades and rapids, and pools boiling
with the force of the current that rushed into them.   It
was, in short, a very trout stream. ʼMy friend's attention was occupied for a moment in giving directions to
a labourer, while I, tempted by the appearance of the
brook, had cut off a long tapering bough from the tree,
and fastening upon it my fishing-line, had taken out my
box of worms and began very leisurely to impale one
of them on the hook.   Just then, Medfield, who had
dismissed the labourer, turned towards me.   As his
eye fell upon me, he started with a look of horror.

"ʼIn the name of mercy what are you doing?"
asked he.

"Only going to try my luck at angling a little in
this brook," answered I, quietly.   "It looks like a
capital stream for trout.   I prepared myself this morning on purpose for a fishing excursion."

"But if you must follow that idle sport," returned
Medfield, "cannot you do it in a manner less inhuman
and disgusting?   Have you forgotten the admonition
of the poet of the Seasons?—

> —— ʼLet not on thy hook the tortured worm,
> Convulsive, twist in agonizing folds !ʼ"

He went on to repeat in his fine way the whole of
the passage, and finally persuaded me to commit my
whole stock of worms to the bosom of the great
mother from which they were taken, and to make him
a kind of promise, that if I continued to follow the profit-
less diversion of angling, I would do it in a less ex-
ceptionable manner.

Other instances of similar behaviour about this time
fell under my observation.   At one time I saw Medfield

buy a supper from a butcher for a strange dog that had come into the village, a lame, half-starved, snappish tyke, whose bad manners, my friend said, were evidently owing to his having nothing in his stomach. On another occasion he gave a wagoner a crown for lightening a load apparently too heavy for his horses. But what most surprised me was the equanimity with which he bore all kinds of reproaches. I once saw him stopped in the street by a person of rather decent appearance, who appeared to enter immediately into earnest and rapid conversation, and as I came up I could perceive that he was censuring him for some action of his, in terms of greater severity than were exactly consistent with good breeding. Medfield answered him mildly, which appeared only to exasperate him the more, and he replied with a torrent of abuse and malediction. My own blood, I confess, was hot with indignation at such epithets applied to my friend, but Medfield heard them with as much serenity as if he had been listening to his own praises, until finding that the man would hearken to no explanation, he put his arm within mine and walked away.

"Poor fellow," said he, "I cannot greatly blame him. He thinks himself injured by an act which I was obliged to perform as a magistrate some years since, and now whenever he sees me, which is not often, he makes a point of telling me, as he says, 'what he thinks of me.' I only wish that the composure with which I hear his opinion of me did not irritate him so much."

One day I took the liberty of remarking to my friend upon the peculiarity of character indicated by the examples I have already mentioned. He acknowledged immediately, that his humanity might seem in many instances overstrained and excessive, and sometimes perhaps affected.

"It is, however, no virtue of mine," continued he, "if

a virtue it be, for I cannot do otherwise than practise
it. I have been disciplined to it by a mysterious cause
apparent to no one but myself. You have been witness to so many of my actions, which must have struck
you as exceedingly singular, that I have been thinking
I ought, as a matter of justice to myself, to give you
the explanation of my behaviour. I have deferred it
the longer on account of the unpleasant nature of some
of the incidents of my story, and perhaps, after all, it
may not be worthy of your attention."

I assured Mr. Medfield, with perfect truth, that I
should be not only a willing, but an interested listener,
and that I should hardly forgive him were he not now
to gratify the curiosity he had excited.

"By what I am about to relate," said he, "I run
the risk of losing ground in your good opinion. I
wish you therefore to understand, once for all, that I
am naturally by no means a credulous or superstitious
man. On the contrary, my disposition has always
been to examine and to doubt, rather than to admit
and believe. An early fondness for mathematical
studies gave my mind the habit of insisting, even too
much perhaps for the common purposes of life, on
strict demonstration of whatever was proposed for my
belief. I took delight in sifting the grounds of a received opinion, and rejecting it peremptorily, when it
seemed to me supported by incomplete evidence. On
some knotty and controverted points I merely con-
tented myself, like the worthy Bishop Watson, with
keeping my opinion in suspense, but my general inclination was to believe too little rather than too much. If,
therefore, any parts of my narrative should strike you as
incredible, you will do me the justice to suppose that
the incidents which you find too extraordinary for belief, appeared as repugnant to my notions of the laws
of nature as they now do to yours; and that it was

only on testimony too strong to be resisted, that I acquiesced in the idea that they were not a delusion.

"About five years ago I was in many respects a different man from what you find me at present. At that time I was the husband of a most beautiful and gentle woman, and the father of a little daughter of three years of age, the loveliest of children. I was a man of strong passions, and a temper that brooked no control, and kindled at the slightest opposition. I was allowed to be generous, and my generosity gained me many friends, but I often lost them by that fierce and imperious temper. If an insult was offered me, I returned it with insults still more intolerable; I repaid scorn by bitterer scorn; I yielded every thing to humble entreaty, but nothing to a frank and bold claim of right, however just. These peculiarities of manners and character I was, however, by no means disposed to tolerate in others; nothing so soon roused my indignation as any conduct which exhibited them, and I was instantly on terms of hostility with any one who had the misfortune to resemble me in this respect. In short I was one of those men of whom if the whole world were composed, society would be a state of perpetual warfare, or at best an armed truce, and who are only tolerated because on important occasions their pugnacious spirit may be turned to use, and because in matters of minor importance the prudent and peaceable part of the community find it a less evil to let them have their way, than to wrangle with them to prevent it.

"My wife lamented this defect in my character, and endeavoured to persuade me to correct it, but in vain. She produced some impression, however, when she showed me how my little daughter, whom I loved with a doting fondness, and who also really bore to me a strong affection, shrunk and trembled before me when in my sterner moods; and a glow of shame came over

my cheek when I witnessed that look of terror in the
countenance of so artless and innocent a being—and
of terror at me. The manners which could produce
such an effect, I felt, must be essentially unamiable and
repulsive; but this reflection was followed by no material amendment.

" My little daughter died, the sweetest blossom ever
mown down by the scythe of death, and my wife in a
little time followed her. On her death-bed she desired
all to withdraw but myself.

" 'My dear Charles,' said she, 'I have a last request to make of your kindness. If you grant it, I
shall die in peace.'

" Such an appeal could not be resisted; I answered
that the request should be fulfilled if it was within the
compass of human power.

" 'It may cost you some effort,' returned she, 'but
you will make it, I am persuaded, both for my sake
and your own. Promise me that you will keep a strict
watch against that severity and impetuosity of temper
which make you less useful and less beloved in the
world than the qualities of your mind and heart would
otherwise make you.'

" I made the promise in sincerity of heart and in
tears.

" Her remains were laid beside those of her little
daughter, and I was left the prey of a grief which I will
not attempt to describe. So strong was the feeling of
desolation which took possession of me, that it sometimes actually seemed to me as if that it was I who
had died; and that I had been translated to another
world, strange, cold, and lonely, and haunted by the
tormenting remembrance of enjoyments fled for ever.
The proud, stern manners of my prosperous days at
first prevented any sympathy with my affliction, but
mankind are good-natured; I at least have found them
so, since they bore so patiently with my caprices and

sallies; and at last, when they saw the sincerity, the depth, the extremity of my sorrow, their behaviour towards me became visibly kinder and more considerate.

"For a while this sorrow absorbed every other feeling, and the usual violence and haughtiness of my temper seemed to be subdued; but life has its duties and its cares, which none of us are at liberty to decline, and to which we must all return from the seclusion of mourning. As I again came forth into the world, I began to assume my former manners.

"Before my late calamity I had consented to become a candidate for a public office. I was now attacked in a newspaper with that coarse invective, too much indulged in by the press of this country; allusions the most unwarrantable and unjustifiable were made to my personal character and history; and actions the most innocent were, by an artful mixture of truth and falsehood, perverted into crimes. I was fiercely indignant; I knew that the shaft came from the hand of a rival candidate, and I resolved that I would send it back to his bosom with tenfold force. I went into my study, and, with the obnoxious article before me, sat down to pen a reply which my adversary must feel, if the sense of indignity were not extinct within him. I had already written part of an article, intended for publication, in which I briefly and explicitly disclaimed the charges brought against me, and I now proceeded to retort the attack. Already thoughts and feelings of supreme and intensest scorn filled my mind; the fitting words came crowding to my pen,—phrases of the bitterest derision, coined by my very heart,—when I felt a touch softly laid on my right arm. I started; and looked round me, but saw nothing. Again I began to write, and again the touch was felt—more strongly than before—again I started, rose, and surveyed the room, but it contained no living thing except myself. A third time I began, and a third time I felt that mysterious pressure. The table at which I was writing stood not far from the window, but at such a distance that I could not easily be reached by an arm from without. The door was closed, and there was no furniture in the room under which a person could effectually conceal himself. Going to the door, I opened it, and looked in every direction, but saw no one; I listened attentively for the sound of retreating footsteps, but heard only the chirp of grasshoppers in the summer-noon. Returning to my study, I carefully scanned a second time every corner of the apartment, removed the table further from the window, and again sat myself down to write. I mused a while to recover the train of ideas which the interruption had caused me to lose; and when I had done so, again attempted to proceed. Before I had finished a single sentence, I felt on the hand which was employed in guiding the pen a distinct, palpable pressure, but at the same time a gentle and delicate one, as if the fingers of a female hand were laid on my own. It was impossible to resist the inclination to turn my head and to inspect narrowly the room around me, in order to be certain whether any person was standing by my side, or behind me. There was no one—all was silence and emptiness. I strove again to write—the pressure grew firmer. I brought my left hand over and passed it along the back of my right—my hair rose on end— and my blood grew-cold in my veins, when I seemed to feel an invisible human hand lying closely on mine. With a convulsive start I dropped the pen, and my hand was instantly released. You may well suppose that I was now in a state of mind which unfitted me from proceeding with the article, even if I had not been restrained by the dread of that mysterious interposition.

" The more I reflected on that incident, the more it embarrassed me. I laboured to convince myself that the sensation I had experienced was owing to some outward cause, independent of the state of my mind, but I was unable satisfactorily to account for it in this manner. That it was an illusion arising from the state of high mental excitement in which I was while writing the article, was a supposition which, independent of other considerations, my pride would not suffer me to embrace. I determined, therefore, to settle the point for myself, by the fullest and most deliberate examination. The next day I went again into my study, closed carefully the door and windows, looked under the table and examined the room thoroughly, to satisfy myself that no person was concealed there. I then sat down to the table, took up the unfinished manuscript, and beginning where I had broken off the day before, proceeded to complete it. In a moment I perceived the well-known pressure of the arm, slight and gentle at first—then firmer—but I disregarded it, and continued to write. Then came the sense of compression and restraint on the fingers of my right hand which I had experienced the day previous, and which now impeded their motion. Applying my left hand to the investigation, I found a set of fingers passing over and clasping my own. I subjected, to the examination of the touch, finger after finger, and joint after joint of that invisible hand; it was delicately moulded, the fingers were tapering, plump and soft, the articulations small and feminine, and it was joined to a round and slender wrist, but beyond that I could feel nothing. I attempted to scrutinize it with my eye, but the sight could not shape for it even the faintest and most shadowy outline. I bowed my forehead towards it, and touched flesh that was not my own. You may judge of the feeling of awe which filled my mind while I was making this investigation. At length, with a shudder, I quitted my grasp of the pen, and immediately I perceived that the invisible hand was gone.

" My perplexity was now greater than ever. I had

hoped that a deliberate and careful examination would have dispelled the mystery, but it ended in setting the evidence of my senses, or rather of one of them, in opposition to the conclusions of my reason. Was I to believe or to distrust that evidence? Was not what I had experienced a reality to me, a substantial verity, whatever it might be, or appear, to the rest of the world? Then, as to the agent in this mysterious interposition, could it be that the spirit of her to whom I had given the solemn promise of watching over my temper, was permitted to remind me of the obligation I had taken, by this appeal to my outward sense? Must I believe what was so repugnant to the whole tenor of my previous opinions? I determined a third time to make the experiment, and it was followed by precisely the same result as in the instances I have already related. Taking the unfinished paper in my hands, I tore it in pieces, and abandoned my design of replying to the attack which had been made upon me.

" For several days the strange event which had happened afforded me food for reflection—reflection deep, continual, absorbing. Firm as were the convictions of my reason that the spiritual part of our nature cannot, without the help of material organs, act upon the perceptions of one to whom it does not belong, I could not, I would not believe, that what I had witnessed was owing to a cause above nature. Still, the uniform recurrence of the same sensation, under the same circumstances, perplexed and confounded me. To divert my thoughts from this subject, I took my fishing-rod and strolled out to the fine noisy brook that flows through my farm. It was a beautiful day in July; the sun was warm, but not powerful, and clouds were now and then floating lazily over his orb. As I approached the stream, which hurried from one clump of softly-waving trees to another, I thought of the lines in the Castle of Indolence :—

—— Softly stealing, with your watery gear,
Along the brooks, the crimson spotted fry
You may delude—the while amused you hear
Now the hoarse stream, and now the zephyr's sigh,
Attuned to the birds and woodland melody.

"I felt a sort of relief from the images of mingled
motion and repose, of activity and ease, of change
without effort, which belong to a fine day in this fine
season of the year; and my mind began to partake,
in some sort, of the serenity of the scene around me.
Standing on the green bank, in the shade of a thicket,
I dropped my line into the water. It was a clear and
glassy little pool of the brook, save at the upper end,
where it was agitated with the current that fell into it
over a mossy rock, and I saw the fish playing in its
transparent depths, noiselessly, and with that easy,
graceful motion which belongs to most creatures of
their element. I was leaning intently forward, waiting
for one of them to approach the fatal hook, when I
felt a touch, a distinct touch, laid on my right arm. So
unexpected was this, in the silence and quiet and utter
solitude of the scene around me, and in the pursuit of
amusement which I had never regarded as otherwise
than innocent—and so irritable had my nervous system
become in consequence of the late extraordinary incidents, that I started at the sensation with the quick-
ness of lightning, wheeling suddenly to the right, and
jerking involuntarily the line from the water. There
was nothing in sight that could have touched me—and
the only living sound to be heard was my own hard
breathing through distended nostrils, mingling with the
murmurs of the water and the sighs of the wind. For
a while I stood lost in astonishment, but at length recovering, I searched the thicket, in the shade of which
I stood, to discover whether it concealed any person
who was idle enough to amuse himself in this manner
at my expense. In this search I was, as usual, unsuccessful.   22*

"I sat on the bank a while to recover my composure. 'I must not,' said I to myself, 'leave the cause of this interruption in uncertainty. I will, if possible, discover whether it be accidental, or whether it be of the same nature with what I have experienced in other instances.' Accordingly I arose and again swung the bait over the stream, and suffered it to sink into the water. At that instant I felt the monitory touch on my right arm just above the elbow. Turning my head in that direction, I suffered the butt-end of the fishing-rod to press against my breast, keeping firm hold of it with my right hand only, and applying my left to the spot where I felt the pressure. There I found the same invisible hand which I had so closely examined the day previous, the same delicate and tapering fingers, gently yet firmly grasping my arm. I threw away my fishing-rod, and have never attempted the sport of angling since. The admonition I had received, whether real or imaginary, induced a train of reflections which brought me to the conclusion that, however justifiable it may be as an occupation, it cannot be defended as an amusement.

"It was at this time that a view of the subject occurred to my mind which, at length, more than any thing else decided my opinion. Of all our senses the touch is the least liable to delusion or mistake. It is the most direct of all our channels of perception; it brings its objects to the closest and minutest scrutiny; it is the least under the control of the imagination, the least liable to be acted upon by delicate and evanescent influences. I never heard of an instance in which the touch became subject to an illusion while the eye remained faithful to reason and the truth of things. In all the idle and silly stories of ghosts and apparitions, in which I believe as little as you do, the supposed supernatural visiter always addresses itself to the eye or the ear; the haunted person sees its form or distinguishes its voice; he rarely ever feels its substance. The spirit is generally said to elude the touch; a blow passes through it as through empty air, the arms stretched to embrace it meet in the midst of its shadowy outlines. The touch is the test by which we prove the truth of the information furnished us by the other senses, and in its decisions the mind acquiesces with undoubting confidence. So universally and fully is this axiom admitted, that some of the commonest phrases in our own and other languages are founded upon it. When we speak of palpable truth, or truth demonstrated by the touch, we mean reality which admits of no dispute; while to the unsubstantial pictures of the imagination which impose upon us by the mere semblance of reality, we give the name of visions, or things apparent to the sight only.

"True it was, that in my own case I had the testimony of but one of my senses, but it was that sense which corrects the errors of the others, and which is never deceived alone. Had the others concurred with it, my perplexity, I thought, would have been less. Had those fallible organs, the eye and the ear, presented to me, the one a definite form, and the other an audible voice, I might have concluded that what wore the appearance of a supernatural interposition was but the hallucination of disturbed nerves, or the phantom of a disordered mind, and I might have inferred that the touch was deceived by a natural sympathy with the other senses. But now my case admitted of no such explanation.

"I again recurred to the arguments which were familiar to me, and which had hitherto appeared to my mind conclusive, against the sensible interference of the spirits of the departed in matters of human action. Shall I confess to you that they appeared to me to have lost somewhat of their force, when I considered the question as one of experience and testimony? The moral purposes which such an interference might serve were apparent; and was it not, I asked myself, as presumptuous in the philosophers of this age to say that they were contrary to the laws of nature, as it would be, in a generation during whose existence a comet had never appeared, to deny that such bodies, eccentric as were their courses, belonged to the system of the universe. I see that you do not agree with me : well, I pray that you may never have reason to do so from your own experience. Do not mistake me, however; I did not immediately pass from disbelief to credulity. I was determined to keep my opinion in suspense until the number and uniformity of instances should leave me no other way of accounting for what had happened than by ascribing it to a cause above nature.

"The incidents I have related took place in solitude, in places and at moments when there was no one to witness the effect they produced upon me ; but I was now to experience the same extraordinary interposition in the midst of a crowd of my fellow-men. In the election to which I have already alluded I had been unsuccessful, principally, I believe, on account of the unpopularity of my manners. My antagonist, the writer of the attack on me in the public prints, who was all smiles and suavity, was returned by a large majority. I had some friends, however, who adhered to me firmly, and who wished to give me a testimony of their respect by the customary compliment of a public dinner. This I declined, alleging, as a principal reason, my late domestic calamities, but offered to meet them in another manner at any time they might appoint. A day was fixed upon, and I made my appearance before an assembly of those who had given me their suffrages. If you have never been a candidate at a country election you can have no idea of the warmth of that feeling of good-will and confidence which subsists between the candidate and his supporters—the hardy, intelligent, independent masters and cultivators of the soil. I looked round on their strong-featured, sun-burnt, honest faces, and shook their hard hands with a pleasure which I cannot describe.

" In obedience to the general expectation, I addressed the meeting. I thanked my friends for the zeal they had shown in my behalf;—fruitless though it had been, it gave them no less a claim on my gratitude than if it had been attended with the accident of success. I alluded to the accusations which had been brought against me—slanders worthy, I said, of the source from which they had proceeded. I vindicated myself from them briefly and concisely, for I was anxious to arrive at a point in my discourse on which I intended to dilate more at length, namely, the conduct of my antagonist and his party. Having come to this topic, I felt myself inspired by that degree of excitement which gives force and fluency of language, and the power of moving the minds of others ; and I thought to utter things which should be remembered, and re-peated, and felt by those against whom they were lev-elled. I had already begun my philippic, and was proceeding with a raised voice and some vehemence of gesture, when I felt myself plucked by the sleeve. Pausing for an instant, I looked round, but saw no one who touched, or appeared to have touched me. I pro-ceeded, and the signal was repeated. It occurred to me that there was probably some creature of my ad-versary near me, who wanted to interrupt and confuse me, and I cast brief and fierce glances to the right and the left, which made my worthy friends who stood near me recede, with looks of anxiety and almost of alarm. Again I began, raising my arm as I spoke, but at that moment it seemed clogged with the weight of a mill-stone, and fell powerless to my side. Eager only to proceed, and careless from what quarter the interruption might come, provided I got clear of it, I made a strong effort to shake off the encumbrance, raising at the same time my voice, and attempting to finish in a full sonorous tone the sentence I had begun. Instantly I felt at my throat a cold rigid grasp, as of a hand of iron—a grasp quite different from the gentle and apparently kind pressure I had sometimes before experienced, choking the voice as it issued from my lungs, and forcing me down into my seat. So completely had I been absorbed in the subject of my harangue that I did not, until the moment that I found myself in my chair, conjecture the real cause of the interruption. The idea then flashed upon my mind that this was an interference of the same nature with that which had withheld me from replying to the newspaper attack of my antagonist. My emotions of awe, alarm, and discouragement, at this stern and mysterious rebuke, were overpowering, and it was with difficulty that I collected myself sufficiently to whisper to a friend who was near me, requesting him to apologize, as well as the case would admit, for my inability to proceed. He arose and attributed what had happened, I believe, to a sudden indisposition, while I retired hastily from the assembly.

"Arriving at my house, I gave myself up to various and distracting reflections. I asked myself whether I, who had ever prided myself on my superiority to vulgar prejudices and superstitions, who had scoffed at stories of supernatural visitations, must now surrender myself to the belief that the ordinary laws of nature were daily broken for my sake, and that I was the object of constant solicitude and care to a being of the other world, who was disquieted for me in the midst of that eternal repose prepared for the spirits of the good? Was not this interference of such a nature as to destroy all liberty of action, and to reduce me to a

state little short of servitude ? Was I to be withstood
even in obeying the instinct of self-defence, which
forms a part of the moral constitution of all the nobler
animal existences, and which was so emphatically a
part of my own ? Could it be the will of the Supreme
Father, could it be the desire of the loved and lost
one, whom haply he permitted to return to this world
in order to watch over and admonish me, that I should
be reduced to a pusillanimous passive being, submitting
tamely to every injury, and leading a life of mere sufferance and inaction, like the plants of the soil, or the animals who are but a degree above them ?

" I did not at that time reflect—I did not even know,
how little the utmost malice of slander avails against
an established reputation for integrity—how the plain
tale of the honest man, related without passion, puts
down the foul calumny of the unprincipled, and how
little it gains, or rather how much it loses, by being
coupled with a retaliatory attack, with words of anger
and phrases of vituperation.

"This restraint upon what seemed to me the necessary
liberty of a rational being, this hindrance in the way of
actions which I esteemed justifiable and laudable, raised
my impatience to a tremendous pitch. I walked my
room rapidly until the sweat started from every pore ; I
chafed like a wild beast caught in the toils. What is
life, said I to myself, if it is to be held on these con-
ditions ? to suffer every indignity from your enemy,
and when you strive to repel him, to be smitten with
impotence, and to retire with defeat, disappointment,
and shame from the contest—nay, more, to be bound
hand and foot, and thrown in his path to be buffeted
and trampled on, without escape, and without redress.
Even if the interference were to a good end, of what
value is the virtue which is the fruit solely of coercion ?
what merit is there in not doing what I am continually
struggling to do, and find myself restrained ?

" Several days and nights passed away in a state of sleepless dejection, from wounded pride, impatience of restraint, and the perplexity arising from the unresolved mystery of my condition.   When I went out, I observed that men seemed to look at me with an air of curiosity, as upon one to whom something extraordinary had happened ; and it was manifest, that my appearance furnished them with a new topic of conversation.   I was wasted almost to a shadow, and I started when I saw myself in the glass, so pale, emaciated, and hollow-eyed.   My friends entreated me to take exercise, and I was persuaded to provide myself with a horse, a fleet animal in the harness, which the man who brought him to me assured me, honestly enough, was the best creature in the world, bating some caprices of temper which only required a little wholesome casti-gation.   ' When the horse refuses to go,' said he, ' you have nothing to do but to take a whip and whip the devil out of him.'

" The horse was put into a light sulky, and I drove out daily.   The rapid motion, and the quick succession of objects, were a sensible relief to the gloomy mo-notony of my reflections.   My excursions compre-hended a considerable extent of country, lying in the sober and mature beauty of September ; and the deep hush of the scene and the season began to communi-cate somewhat of a correspondent tranquillity to my feelings.   My horse had as yet shown none of the ca-prices of which the seller had given me notice, and I began to think that they were occasioned merely by unskilful management on his part ; when at length, one day as I was returning in some haste from a morning drive of greater length than usual, he gave me a spe-cimen of his humours.   All at once he stopped short in the middle of the road.   I shook the reins over his neck, cracked the whip about his ears, touched him with the end of the lash, spoke to him, chirrupped, whistled, and used every means of encouragement and stimulus usual in such cases, but in vain. The only effect they had was to make the animal break, at times, into a short bouncing gallop, which he performed with such a wonderful economy of space as not to get forward more than a rod in a minute. I had engaged a friend to dine with me that day, and remembering the prescription of the owner of the horse, I got out of my carriage in no little indignation to ' whip the devil out of him.'

" I struck him smartly with the lash, and as I did so I felt the monitory pressure on my arm, but I paid no attention to it at the time, thinking it occasioned by some accidental entanglement of the reins which I was holding. The animal answered the blow by running a few steps backward. Taking the whip in my left hand, I wound the lash spirally round the handle, and restoring it to the right, I raised it to deal a series of heavier and severer blows with the stock, but immediately I perceived a force which I could not resist pulling it down to my side. Shuddering, I desisted from my intention, and after a pause of a few moments, to recover from the shock caused by this new interposition, I took the animal by the bridle to lead him forwards ; he obeyed the motion without hesitation ; and after leading him a few rods I again got into the carriage, and he proceeded at his usual pace.

" After this I took little pleasure in my rides, in consequence of the perpetual apprehension of a check from my invisible monitor, fearing as I did to urge my horse beyond his voluntary speed, lest I should incur a repetition of these ghostly admonitions, of which I now entertained a kind of nervous dread, and which, instead of becoming more indifferent to them as they grew more frequent, I only regarded with greater terror. Instead of driving out, therefore, I began to take long walks, wandering into unfre-

quented places, traversing forests, and climbing mountains.   It was a fine season, about the beginning of October ; a few light early frosts had fallen, the days were
soft and sunny, and the woods glorious with the splendours of their annual decay.   My walks, begun at
early sunrise, were often protracted to nightfall.
Sometimes I carried a fowling-piece, but I had not
yet thought of using it, when once straying into a deep
unfrequented wood, I observed, not far distant from me,
sitting on the prostrate trunk of a tree, a partridge or
pheasant, as it is differently called in this country,
though like neither of the birds known in England by
these names.   The shy and beautiful bird, unaware of
my near approach, yet roused to attention by the
rustling of the leaves, stood with his crested head and
ruffed neck erect, as if listening to the sound, in order
to determine whether it boded danger.   I raised my
fowling-piece to my eye and levelled it, and immediately I felt the muzzle drawn towards the ground as if
loaded with a sudden weight.   I raised it again, taking
fresh aim, but before I could discharge the piece, it was
drawn downwards a second time.   Was this the effect
of an excited imagination, or of my own want of skill,
or was it in fact a supernatural admonition ?   The
worst certainly could not be so painful as this state of
doubt ; and in conformity with the habit and inclination of my mind, I instantly resolved that I would obtain all the certainty of which the case admitted.
Kneeling down, therefore, I rested my fowling-piece
on a log which lay before me, and placing my hands,
one on the stock, and the other under the lock, with its
forefinger on the trigger, I directed the muzzle towards
the object.   Before I could take accurate aim, I felt
my right arm suddenly pulled back, the piece was discharged, and the ball passed over the head of the
bird, which, spreading its mottled wings, rose with a

whirr from the ground, and flying a few rods, alighted and ran from my sight.

" Here was what appeared to me a clear interposition of some external power which had caused me to discharge the piece before I was prepared. But who or what was the agent by whom I had been restrained? In the present case it was an interposition of benevolence, and effected its end by mild methods. But what was I to think of the chill and iron grasp which had stifled my utterance, and nearly deprived me of the breath of life when I strove to speak in my own defence? And in what light should I regard the force which but a day or two previous had struck my arm powerless to my side? Could it be that the gentle being who once shared my fortunes was the agent of such violence,— or was another employed in the ungrateful task of subduing my more obstinate moods, while to her was left the care of admonishing me by light pressures, and soft touches of her own delicate hand?

" There was nothing less fitted to awaken or keep up the idea of communication with the supernatural world than the aspect of nature around me. The woods were all yellow with autumn, or rather the prevailing colour was a bright golden tinge, here and there interspersed with flushes of crimson, purple, and orange. There was no shadow throughout this wide extent of forest, at least there appeared to be none, for the light came through the semi-transparent leaves, or was reflected from their glowing surfaces, with the same golden hue as when it left the orb of the sun. It was a scene of universal warmth and cheerfulness. In the broad glare of the common sunshine, to an imagination excited by the idea of a spectral visitant, the sight of one's own shadow keeping pace with him, and mimicking all his actions, has something in it actually frightful. The wild motions of the clouds

also, on a stormy day, have the same effect; and from
the uncertain outlines of things seen by a feeble light,
the alarmed fancy shapes for itself images of terror.
But here was no shadow, no dimness, all was brightness and glory around me. Yet even here, said I to
myself, alone as I seem, I have my companions. Invisible beings are ever at my side, they glide with me
among the trunks of these trees; they float on the
soft pulsations of the air which detach the yellow
leaves from the boughs; they watch every motion of
my frame, and every word of my lips. Never was
prisoner, suspected of having formed a plan to escape
from his captivity, so vigilantly guarded and observed.

"As I walked slowly homeward, I came to an opening in the forest, on the top of a little eminence, where
I stopped and turned to take a last look of the sun as
he descended. His mild golden rays were streaming
with a sweet and sleepy languor, as if the lids of that
great eye of heaven were half-closed over it, softening
but not veiling its brightness; while beneath, the earth
slept in Sabbath stillness, as if yielding itself up to
the sole enjoyment of that genial splendour. I sighed,
as I thought of the contrast thus presented between
my own enthralled and agitated spirit, and the repose
and liberty of every thing around me. As I proceeded,
sunset came on, and twilight stole over the woods.
Sometimes I passed through a gloomy thicket of ever-
greens; and as darkness always heightens the feeling
of the marvellous, I almost expected to descry some
dim half-defined form in the shadow, the visible pre-
sentation of my ghostly attendant. I saw, however,
nothing; powerfully as I had been affected by the incident I have just related, my imagination refused to
body forth a visionary shape from the indistinct outlines of things around me; but I reached home in a
state of extreme excitement.

"I went to my chamber, but I was too much agitated to think of sleep. For hours I paced the floor, revolving in my mind circumstances of the mysterious visitation of which I was the subject; I watched the moon as she rose, and saw her climb the zenith; and I said to myself, though half ashamed of the thought, 'Will not the dead of night, the witching hour at which our forefathers believed the dead were permitted to leave their graves and walk the earth visible to men, show me the form of that being which keeps perpetual watch over me? Must even the light of the moon, powerful as it is to endue things with strange shapes,—that light which the Mantuan poet called malignant, from its being peopled with terrifying phantoms,—show me only the accustomed and familiar objects of day? Shall I never be permitted to behold the external shape of the mysterious existence which so often manifests itself to another of my senses, that I may determine with more certainty its nature, and whether its interposition be for good or evil? But it must be for good, for it interposes only to prevent some act of cruelty or passion.' These reflections, it will easily be imagined, did not dispose me to slumber. It was not until the stars began to grow pale that a sense of fatigue compelled me to throw myself on the bed, nor even then were my eyes soon closed in sleep. It was late, however, very late when I awoke, the light streaming into my windows pained my eyes as I opened them. My black man, an honest, faithful creature, who had grown old in the family of my wife's father, and whom at her request I had taken into my service, was just opening the door.

" ' What o'clock is it?' said I; 'look at my watch on the table.'

" He took up the watch, but appeared to find some difficulty in distinguishing the hour.

" ' Hand it to me, you stupid creature,' said I, ' and let me see for myself.'

23*

" I looked at the dial, which informed me that it was half-past ten o'clock.

." 'Rascal !' exclaimed I, 'have you not been positively directed never to neglect calling me at seven o'clock, if I were not already up?'

" ' Yes, master, but I thought you might have need of rest. I am certain that I heard master walking his room till very late, and I was afraid he would not like to be disturbed.'

" ' What business had you to set your thoughts or your fears against my orders? How did you know that I had not some appointment to keep, or some important business to transact before this hour? I had actually an appointment, and your negligence has caused me to break it. But I will take care to teach you a lesson that you will remember. Leave the room instantly, call again in half an hour, and I will pay you your wages, and you shall—'

" I was going to add that he should immediately quit my service, but at that moment I felt the bed-clothes, which lay across my shoulders and the lower part of my face, pressed over them so tightly and closely, and with such a prodigious weight, as to smother my voice, or at least to reduce it to sounds choked and inarticulate. In vain I struggled to free myself; the sheets seemed, as we sometimes fancy them in a fit of the nightmare, to be thick plates of the heaviest and hardest of metals, and lay upon me with an immoveable rigidity. The black man retreated from the room with a face of blank astonishment; but as soon as he was gone, the enormous weight ceased to press upon me, and I again breathed freely. I arose and put on my clothes ; in a short time the negro presented himself, and I paid him his wages up to that morning. He looked surprised, but I sent him about some ordinary service, without entering into any explanation,

"It might be thought that these successive admonitions, manifest as their design had become, would have made me cautious of transgressing the bounds of a just moderation of temper, and have restrained me from every act bordering on inhumanity. I was not yet, however, wholly cured. One day, as I was returning from one of my usual walks, I chanced to pass by a farm of which I was the proprietor. I had been of late so entirely absorbed in other matters that I had not visited it to inspect its condition, but I now observed that the house was in bad repair, the shutters dropping from the hinges, the windows broken and patched with rags, and the fences everywhere falling down. The tenant had taken the farm on condition of rendering me half the annual product. The portion I had already received was not equal to my expectations; and the autumnal crops, then ready for gathering, exposed as they were to the depredations of animals, I thought would be little or nothing.

"I sent for the man as soon as I got home. He made no haste to come; but in a day or two, after a second message, he deigned to make his appearance, He was a stout, broad-shouldered, dark-complexioned man, with a blackguard cast of the eye, and a resolute demeanour. His beard was of some ten days' growth; he wore a tattered hat, and an old great-coat tied round his middle with a fragment of an old silk handkerchief. In short, he had every mark of being an idle, saucy, good-for-nothing fellow, and a very unpromising subject for a quarrel.

"'Johnston,' said I to him, 'I fear you do not keep your farm in the best order.'

"'I do the best I can, squire,' was the laconic answer.

"'But I saw the fences down the other day, and observed strange cattle feeding in my meadows and spoiling the next year's crop of grass.'

" ' I have nothing to do with the next year's crop, squire, till I know whether I am to stay another year on the place.'

" ' That you may know from this moment. Your lease is from the twentieth of November to the twentieth of November; so you may make up your mind to leave the premises the very day your lease expires; for I am determined that so worthless a tenant shall remain on the farm no longer.'

" The man laughed in my face. ' I rather guess, squire,' returned he, ' that you will be troubled to git me out quite as soon as you expect. I believe there was no writing in the business; and as for the law about them matters, I know what it is as well as you, for I heard the judge lay it down once in court. No, squire, I thank you; I shall not budge a foot; I shall stay in that house for the winter. I will not be turned out, wife and children and all, in the cold weather, just because you ha'n't made so much money by me as you meant to do—and what is more, you can't turn me out. I know what the law is as well as you.'

" I was provoked beyond measure at the man's insolence. ' Scoundrel!' said I; ' do you set me at defiance? Did I not put you on that farm out of charity ?'

" ' And now you would turn me into the street to starve, out of charity, I s'pose. There is just as much charity in one case as in the other. I was needy, and you thought to take advantage of my situation for your own profit; you have been disappointed, and now you want to be rid of me.'

" ' Fellow,' said I to Johnston, ' your dishonesty and ingratitude are bad enough, but your ill-manners are past all bearing. Leave the house instantly.'

" I shall never forget the look of cool impudence which the man gave me, as he answered, that having come at my request on a matter of business, he should not think of taking his leave until it was settled; that he was no lackey of mine, to come and go at my bidding, and that having entered the house by my special invitation, he should take his own time for leaving it.

" ' Then I must endeavour to quicken your speed,' said I, reaching my hand to the wall near me, where hung a large horsewhip; with which, in the extremity of my anger, I resolved to chastise the insolence of the plebeian. Immediately I felt a soft pressure on the wrist, as if a gentle hand strove to detain my own. This was no time, however, nor was I in a mood, to be withheld from my purpose by any thing short of irresistible force. There stood the insolent and ragged rascal who had provoked me; he had thrown off his great-coat, and stood in the only garments left, a tattered shirt and pantaloons, placing himself in an attitude of defence, looking as if ready to spring upon me, and watching me with a quick eye and a determined look, which, however, indicated no more passion than might give firmness to his purpose and vigour to its execution. I broke impatiently from the soft restraint which impeded me, raised my hand to the whip, seized it, and had already lifted it over Johnston's head, when I felt my arm suddenly arrested by a firm, rigid, painful grasp. I strove to move forward, but could not: it seemed as if every part of my frame was imprisoned with bars and shackles of iron; I felt them on my breast, my sides, my arms, and my thighs. No words can describe the tumult of feelings in my bosom—indignation, surprise, disappointment, all wrought to the highest pitch, and all subsiding into horror. Johnston, who was waiting to repel and return my blow, and who evidently intended to fell me to the earth, if possible, had I struck him, grew pale as he looked at me, and walked away, turning once or twice as he left the room to fix his eyes upon me. I heard afterward that he had acknowledged that, fearless

M 3

as he was, the expression of my countenance daunted him—with such a frightful and demoniac energy did it speak of the violent passions which raged within me.

"I was now left alone; but not as formerly was I released as soon as the occasion for restraint had ceased. On the contrary, the rigid pressure still continued to impede my motions on every side. My left hand, however, was at liberty, and as somewhat of my presence of mind returned, I began to investigate the nature of the strange invisible shackles which confined me. That powerful grasp was still on my right arm. I searched it—it was not a hand of flesh—I felt the smooth, cold articulations of a skeleton. The gentle being who had given me the first admonition, had resigned me for the time to severer guardianship. I endeavoured to move my hand forward and towards either side,—it was obstructed by a kind of irregular lattice-work, which, on examining it closely, proved to be the bones of a skeleton. I felt the parallel ribs; I passed my hand through them, and touched the column of the spine. Words cannot describe my horror. I did not swoon; I did not lose consciousness; but with dilated eyes, and erected hair, and cold shudderings passing over my whole frame, I explored the mysterious objects which surrounded me; I continued the examination until not a doubt remained, and I came to the conclusion that I was surrounded by a group of skeletons, one of which held my arm, and another clasped me in its horrible embraces. Shortly afterward my arm was released—the stricture around my chest was gone, and I could move my limbs without difficulty. In a state of extreme exhaustion, I sank down upon the nearest seat.

"My incredulity with respect to these interpositions had previously to this, as I think I have intimated, been overcome; and it now remained for me to consider whether I would incur a repetition of such ad-

monitions as the last, administered doubtless in that
terrible manner because it was manifest that milder
means had no effect upon me. I began to watch all
my actions and words, to abstain from the utterance of
every thing unkind or angry, and from the doing of
every thing which could give pain to a living creature.
I have in some measure reaped the reward of my cir-
cumspection in the complacent feeling which attends
the overcoming of temptation, or, in perhaps better
phrase, the sense of gratitude at having been preserved
from odious and mischievous actions. My life has
since been passed with great tranquillity, though still
saddened with the memory of my loss. Yet I confess to you that with this perpetual restraint upon my
actions, this sense of a presence which checks and
chastises what is wrong, I am far from happy. I feel
like a captive in chains, and my spirit yearns after its
former freedom. My sole desire and hope is, that by
a patient submission to the guidance appointed me, I
may become fitted for a state where liberty and virtue
are the same, and where in following the rules of duty
we shall only pursue a natural and unerring inclination."

Here Medfield ended. I endeavoured to reason with
him on the subject of his story, and to show him that
what he had experienced was only a delusion of the
imagination, a *monomania*, as it is termed by the phy-
sicians,—though I did not venture to call it by that
name,—a diseased relation between the mind and one
of the senses, to which a man of the soundest and
clearest judgment might be subject.

He heard me for a little while, and then interrupting
me, said, "All that you say is only what has occurred
to my own mind. I am willing to believe you as ingenious in argument as most men, but I can scarcely
suppose that you will advance any thing new in favour
of incredulity on this point, which I have not already

considered, and to which I did not sedulously endeavour to allow its utmost weight. It was all in vain.
Skeptical as I naturally was on such subjects, I could
not bring myself to set aside the evidence of the most
scrutinizing and least fallible of our senses, the sense
which conveys to us the most certain information of
the world about us. You will only weary me by the
revival of a dispute which I long ago settled for myself. Let us, my dear sir, talk of something else."

After some conversation on indifferent topics, I
parted from Medfield, with a full conviction that his
melancholy had produced some alienation of mind. I
returned in a few days afterward to New-York. In the
course of the winter I had a letter from him, somewhat melancholy in its tenor. He spoke of ill-health,
and impaired spirits, and complained of the monotony
and weariness of the season. In the month of June
afterward, as I was looking over the columns of a
newspaper, I saw announced in the obituary the death
of Charles Medfield, of ——, aged 36 years.

END OF VOL. I.